Jeremy Taylor

Selections from the Works of Jeremy Taylor

with some account of the author and his writings

Jeremy Taylor

Selections from the Works of Jeremy Taylor
with some account of the author and his writings

ISBN/EAN: 9783337276928

Printed in Europe, USA, Canada, Australia, Japan

Cover: Foto ©Andreas Hilbeck / pixelio.de

More available books at **www.hansebooks.com**

SELECTIONS

FROM THE

WORKS OF JEREMY TAYLOR.

WITH

SOME ACCOUNT OF THE AUTHOR
AND HIS WRITINGS.

BOSTON:

LITTLE, BROWN AND COMPANY.

1863.

CONTENTS.

SOME ACCOUNT

OF THE LIFE AND WRITINGS OF

JEREMY TAYLOR.*

JEREMY TAYLOR was the son of a barber, and was born at Cambridge in the year 1613. He was brought up in the free-school there, and was ripe for the university before custom would allow of his admittance; but by the time he was thirteen years old he was entered into Caius College. Had he lived among the ancient pagans, he had been ushered into the world with a miracle, and swans must have danced and sung at his birth; and he must have been a great hero, and no less than the son of Apollo, the god of wisdom and eloquence.†

He was a man long before he was of age, and knew little more of the state of childhood than its innocency and pleasantness. From the university, by that time he was Master of Arts, he removed to

---

* This account consists chiefly of Dr. Rust's Sermon, preached at Taylor's funeral. For the minuter details the reader is referred to *Heber's Life of Taylor.*

† Anthony Wood, speaking of his birth, says, "Jeremy Taylor tumbled into the lap of the muses at Cambridge."

London, and became public lecturer in the church of St. Paul's, where he preached to the admiration and astonishment of his auditory, and by his florid and youthful beauty, and sweet and pleasant air, and sublime and raised discourses, he made his hearers take him for some young angel, newly descended from the visions of glory. The fame of this new star, that outshone all the rest of the firmament, quickly came to the notice of the great Archbishop of Canterbury,* who would needs have him preach before him, which he performed not less to his wonder than satisfaction; his discourse was beyond exception and beyond imitation : yet the wise prelate thought him too young; but the great youth humbly begged his Grace to pardon that fault, and promised. if he lived, he would mend it. However, the grand patron of learning and ingenuity thought it for the advantage of the world, that such mighty parts should be afforded better opportunities of study and improvement than a course of constant preaching would allow of ; and to that purpose he placed him in All-Souls College, in Oxford ; where love and admiration still waited upon him : which, so long as there is any spark of ingenuity in the breasts of men, must needs be the inseparable attendants of so extraordinary a worth and sweetness. He had not been long here, before my Lord of Canterbury bestowed upon him the rectory of Uppingham in Rutlandshire, and soon after preferred him to be chaplain to King Charles the Martyr, of blessed and immortal memory. Thus were preferments heaped

* Laud.

upon him, but still less than his deserts; and that
not through the fault of his great masters, but because the amplest honors and rewards were poor
and inconsiderable compared with the greatness of
his worth and merit.

This great man had no sooner launched into the
world, but a fearful tempest arose, and a barbarous
and unnatural war disturbed a long and uninter-
rupted peace and tranquillity, and brought all things
into disorder and confusion. But his religion taught
him to be loyal, and engaged him on his prince's
side, whose cause and quarrel he always owned and
maintained with a great courage and constancy: till
at last he and his little fortune were shipwrecked in
that great hurricane that overturned both Church
and State. This fatal storm cast him ashore in a
private corner of the world, and a tender Providence
shrouded him under her wings, and the prophet was
fed in the wilderness; and his great worthiness procured him friends, that supplied him with bread and
necessaries. In this solitude he began to write those
excellent Discourses, which are enough of themselves to furnish a library, and will be famous to
all succeeding generations for their greatness of
wit, and profoundness of judgment, and richness of
fancy, and clearness of expression, and copiousness
of invention, and general usefulness to all the purposes of a Christian. And by these he soon got a
great reputation among all persons of judgment and
indifferency, and his name will grow greater still as
the world grows better and wiser.

When he had spent some years in this retirement,

it pleased God to visit his family with sickness, and to take to himself the dear pledges of his favor,—three sons of great hopes and expectations,—within the space of two or three months: and though he had learned a quiet submission unto the divine will, yet the affliction touched him so sensibly, that it made him desirous to leave the country; and going to London, he there met my Lord Conway, a person of great honor and generosity, who making him a kind proffer, the good man embraced it; and that brought him over into Ireland, and settled him at Portmore, a place made for study and contemplation, which he, therefore, dearly loved; and here he wrote his " Cases of Conscience," a book that is able alone to give its author immortality.

By this time the wheel of Providence brought about the king's happy restoration, and there began a new world, and the Spirit of God moved upon the face of the waters. and out of a confused chaos brought forth beauty and order, and all the three nations were inspired with a new life, and became drunk with an excess of joy: among the rest this loyal subject went over to congratulate the prince and people's happiness, and bear a part in the universal triumph.

It was not long ere his sacred Majesty began the settlement of the Church. and the great Doctor Jeremy Taylor was resolved upon for the bishopric of Down and Connor; and not long after, Dromore was added to it; and it was but reasonable that the king and Church should consider their champion, and reward the pains and sufferings he underwent in the

defence of their cause and honor. With what care
and faithfulness he discharged his office, we are all
his witnesses; what good rules and directions he
gave his clergy, and how he taught us the practice
of them by his own example. Upon his coming
over bishop, he was made a privy-counsellor; and
the University of Dublin gave him their testimony
by recommending him for their vice-chancellor:
which honorable office he kept to his dying day.

During his being in this see, he wrote several excellent discourses, particularly his " Dissuasive from
Popery," which was received by a general approba-
tion; and a " Vindication " of it from some impertinent cavillers, that pretend to answer books when
there is nothing towards it more than the very title-
page. This great prelate improved his talent with
a mighty industry, and managed his stewardship
rarely well; and his Master, when he called for his
accounts, found him busy and at his work, and employed upon an excellent subject, "A Discourse
upon the Beatitudes "; which, if finished, would
have been of great use to the world, and solve most
of the cases of conscience that occur to a Christian
in all the varieties of states and conditions. But
the all-wise God hath ordained it otherwise, and
hath called home his good servant, to give him a
portion in that blessedness that Jesus Christ hath
promised to all his faithful disciples and followers.

Thus having given you a brief account of his life,
I know you will now expect a character of his person; but, I foresee, it will befall him as it does all
glorious subjects that are but disparaged by a com-

mendation. One thing I am secure of, that I shall
not be thought to speak hyperboles; for the subject
can hardly be reached by any expressions; for he
was none of God's ordinary works, but his endowments were so many, and so great, as really made
him a miracle.

Nature had befriended him much in his constitution; for he was a person of most sweet and oblig-
ing humor, of great candor and ingenuity; and there
was so much of salt and fineness of wit, and prettiness of address, in his familiar discourses, as made
his conversation have all the pleasantness of a comedy, and all the usefulness of a sermon. His soul
was made up of harmony; and he never spake but
he charmed his hearer, not only with the clearness
of his reason, but all his words, and his very tone
and cadences, were strangely musical.

But that which did most of all captivate and en-
ravish, was, the gayety and richness of fancy; for
he had much in him of that natural enthusiasm that
inspires all great poets and orators; and there was a
generous ferment in his blood and spirits that set his
fancy bravely a-work, and made it swell and teem
and become pregnant to such degrees of luxuriancy
as nothing but the greatness of his wit and judgment could have kept it within due bounds and
measures.

And, indeed, it was a rare mixture, and a single
instance, hardly to be found in an age: for the great
trier of wits has told us, that there is a peculiar and
several complexion required for wit, and judgment,
and fancy; and yet you might have found all these

in this great personage in their eminency and perfection. But that which made his wit and judgment
so considerable, was the largeness and freedom of
his spirit; for truth is plain and easy to a mind dis-
entangled from superstition and prejudice. He was
one of the Eclectics, a sort of brave philosophers
that Laertius speaks of, that did not addict themselves to any particular sect, but ingenuously sought
for truth among all the wrangling schools; and they
found her miserably torn and rent to pieces, and
parcelled into rags, by the several contending parties,
and so disfigured and misshapen that it was hard to
know her; but they made a shift to gather up her
scattered limbs, which, as soon as they came together, by a strange sympathy and connaturalness,
presently united into a lovely and beautiful body.
This was the spirit of this great man; he weighed
men's reasons and not their names, and was not
scared with the ugly visors men usually put upon
persons they hate and opinions they dislike, — not
affrighted with the anathemas and execrations of an
infallible chair, which he looked upon only as bug-
bears to terrify weak and childish minds. He considered that it is not likely any one party should
wholly engross truth to themselves; that obedience
is the only way to true knowledge; which is an argument that he has managed rarely well in that
excellent sermon of his, which he calls " Via Intel-
ligentiæ "; that God always, and only, teaches do-
cible and ingenuous minds, that are willing to hear
and ready to obey according to their light; that it
is impossible a pure, humble, resigned, God-like

soul should be kept out of heaven, whatever mistakes it might be subject to in this state of mortality; that the design of heaven is not to fill men's heads and feed their curiosities, but to better their hearts and mend their lives. Such considerations as these made him impartial in his disquisitions, and give a due allowance to the reasons of his adversary, and contend for truth, and not for victory.

And now you will easily believe that an ordinary diligence would be able to make great improvements upon such a stock of parts and endowments; but to these advantages of nature and excellency of his spirit he added an indefatigable industry, and God gave a plentiful benediction: for there were very few kinds of learning but he was a " Mystes," and a great master in them; he was a rare humanist, and hugely versed in all the polite arts of learning; and had thoroughly concocted all the ancient moralists, Greek and Roman, poets and orators ; and was not unacquainted with the refined wits of later ages, whether French or Italian.

But he had not only the accomplishments of a gentleman, but so universal were his parts, that they were proportioned to everything ; and though his spirit and humor were made up of smoothness and gentleness, yet he could bear with the harshness and roughness of the schools ; and was not unseen in their subtilties and spinosities, and, upon occasion, could make them serve his purpose ; and yet, I believe, he thought many of them very near akin to the famous Knight de la Mancha, and would make sport sometimes with the romantic sophistry and

fantastic adventures of school-errantry. His skill
was great, both in the civil and canon law, and casu-
istical divinity; and he was a rare conductor of
souls, and knew how to counsel and to advise, — to
solve difficulties, and determine cases, and quiet
consciences. And he was no novice in Mr. I. S.'s
new science of controversy ; but could manage an
argument and repartees with a strange dexterity;
he understood what the several parties in Christen-
dom have to say for themselves, and could plead
their cause to better advantage than any advocate
of their tribe: and when he had done, he could confute them too, and show that better arguments
than ever they could produce for themselves would
afford no sufficient ground for their fond opinions.

It would be too great a task to pursue his accomplishments through the various kinds of literature.
I shall content myself to add only his great acquaintance with the Fathers and ecclesiastical writers, and
the doctors of the first and purest ages both of the
Greek and Latin Church ; which he has made use
of against the Romanists, to vindicate the Church of
England from the challenge of innovation, and prove
her to be truly ancient, catholic, and apostolical.

But religion and virtue is the crown of all other
accomplishments ; and it was the glory of this great
man to be thought a Christian, and whatever you
added to it, he looked upon as a term of diminution ;
and he was a zealous son of the Church of England ; but that was because he judged her (and
with great reason) a Church the most purely Christian of any in the world. In his younger years he

met with some assaults from popery; and the high pretensions of their religious orders were very accommodate to his devotional temper: but he was always so much master of himself, that he would never be governed by anything but reason, and the evidence of truth, which engaged him in the study of those controversies; and to how good purpose, the world is by this time a sufficient witness: but the longer and the more he considered, the worse he liked the Roman cause, and became at last to censure them with some severity; but I confess I have so great an opinion of his judgment, and the charitableness of his spirit, that I am afraid he did not think worse of them than they deserve.

But religion is not a matter of theory and orthodox notions; and it is not enough to believe aright, but we must practise accordingly; and to master our passions, and to make a right use of that power that God has given us over our own actions, is a greater glory than all other accomplishments that can adorn the mind of man; and, therefore, I shall close my character of this great personage with a touch upon some of those virtues for which his memory will be precious to all posterity. He was a person of great humility; and notwithstanding his stupendous parts, and learning, and eminency of place, he had nothing in him of pride and humor, but was courteous and affable, and of easy access, and would lend a ready ear to the complaints, yea, to the impertinencies of the meanest persons. His humility was coupled with an extraordinary piety; and, I believe, he spent the greatest part of his time in heaven; his solemn hours of prayer took up a considerable portion of his life; and we are not to doubt but he had learned of St. Paul to pray continually; and that occasional ejaculations, and frequent aspirations and emigrations of his soul after God, made up the best part of his devotions. But he was not only a good man Godward, but he was come to the top of St. Peter's gradation, and to all his other virtues added a large and diffusive charity: and whoever compares his plentiful incomes with the inconsiderable estate he left at his death, will be easily convinced that charity was steward for a great proportion of his revenue. But the hungry that he fed, and the naked that he clothed, and the distressed that he supplied, and the fatherless that he provided for, — the poor children that he put to apprentice, and brought up at school, and maintained at the university, — will now sound a trumpet to that charity which he dispersed with his right hand, but would not suffer his left hand to have any knowledge of it.

To sum up all in a few words: this great prelate had the good-humor of a gentleman, the eloquence of an orator, the fancy of a poet, the acuteness of a schoolman, the profoundness of a philosopher, the wisdom of a chancellor, the sagacity of a prophet, the reason of an angel, and the piety of a saint; he had devotion enough for a cloister, learning enough for a university, and wit enough for a college of virtuosi; and had his parts and endowments been parcelled out among his poor clergy that he left behind him, it would, perhaps, have made one of the

2

best dioceses in the world. But, alas! "Our father! our father! the horses of our Israel, and the chariot thereof!" he is gone, and has carried his mantle and his spirit along with him up to heaven; and the sons of the prophets have lost all their beauty and lustre, which they enjoyed only from the reflection of his excellencies, which were bright and radiant enough to cast a glory upon a whole order of men. But the sun of this our world, after many attempts to break through the crust of an earthly body, is at last swallowed up in the great vortex of eternity, and there all his *maculæ* are scattered and dissolved, and he is fixed in an orb of glory, and shines among his brethren stars, that, in their several ages, gave light to the world, and turned many souls unto righteousness; and we that are left behind, though we can never reach his perfections, must study to imitate his virtues, that we may at last come to sit at his feet in the mansions of glory.

After a short illness of ten days, this man of extraordinary gifts and attainments finished his earthly course, on the 13th of August, 1667, at the age of fifty-five years.

The critical remarks that follow are from the pen of Bishop Heber.

The comeliness of Taylor's person has been often noticed, and he himself appears to have been not insensible of it. Few authors have so frequently introduced their own portraits, in different characters

and attitudes, as ornaments to their printed works.
So far as we may judge from these, he appears to
have been above the middle size, strongly and hand-
somely proportioned, with his hair long and grace-
fully curling on his cheeks, large dark eyes, full of
sweetness, an aquiline nose, and an open and intel-
ligent countenance.

Of Taylor's domestic habits and private character
much is not known, but all which is known is amiable. " Love," as well as " admiration," is said to
have " waited on him " in Oxford. In Wales, and
amid the mutual irritation and violence of civil and
religious hostility, we find him conciliating, when a
prisoner, the favor of his keepers, at the same time
that he preserved, undiminished, the confidence and
esteem of his own party. Laud, in the height of
his power and full-blown dignity ; Charles, in his
deepest reverses ; Hatton, Vaughan, and Conway,
amid the tumults of civil war ; and Evelyn, in the
tranquillity of his elegant retirement ; seem alike to
have cherished his friendship, and coveted his society. The same genius which extorted the com-
mendation of Jeanes, for the variety of its research
and the vigor of its argument, was also an object of
interest and affection with the young and rich and
beautiful Katharine Philips ; and few writers, who
have expressed their opinions so strongly, and,
sometimes, so unguardedly as he has done, have
lived and died with so much praise and so little censure. Much of this felicity may be probably referred to an engaging appearance and a pleasing
manner ; but its cause must be sought, in a still

greater degree, in the evident kindliness of heart,
which, if the uniform tenor of a man's writings is
any index to his character, must have distinguished
him from most men living; in a temper, to all appearance warm, but easily conciliated; and in that
which, as it is one of the least common, is of all
dispositions the most attractive, not merely a neglect,
but a total forgetfulness of all selfish feeling. It is
this, indeed, which seems to have constituted the
most striking feature of his character. Other men
have been, to judge from their writings and their
lives, to all appearance, as religious, as regular in
their devotions, as diligent in the performance of all
which the laws of God or man require from us ;
but with Taylor his duty seems to have been a delight, his piety a passion. His faith was the more
vivid in proportion as his fancy was more intensely
vigorous ; with him the objects of his hope and reverence were scarcely unseen or future ; his imagination daily conducted him to " diet with gods," and
elevated him to the same height above the world,
and the same nearness to ineffable things, which
Milton ascribes to his allegorical " cherub Contemplation."

Of the broader and more general lines of Taylor's
literary character a very few observations may be
sufficient. The greatness of his attainments, and
the powers of his mind, are evident in all his writings, and to the least attentive of his readers. It is
hard to point out a branch of learning, or of scien-
tific pursuit, to which he does not occasionally al-
lude ; or any author of eminence, either ancient or

modern, with whom he does not evince himself acquainted. And it is certain, that, as very few other
writers have equal riches to display, so he is apt to
display his stores with a lavish exuberance which
the severer taste of Hooker or of Barrow would
have condemned as ostentatious, or rejected as cum-
bersome. Yet he is far from a mere reporter of
other men's arguments, — a textuary of fathers and
schoolmen, — who resigns his reason into the hands
of his predecessors, and who employs no other instrument for convincing his readers than a length-
ened string of authorities. His familiarity with the
stores of ancient and modern literature is employed
to illustrate more frequently than to establish his
positions; and may be traced, not so much in direct
citation, (though of this, too, there is, perhaps, more
than sufficient,) as in the abundance of his allusions,
the character of his imagery, and the occurrence of
terms of foreign derivation, or employed in a foreign
and unusual meaning.

It is thus that he more than once refers to obscure
stories in ancient writers, as if they were, of necessity, as familiar to all his readers as himself; that he
talks of " poor Attilius Aviola," or " the Lybian
lion," that " brake loose into his wilderness and
killed two Roman boys"; as if the accidents of
which he is speaking had occurred in London a few
weeks before. It is thus that, in warning an English (or a Welsh) auditory against the brief term of
mortal luxury, he enumerates a long list of ancient
dainties, and talks of " the condited bellies of the
scarus," and " drinking of healths by the numeral

letters of Phileninm's name." It is thus that one of
his strangest and harshest similes, where he compares an ill-sorted marriage to " going to bed with a
dragon," is the suggestion of a mind familiar with
those *lamiæ* with female faces and extremities like
a serpent, of whose enticements strange stories are
told, in the old demonologies. And thus that he
speaks of the " justice," instead of the " juice " of
fishes ; of an " excellent " pain ; of the gospel being
preached, not " to the common people," but to
" idiots " ; and of " serpents," (meaning " creeping
things,") devouring our bodies in the grave. It is
this which gives to many of his most striking passages
the air of translations, and which, in fact, may well
lead us to believe, that some of them are indeed the
selected members of different and disjointed classics.

On the other hand, few circumstances can be
named, which so greatly contribute to the richness
of his matter, the vivacity of his style, and the harmony of his language, as those copious drafts on all
which is wise, or beautiful, or extraordinary, in ancient writers or in foreign tongues ; and the very
singularity and hazard of his phrases has not unfre-
quently a peculiar charm, which the observers of a
tamer and more ordinary diction can never hope to
inspire. One of these archaisms, and a very grace-
ful one, is the introduction of the comparative degree, simply and without its contrasted quantity, of
which he has made a very frequent use, but which
he has never employed without producing an effect
of striking beauty. Thus, he tells us " of a *more*
healthy sorrow "; of " the air's *looser* garment," or

" the *wilder* fringes of the fire "; which, though in
a style purely English they would be probably re-
placed by positive or superlative epithets, could
hardly suffer this change without a considerable
detraction from the spirit and raciness of the sentence. The same observation may apply to the use
of " prevaricate." in an active sense; to " the *tem-
eration* of ruder handling " ; and to many similar
expressions, which, if unusual, are at least expres-
sive and sonorous, and which could hardly be re-
placed by the corresponding vernacular phrases
without a loss of brevity or beauty. Of such expressions as these it is only necessary to observe
that their use, to be effectual or allowable, should be
more discreet. perhaps, and infrequent, than is the
case in the works of Taylor.

I have already noticed the familiarity which he
himself displays,—and which he apparently expected
to find. in an almost equal degree. in his readers or
hearers, — with the facts of history. the opinions of
philosophy. the productions of distant climates, and
the customs of distant nations. Nor. in the allusions
or examples which he extracts from such sources, is
he always attentive to the weight of authority, or
the probability of the fact alleged. The age, indeed, in which he lived was, in many respects, a
credulous one. The discoveries which had been
made by the enterprise of travellers, and the unskilful and as yet immature efforts of the new philosophy, had extended the knowledge of mankind
just far enough to make them know that much yet
remained uncertain, and that many things were true

which their fathers had held for impossible. Such absence of skepticism is, of all states of the human mind, most favorable to the increase of knowledge ; but for the preservation of truths already acquired, and the needful separation of truth from falsehood, it is necessary to receive the testimony of men, however positive, with more of doubt than Boyle, Wilkins, or even Bacon, appear to have been accustomed to exercise.

But Taylor was anything rather than a critical inquirer into facts (however strange) of history or philosophy. If such alleged facts suited his purpose, he received them without examination, and retailed them without scruple ; and we therefore read in his works of such doubtful or incredible examples as that of a single city containing fifteen millions of inhabitants; of the Neapolitan manna, which failed as soon as it was subjected to a tax ; and of the monument "nine furlongs high," which was erected by Ninus, the Assyrian. Nor in his illustrations, even where they refer to matters of daily observation or of undoubted truth, is he always attentive to accuracy.

"When men sell a mule," he tells us, "they speak of the horse that begat him, not of the ass that bore him." It is singular that he should forget that, of mules, the ass is always the father. What follows is still more extraordinary, inasmuch as it shows a forgetfulness of the circumstances of two of the most illustrious events in the Old Testament. "We should fight," says he, "as Gideon did, with three hundred hardy brave fellows that would stand

against all violence. rather than to make a noise
with rams' horns and broken pitchers, like the men
at the siege of Jericho." Had he thought twice, he
must have recollected that "making a noise" was
at least one principal part of the service required
from Gideon's troops, and that the "broken pitchers" were their property alone, and a circumstance
of which the narrative of the siege of Jericho affords
not the least mention. An occasional occurrence of
such errors is indeed unavoidable ; and, irrelevant
as some of his illustrations are, and uncertain as
may be the truth of others, there is none, perhaps,
of his readers who would wish those illustrations
fewer, to which his works owe so much of their
force, their impressiveness, and their entertainment.
As a reasoner, I do not think him matchless. He is,
indeed, always acute, and. in practical questions,
almost always sensible. His knowledge was so vast,
that on every point of discussion he set out with
great advantage, as being familiar with all the necessary preliminaries of the question, and with every
ground or argument which had been elicited on
either side by former controversies. But his own
understanding was rather inventive than critical.
He never failed to find a plausible argument for any
opinion which he himself entertained ; he was as
ready with plausible objections to every argument
which might be advanced by his adversaries ; and
he was completely acquainted with the whole detail
of controversial attack and defence, and of every
weapon of eloquence, irony, or sarcasm, which was
most proper to persuade or to silence. But his own

views were sometimes indistinct, and often hasty. His opinions, therefore, though always honest and ardent, he had sometimes occasion, in the course of his life, to change : and instances have been already pointed out, not only where his reasoning is inconclusive, but where positions ardently maintained in some of his writings are doubted or denied in others. But it should be remembered how much he wrote during a life in itself not long, and in its circumstances by no means favorable to accurate research or calm reasoning. Nor can it be a subject of surprise that a poor and oppressed man should be sometimes hurried too far in opposition to his persecutors, or that one who had so little leisure for the correction of his works should occasionally be found to contradict or repeat himself.

I have already had occasion to point out the versatility of his talents, which, though uniformly exerted on subjects appropriate to his profession, are distinguished, where such weapons are needed, by irony and caustic humor, as well as by those milder and sublimer beauties of style and sentiment which are his more familiar and distinguishing characteristics. Yet to such weapons he has never recourse wantonly or rashly. Nor do I recollect any instance in which he has employed them in the cause of private or personal, or even polemical hostility, or any occasion where their fullest severity was not justified and called for by crimes, by cruelty, by interested superstition, or base and sordid hypocrisy. His satire was always kept in check by the depth and fervor of his religious feelings, his charity, and his humility. It is on devotional and moral subjects, however, that the peculiar character of his mind is most, and most successfully, developed. To this service he devotes his most glowing language; to this his aptest illustrations; his thoughts, and his words at once burst into a flame, when touched by the coals of this altar; and whether he describes the duties, or dangers, or hopes of man, or the mercy, power, and justice of the Most High, — whether he exhorts or instructs his brethren, or offers up his supplications in their behalf to the common Father of all, — his conceptions and his expressions belong to the loftiest and most sacred description of poetry, of which they only want, what they cannot be said to need, the name and the metrical arrangement.

It is this distinctive excellence, still more than the other qualifications of learning and logical acuteness, which has placed him, even in that age of gigantic talent, on an eminence superior to any of his immediate contemporaries; which has exempted him from the comparative neglect into which the dry and repulsive learning of Andrews and Sanderson has fallen; which has left behind the acuteness of Hales, and the imaginative and copious eloquence of Bishop Hall, at a distance hardly less than the cold elegance of Clarke, and the dull good sense of Tillotson; and has seated him, by the almost unanimous estimate of posterity, on the same lofty elevation with Hooker and with Barrow.

Of such a triumvirate, who shall settle the precedence? Yet it may, perhaps, be not far from the truth, to observe, that Hooker claims the foremost

rank in sustained and classic dignity of style, in
political and pragmatical wisdom ; that to Barrow
the praise must be assigned of the closest and the
clearest views, and of a taste the most controlled
and chastened ; but that in imagination, in interest,
in that which more properly and exclusively deserves
the name of genius, Taylor is to be placed before
either. The first awes most, the second convinces
most, the third persuades and delights most ; and
(according to the decision of one * whose own rank
among the ornaments of English literature yet remains to be determined by posterity) Hooker is the
object of our reverence, Barrow of our admiration,
and Jeremy Taylor of our love.

* Dr. Parr.

SELECTIONS

FROM

JEREMY TAYLOR.

SELECTIONS.

———◆———

THE DAY OF JUDGMENT.

VIRTUE and vice are so essentially distinguished, and the distinction is so necessary to be observed in order to the well-being of men in private and in societies, that, to divide them in themselves, and to separate them by sufficient notices, and to distinguish them by rewards, hath been designed by all laws, by the sayings of wise men, by the order of things, by their proportions to good or evil. And the expectations of men have been framed accordingly: that virtue may have a proper seat in the will and in the affections, and may become amiable by its own excellency and its appendant blessing; and that vice may be as natural an enemy to a man, as a wolf to the lamb, and as darkness to light, — destructive of its being, and a contradiction of its nature. But it is not enough that all the world hath armed itself against vice, and, by all that is wise and sober among men, hath taken the part of virtue, adorning it with glorious appellatives, encouraging it by rewards, entertaining it by sweetness, and commanding it by edicts, fortifying it with defensatives, and twining with it in all artificial compliances. All this is short of man's necessity; for this will, in all modest men, secure their actions in theatres and highways, in markets and churches, before the eye of judges, and in the society of witnesses: but the actions of closets and chambers, the designs and thoughts of men, their discourses in dark places, and the actions of retirements and of the night, are left indifferent to virtue or to vice; and of these, as man can take no cognizance, so he can make no coercitive; and therefore above one half of human actions is by the laws of man left unregarded and unprovided for. And besides this, there are some men who are bigger than laws, and some are bigger than judges; and some judges have lessened themselves by fear and cowardice, by bribery and flattery, by iniquity and compliance; and where they have not, yet they have notices but of few causes. And there are some sins so popular and universal, that to punish them is either impossible or intolerable; and to question such, would betray the weakness of the public rods and axes, and represent the sinner to be stronger than the power that is appointed to be his bridle. And after all this, we find sinners so prosperous that they escape, so potent that they fear not; and sin is made safe when it grows great,

—— Facere omnia sævè
Non impunè licet, nisi dum facis ——

and innocence is oppressed, and the poor cries, and he hath no helper, and he is oppressed, and he wants a patron. And for these and many other concurrent causes, if you reckon all the causes that come before all the judicatories of the world, though the litigious are too many, and the matters of instance are intricate and numerous, yet the personal and criminal are so few, that of two thousand sins that cry aloud to God for vengeance, scarce two are noted by the public eye, and chastised by the hand of justice. It must follow from hence, that it is but reasonable, for the interest of virtue and the necessities of the world, that the private should be judged, and virtue should be tied upon the spirit, and the poor should be relieved, and the oppressed should appeal, and the noise of widows should be heard, and the saints should stand upright, and the cause that was ill-judged should be judged over again, and tyrants should be called to account, and our thoughts should be examined, and our secret actions viewed on all sides, and the infinite number of sins which escape here should not escape finally. And therefore God hath so

3

ordained it, that there shall be a day of doom, wherein all that are let alone by men shall be questioned by God, and every word and every action shall receive its just recompense of reward. " For we must all appear before the judgment-seat of Christ, that every one may receive the things done in his body, according to that he hath done, whether it be good or bad."

" The things done in the body," so we commonly read it; the things proper or due to the body, so the expression is more apt and proper; for not only what is done by the body, but even the acts of abstracted understanding and volition, the acts of reflection and choice, acts of self-love and admiration, and whatever else can be supposed the proper and peculiar act of the soul or of the spirit, is to be accounted for at the day of judgment : and even these may be called " the things done in the body," because these are the acts of the man in the state of conjunction with the body. The words have in them no other difficulty or variety, but contain a great truth of the biggest interest, and one of the most material constitutive articles of the whole religion, and the greatest endearment of our duty in the whole world. Things are so ordered by the great Lord of all the creatures, that whatsoever we do or suffer shall be called to account, and this account shall be exact, and the sentence shall be just, and the reward shall be great; all the evils of the world shall be amended, and the injustices shall be repaid, and the divine Providence shall be vindicated, and virtue and vice shall forever be remarked by their separate dwellings and rewards.

We will consider the persons that are to be judged, with the circumstances of our advantages or our sorrows. " We must all appear," even you, and I, and all the world; kings and priests, nobles and learned, the crafty and the easy, the wise and the foolish, the rich and the poor, the prevailing tyrant and the oppressed party, shall all appear to receive their symbol. And this is so far from abating anything of its terror and our dear concernment, that it much increases it : for, although concerning precepts and discourses we are apt to neglect in particular what is recommended in general, and in incidencies of mortality and sad events, the singularity of the chance heightens the apprehension of the evil; yet it is so by accident, and only in regard of our imperfection ; it being an effect of self-love, or some little creeping envy which adheres too often to the unfortunate and miserable; or else because the sorrow is apt to increase, by being apprehended to be a rare case, and a singular unworthiness in him who is afflicted, otherwise than is common to the sons of men, companions of his sin, and brethren of his nature, and partners of his usual accidents. Yet in final and extreme events, the multitude of sufferers does not lessen, but increase the sufferings; and when the first day of judgment happened, that, I mean, of the universal deluge of waters upon the old world, the calamity swelled like the flood, and every man saw his friend perish, and the neighbors of his dwelling, and the relatives of his house, and the sharers of his joys, and yesterday's bride, and the new-born heir, the priest of the family, and the honor of the kindred, all dying or dead, drenched in water and the divine vengeance; and then they had no place to flee unto, no man cared for their souls; they had none to go unto for counsel, no sanctuary high enough to keep them from the vengeance that rained down from heaven. And so it shall be at the day of judgment, when that world and this, and all that shall be born hereafter, shall pass through the same Red Sea, and be all baptized with the same fire, and be involved in the same cloud, in which shall be thunderings and terrors infinite. Every man's fear shall be increased by his neighbor's shrieks; and the amazement that all the world shall be in, shall unite as the sparks of a raging furnace into a globe of fire, and roll upon its own principle, and increase by direct

appearances, and intolerable reflections. He
that stands in a churchyard in the time of a
great plague, and hears the passing-bell perpetually telling the sad stories of death, and sees
crowds of infected bodies pressing to their
graves, and others sick and tremulous, and
death dressed up in all the images of sorrow
round about him, is not supported in his spirit
by the variety of his sorrow. And at doomsday, when the terrors are universal, besides
that it is in itself so much greater, because it
can affright the whole world, it is also made
greater by communication and a sorrowful influence ; grief being then strongly infectious
when there is no variety of state, but an entire
kingdom of fear; and amazement is the king
of all our passions, and all the world its subjects. And that shriek must needs be terrible,
when millions of men and women at the same
instant shall fearfully cry out, and the noise
shall mingle with the trumpet of the archangel,
with the thunders of the dying and groaning
heavens, and the crack of the dissolving world;
when the whole fabric of nature shall shake
into dissolution and eternal ashes. But this
general consideration may be heightened with
four or five circumstances.

1. Consider what an infinite multitude of
angels and men and women shall then appear.
It is a huge assembly, when the men of one

kingdom, the men of one age in a single province, are gathered together into heaps and confusion of disorder. But then all kingdoms of all ages, all the armies that ever mustered, all the world that Augustus Cæsar taxed, all those hundreds of millions that were slain in all the Roman wars from Numa's time till Italy was broken into principalities and small exarchates; all these, and all that can come into numbers, and that did descend from the loins of Adam, shall at once be represented. To which account if we add the armies of heaven, the nine orders of blessed spirits, and the infinite numbers in every order, we may suppose the numbers fit to express the majesty of that God, and terror of that Judge, who is the Lord and Father of all that unimaginable multitude. *Erit terror ingens tot simul tantorumque populorum.**

2. In this great multitude we shall meet all those who by their example and their holy precepts have, like tapers, enkindled with a beam of the sun of righteousness, enlightened us, and taught us to walk in the paths of justice. There we shall see all those good men whom God sent to preach to us, and recall us from human follies and inhuman practices; and when we espy the good man, that chid us for our last drunkenness or adulteries, it shall then

* Florus.

also be remembered, how we mocked at counsel, and were civilly modest at the reproof, but
laughed when the man was gone, and accepted
it for a religious compliment, and took our
leaves, and went and did the same again. But
then things shall put on another face, and that
we smiled at here, and slighted fondly, shall
then be the greatest terror in the world; men
shall feel that they once laughed at their own
destruction, and rejected health, when it was
offered by a man of God upon no other condition but that they would be wise, and not be
in love with death. Then they shall perceive,
that, if they had obeyed an easy and a sober
counsel, they had been partners of the same
felicity which they see so illustrious upon the
heads of those preachers whose work is with
the Lord, and who by their life and doctrine
endeavored to snatch the soul of their friend
or relative from an intolerable misery. But
he that sees a crown put upon their heads that
give good counsel, and preach holy and severe
sermons with designs of charity and piety, will
also then perceive that God did not send
preachers for nothing, on trifling errands and
without regard ; but that work, which he
crowns in them, he purposed should be effective to us, persuasive to the understanding, and
active upon our consciences. Good preachers by their doctrine, and all good men by

their lives, are the accusers of the disobedient;
and they shall rise up from their seats, and
judge and condemn the follies of those who
thought their piety to be want of courage, and
their discourses pedantical, and their reproofs
the priest's trade, but of no signification, because they preferred moments before eternity.

3. There in that great assembly shall be
seen all those converts, who, upon easier terms,
and fewer miracles, and a less experience, and
a younger grace, and a seldomer preaching,
and more unlikely circumstances, have suffered
the work of God to prosper upon their spirits,
and have been obedient to the heavenly calling. There shall stand the men of Nineveh,
and they shall stand upright in judgment, for
they at the preaching of one man in a less
space than forty days returned unto the Lord
their God; but we have heard him call all our
lives, and like the deaf adder stopped our ears
against the voice of God's servants, charm they
never so wisely. There shall appear the men
of Capernaum, and the Queen of the South,
and the men of Berea, and the first fruits of
the Christian Church, and the holy martyrs,
and shall proclaim to all the world, that it was
not impossible to do the work of grace in the
midst of all our weaknesses, and accidental
disadvantages; and that the obedience of faith,
and the labor of love, and the contentions of

chastity, and the severities of temperance and self-denial, are not such insuperable mountains, but that an honest and sober person may perform them in acceptable degrees, if he have but a ready ear, and a willing mind, and an honest heart. And this scene of honest persons shall make the divine judgment upon sinners more reasonably and apparently just, in passing upon them the horrible sentence; for why cannot we as well serve God in peace, as others served him in war? Why cannot we love him as well, when he treats us sweetly, and gives us health and plenty, honors our fair fortunes, reputation, or contentedness, quietness and peace, as others did upon gibbets and under axes, in the hands of tormentors and in hard wildernesses, in nakedness and poverty, in the midst of all evil things and all sad discomforts? Concerning this no answer can be made.

4. But there is a worse sight than this yet, which, in that great assembly, shall distract our sight and amaze our spirits. There men shall meet the partners of their sins, and them that drank the round, when they crowned their heads with folly and forgetfulness, and their cups with wine and noises. There shall ye see that poor, perishing soul, whom thou didst tempt to adultery and wantonness, to drunkenness or perjury, to rebellion or an evil interest, by power or craft, by witty discourses or deep

dissembling, by scandal or a snare, by evil
example or pernicious counsel, by malice or
unwariness; and when all this is summed up,
and from the variety of its particulars is drawn
into an uneasy load and a formidable sum, possibly we may find sights enough to scare all
our confidences, and arguments enough to press
our evil souls into the sorrows of a most intolerable death.   For, however we make now
but light accounts and evil proportions concerning it, yet it will be a fearful circumstance of
appearing, to see one, or two, or ten, or twenty
accursed souls, despairing, miserable, infinitely
miserable, roaring and blaspheming, and fearfully cursing thee as the cause of its eternal
sorrows.   Thy lust betrayed and rifled her
weak, unguarded innocence; thy example made
thy servant confident to lie, or to be perjured;
thy society brought a third into intemperance
and the disguises of a beast: and when thou
seest that soul, with whom thou didst sin,
dragged into hell, well mayest thou fear to
drink the dregs of thy intolerable potion.   And
most certainly, it is the greatest of evils to
destroy a soul, for whom the Lord Jesus died,
and to undo that grace which our Lord purchased with so much sweat and blood, pains,
and a mighty charity.   And because very many
sins are sins of society and confederation, —
such are fornication, drunkenness, bribery, sim-

ony, rebellion, schism, and many others, — it
is a hard and a weighty consideration, what
shall become of any one of us, who have
tempted our brother or sister to sin and death.
For though God hath spared our life, and they
are dead, and their debt-books are sealed up till
the day of account; yet the mischief of our
sin is gone before us, and it is like a murder,
but more execrable : the soul is dead in trespasses and sins, and sealed up to an eternal
sorrow; and thou shalt see, at doomsday, what
damnable uncharitableness thou hast done.
That soul that cries to those rocks to cover her,
if it had not been for thy perpetual temptations,
might have followed the Lamb in a white robe ;
and that poor man, that is clothed with shame
and flames of fire, would have shined in glory,
but that thou didst force him to be partner of
the baseness. And who shall pay for this loss ?
A soul is lost by thy means ; thou hast defeated
the holy purposes of the Lord's bitter passion
by thy impurities ; and what shall happen to
thee, by whom thy brother dies eternally ?

Of all the considerations that concern this
part of the horrors of doomsday, nothing can
be more formidable than this, to such whom it
does concern : and truly it concerns so many,
and amongst so many perhaps some persons
are so tender, that it might affright their hopes,
and discompose their industries and spiritual

labors of repentance ; but that our most merciful Lord hath, in the midst of all the fearful circumstances of his second coming, interwoven this one comfort relating to this, which to my sense seems the most fearful and killing circumstance : " Two shall be grinding at one mill ; the one shall be taken, and the other left: two shall be in a bed ; the one shall be taken, and the other left " ; that is, those who are confederate in the same fortunes, and interests, and actions, may yet have a different sentence ; for an early and an active repentance will wash off this account, and put it upon the tables of the cross : and though it ought to make us diligent and careful, charitable and penitent, hugely penitent, even so long as we live ; yet when we shall appear together, there is a mercy that shall there separate us, who sometimes had blended each other in a common crime. Blessed be the mercies of God, who hath so carefully provided a fruitful shower of grace, to refresh the miseries and dangers of the greatest part of mankind. Thomas Aquinas was used to beg of God, that he might never be tempted from his low fortune to prelacies and dignities ecclesiastical ; and that his mind might never be discomposed or polluted with the love of any creature ; and that he might, by some instrument or other, understand the state of his deceased brother : and the story says, that he was heard in all. In him it was a great curiosity, or the passion and impertinencies of a useless charity to search after him, unless he had some other personal concernment than his relation of kindred. But truly, it would concern very many to be solicitous concerning the event of those souls, with whom we have mingled death and sin ; for many of those sentences, which have passed and decreed concerning our departed relatives, will concern us dearly, and we are bound in the same bundles, and shall be thrown into the same fires, unless we repent for our own sins, and double our sorrows for their damnation.

5. We may consider that this infinite multitude of men and women, angels and devils, is not ineffective as a number in Pythagoras's tables, but must needs have influence upon every spirit that shall there appear : for the transactions of that court are not like orations spoken by a Grecian orator in the circles of his people, heard by them that crowd nearest him, or that sound limited by the circles of air, or the enclosure of a wall ; but everything is represented to every person. And then let it be considered, when thy shame and secret turpitude, thy midnight revels and secret hypocrisies, thy lustful thoughts and treacherous designs, thy falsehood to God and startings from thy holy promises, thy follies and impieties,

shall be laid open before all the world, and
that then shall be spoken by the trumpet of an
archangel upon the house-top, the highest battlements of heaven, all those filthy words and
lewd circumstances which thou didst act secretly, thou wilt find that thou wilt have reason strangely to be ashamed. All the wise
men in the world shall know how vile thou
hast been ; and then consider with what confusion of face wouldst thou stand in the presence of a good man and a severe, if peradventure he should suddenly draw thy curtain, and
find thee in the sins of shame and lust ; it must
be infinitely more, when God and all the angels
of heaven and earth, all his holy myriads, and
all his redeemed saints, shall stare and wonder
at thy impurities and follies.

I have read a story, that a young gentleman,
being passionately by his mother dissuaded from
entering into the severe courses of a religious
and single life, broke from her importunity by
saying, "*Volo servare animam meam*": I am
resolved by all means to save my soul. But
when he had undertaken a rule with passion,
he performed it carelessly and remissly, and
was but lukewarm in his religion, and quickly
proceeded to a melancholy and wearied spirit,
and from thence to a sickness and the neighborhood of death : but, falling into an agony
and a fantastic vision, dreamed that he saw

himself summoned before God's angry throne,
and from thence hurried into a place of torments, where espying his mother, full of scorn
she upbraided him with his former answer, and
asked him, " Why he did not save his soul by
all means, according as he undertook ? " But
when the sick man awakened and recovered,
he made his words good indeed, and prayed
frequently, and fasted severely, and labored
humbly, and conversed charitably, and morti-
fied himself severely, and refused such secular
solaces which other good men received to refresh and sustain their infirmities ; and gave no
other account to them that asked him but this :
" If I could not, in my ecstasy or dream, endure my mother's upbraiding my follies and
weak religion, how shall I be able to suffer,
that God should redargue me at doomsday,
and the angels reproach my lukewarmness, and
the devils aggravate my sins, and all the saints
of God deride my follies and hypocrisies ? "

The effect of that man's consideration may
serve to actuate a meditation in every one of
us : for we shall all be at that pass, that unless
our shame and sorrows be cleansed by a timely
repentance, and covered by the robe of Christ,
we shall suffer the anger of God, the scorn of
saints and angels, and our own shame in the
general assembly of all mankind. This argument is most considerable to them who are

tender of their precious name, and sensible of
honor ; if they rather would choose death than
a disgrace, poverty rather than shame, let them
remember that a sinful life will bring them to
an intolerable shame at that day, when all that
is excellent in heaven and earth shall be summoned as witnesses and parties in a fearful
scrutiny.

The sum is this : all that are born of Adam
shall appear before God and his Christ ; and
all the innumerable companies of angels and
devils shall be there : and the wicked shall be
affrighted with everything they see ; and there
they shall see those good men, that taught them
the ways of life, and all those evil persons,
whom themselves have tempted into the ways
of death, and those who were converted upon
easier terms ; and some of these shall shame
the wicked, and some shall curse them, and
some shall upbraid them, and all shall amaze
them.

The majesty of the Judge, and the terrors
of the judgment, shall be spoken aloud by the
immediate forerunning accidents, which shall
be so great violences to the old constitutions
of nature, that it shall break her very bones,
and disorder her till she be destroyed. Saint
Jerome relates out of the Jews' books, that
their Doctors use to account fifteen days of
prodigy immediately before Christ's coming.

and to every day assign a wonder, any one
of which, if we should chance to see in the
days of our flesh, it would affright us into the
like thoughts which the old world had when
they saw the countries round about them covered with water and the divine vengeance ; or
as those poor people near Adria, and the Medi-
terranean Sea, when their houses and cities
are entering into graves, and the bowels of
the earth rent with convulsions and horrid
tremblings. The sea, they say, shall rise fifteen cubits above the highest mountains, and
thence descend into hollowness, and a prodigious drought ; and when they are reduced
again to their usual proportions, then all the
beasts and creeping things, the monsters and
the usual inhabitants of the sea, shall be gathered together, and make fearful noises to distract mankind. The birds shall mourn and
change their songs into threnes and sad accents. Rivers of fire shall rise from east to
west, and the stars shall be rent into threads
of light, and scatter like the beards of comets.
Then shall be fearful earthquakes, and the
rocks shall rend in pieces, the trees shall dis-
til blood, and the mountains and fairest struc-
tures shall return into their primitive dust.
The wild beasts shall leave their dens, and
come into the companies of men, so that you
shall hardly tell how to call them, herds of
4

men, or congregations of beasts. Then shall
the graves open and give up their dead ; and
those which are alive in nature and dead in
fear, shall be forced from the rocks whither
they went to hide them, and from caverns of
the earth, where they would fain have been
concealed ; because their retirements are dismantled, and their rocks are broken into wider
ruptures, and admit a strange light into their
secret bowels ; and the men being forced
abroad into the theatre of mighty horrors,
shall run up and down distracted and at their
wits' end ; and then some shall die, and some
shall be changed.

We may guess at the severity of the Judge
by the lesser strokes of that judgment, which
he is pleased to send upon sinners in this
world, to make them afraid of the horrible
pains of doomsday : I mean the torments of
an unquiet conscience, the amazement and
confusions of some sins and some persons.
For I have sometimes seen persons surprised
in a base action, and taken in the circumstances of a crafty theft, and secret injustices,
before their excuse was ready ; they have
changed their color, their speech hath fal-
tered, their tongue stammered, their eyes did
wander and fix nowhere, till shame made
them sink into their hollow eyepits, to retreat
from the images and circumstances of discov-

ery; their wits are lost, their reason useless,
the whole order of the soul is discomposed,
and they neither see, nor feel, nor think, as
they used to do, but they are broken into
disorder by a stroke of damnation and a lesser
stripe of hell. But then if you come to observe
a guilty and a base murderer, a condemned
traitor, and see him harassed first by an evil
conscience, and then pulled in pieces by the
hangman's hooks, or broken upon sorrows and
the wheel, we may then guess (as well as we
can in this life) what the pains of that day
shall be to accursed souls. But those we
shall consider afterwards in their proper scene;
now only we are to estimate the severity of
our Judge by the intolerableness of an evil
conscience. If guilt will make a man despair,
and despair will make a man mad, confounded
and dissolved in all the regions of his senses
and more noble faculties, that he shall neither
feel, nor hear, nor see anything but spectres
and illusions, devils and frightful dreams, and
hear noises, and shriek fearfully, and look pale
and distracted, like a hopeless man from the
horrors and confusions of a lost battle upon
which all his hopes did stand, then the wicked
must at the day of judgment expect strange
things and fearful, and such now which no
language can express, and then no patience
can endure.

The Lord shall judge concerning those judgments which men here make of things below;
and the fighting men shall perceive the noise
of drunkards and fools, that cried him up for
daring to kill his brother, to have been evil
principles; and then it will be declared by
strange effects, that wealth is not the greatest
fortune; and ambition was but an ill counsellor; and to lie for a good cause was no piety;
and to do evil for the glory of God was but an
ill worshipping him; and that good-nature was
not well employed, when it spent itself in vicious company and evil compliances; and that
piety was not softness and want of courage;
and that poverty ought not to have been contemptible; and the cause that is unsuccessful is
not therefore evil; and what is folly here shall
be wisdom there. Then shall men curse their
evil guides, and their accursed superinduced
necessities, and the evil guises of the world;
and then when silence shall be found innocence, and eloquence in many instances condemned as criminal; when the poor shall reign,
and generals and tyrants shall lie low in horrible regions; when he that lost all shall find
a treasure, and he that spoiled him shall be
found naked and spoiled by the destroyer;
then we shall find it true that we ought here
to have done what our Judge, our blessed
Lord, shall do there; that is, take our meas-

ures of good and evil by the severities of the
word of God, by the sermons of Christ, and
the four Gospels, and by the Epistles of St.
Paul, by justice and charity, by the laws of
God and the laws of wise princes and republics, by the rules of nature and the just proportions of reason, by the examples of good
men and the proverbs of wise men, by severity and the rules of discipline; for then it
shall be, that truth shall ride in triumph, and
the holiness of Christ's sermons shall be manifest to all the world; that the word of God
shall be advanced over all the discourse of
men, and "wisdom shall be justified by all
her children."

The devil shall accuse "the brethren," that
is, the saints and servants of God, and shall tell
concerning their follies and infirmities, the sins
of their youth and the weakness of their age,
the imperfect grace and the long schedule
of omissions of duty, their scruples and their
fears, their diffidences and pusillanimity, and
all those things which themselves by strict examination find themselves guilty of and have
confessed, all their shame and the matter of
their sorrows, their evil intentions and their
little plots, their carnal confidences and too
fond adherences to the things of this world,
their indulgence and easiness of government,
their wilder joys and freer meals, their loss of

time and their too forward and apt compliances,
their trifling arrests and little peevishnesses,
the mixtures of the world with the things of
the spirit, and all the incidences of humanity
he will bring forth, and aggravate them by the
circumstance of ingratitude, and the breach of
promise, and the evacuating of their holy purposes, and breaking their resolutions, and rifling
their vows.   And all these things being drawn
into an entire representment, and the bills clogged by numbers, will make the best men in the
world seem foul and unhandsome, and stained
with the characters of death and evil dishonor.
But for these there is appointed a defender ;
the Holy Spirit, that maketh intercession for
us, shall then also interpose, and against all
these things shall oppose the passion of our
blessed Lord, and upon all their defects shall
cast " the robe of his righteousness " ; and the
sins of their youth shall not prevail so much as
the repentance of their age ; and their omissions
be excused by probable intervening causes ;
and their little escapes shall appear single and
in disunion, because they were always kept
asunder by penitential prayers and sighings,
and their seldom returns of sin by their daily
watchfulness, and their often infirmities by the
sincerity of their souls, and their scruples by
their zeal, and their passions by their love, and
all by the mercies of God and the sacrifice

which their Judge offered, and the Holy Spirit made effective by daily graces and assistances.

PRAYER.

I KNOW not which is the greater wonder, either that prayer, which is a duty so easy and facile, so ready and adapted to the powers and skill and opportunities of every man, should have so great effects, and be productive of such mighty blessings ; or, that we should be so unwilling to use so easy an instrument of procuring so much good. The first declares God's goodness, but this publishes man's folly and weakness, who finds in himself so much difficulty to perform a condition so easy and full of advantage. But the order of this felicity is knotted like the foldings of a serpent ; all those parts of easiness which invite us to do the duty are become like the joints of a bulrush, not bendings, but consolidations and stiffenings ; the very facility becomes its objection, and in every of its stages we make or find a huge uneasiness. At first we do not know what to ask ; and when we do, then we find difficulty to bring our will to desire it ; and when that is instructed and kept in awe, it mingles interest, and confounds the purposes ; and when it is forced to ask honestly and severely, then it wills so coldly, that God hates the prayer; and if it desires fervently, it sometimes turns that into passion, and that passion breaks into murmurs or unquietness; or if that be avoided, the indifferency cools into death, or the fire burns violently and is quickly spent; our desires are dull as a rock, or fugitive as lightning: either we ask ill things earnestly, or good things remissly; we either court our own danger, or are not zealous for our real safety; or if we be right in our matter, or earnest in our affections, and lasting in our abode, yet we miss in the manner; and either we ask for evil ends, or without religious and awful apprehensions; or we rest in the words and signification of the prayer, and never take care to pass on to action; or else we sacrifice in the company of Corah, being partners of a schism, or a rebellion in religion; or we bring unhallowed censers, our hearts send up to God an unholy smoke, a cloud from the fires of lust, and either the flames of lust or rage, of wine or revenge, kindle the beast that is laid upon the altar; or we bring swine's flesh, or a dog's neck; whereas God never accepts, or delights in a prayer, unless it be for a holy thing, to a lawful end, presented unto him upon the wings of zeal and love, of religious sorrow, or religious joy, by sanctified lips, and pure hands, and a sincere heart. It must be the prayer of a gracious man; and he is only gracious before God, and acceptable, and effective in his prayer, whose life is holy, and whose prayer is holy; for both these are necessary ingredients to the constitution of a prevailing prayer; there is a holiness peculiar to the man, and a holiness peculiar to the prayer, that must adorn the prayer before it can be united to the intercession of the holy Jesus, in which union alone our prayers can be prevailing.

Lust and uncleanness are a direct enemy to the praying man, an obstruction to his prayers; for this is not only a profanation, but a direct sacrilege; it defiles a temple to the ground; it takes from a man all affection to spiritual things, and mingles his very soul with the things of the world; it makes his understanding low, and his reasonings cheap and foolish, and it destroys his confidence, and all his manly hopes; it makes his spirit light, effeminate, and fantastic, and dissolves his attention; and makes his mind so to disaffect all the objects of his desires, that when he prays he is as uneasy as an impaled person, or a condemned criminal upon the hook or wheel; and it hath in it this evil quality, that a lustful person cannot pray heartily against his sin; he cannot desire his cure, for his will is contradictory to his collect, and he would not that God should hear the words of his prayer, which he, poor man, never intended. For no crime so seizes upon the will as that ; some sins steal an affection, or obey a temptation, or secure an interest, or work by the way of understanding, but lust seizes directly upon the will, for the devil knows well that the lusts of the body. are soon cured ; the uneasiness that dwells there is a disease very tolerable, and every degree of patience can pass under it. But therefore the devil seizes upon the will, and that is it that makes adulteries and all the species of uncleanness; and lust grows so hard a cure, because the formality of it is, that it will not be cured ; the will loves it, and, so long as it does, God cannot love the man ; for God is the prince of purities, and the Son of God is the king of virgins, and the Holy Spirit is all love, and that is all purity, and all spirituality : and therefore the prayer of an adulterer, or an unclean person, is like the sacrifices to Moloch, or the rites of Flora, *" ubi Cato spectator esse non potuit."* A good man will not endure them ; much less will God entertain such reekings of the Dead Sea and clouds of Sodom. For so an impure vapor, begotten of the slime of the earth by the fevers and adulterous heats of an intemperate summer-sun, striving by the ladder of a mountain to climb up to heaven, and rolling into various figures by an uneasy, unfixed revolution, and

stopped at the middle region of the air, being
thrown from his pride and attempt of passing
towards the seat of the stars, turns into an unwholesome flame, and, like the breath of hell, is
confined into a prison of darkness, and a cloud,
till it breaks into diseases, plagues, and mil-
dews, stink and blastings : so is the prayer of
an unchaste person ; it strives to climb the battlements of heaven, but because it is a flame of
sulphur, salt, and bitumen, and was kindled in
the dishonorable regions below, derived from
hell, and contrary to God, it cannot pass forth
to the element of love, but ends in barrenness
and murmur, fantastic expectations, and trifling
imaginative confidences ; and they at last end
in sorrows and despair. Every state of sin is
against the possibility of a man's being accepted ; but these have a proper venom against
the graciousness of the person, and the power
of the prayer. God can never accept an unholy prayer, and a wicked man can never send
forth any other ; the waters pass through impure aqueducts and channels of brimstone, and
therefore may end in brimstone and fire, but
never in forgiveness and the blessings of an
eternal charity.

Henceforth, therefore, never any more wonder that men pray so seldom ; there are few
that feel the relish, and are enticed with the
deliciousness, and refreshed with the comforts,

and instructed with the sanctity, and acquainted with the secrets of a holy prayer : but cease also to wonder, that of those few that say many prayers, so few find any return of any at all. To make up a good and a lawful prayer, there must be charity, with all its daughters, alms, forgiveness, not judging, uncharitably ; there must be purity of spirit, that is, purity of intention ; and there must be purity of the body and soul, that is, the cleanness of chastity ; and there must be no vice remaining, no affection to sin : for he that brings his body to God, and hath left his will in the power of any sin, offers to God the calves of his lips, but not a whole burnt-offering ; a lame oblation, but not a " reasonable sacrifice "; and therefore their portion shall be amongst them whose prayers were never recorded in the book of life, whose tears God never put into his bottle, whose desires shall remain ineffectual to eternal ages.

Plutarch reports, that the Tyrians tied their gods with chains, because certain persons did dream that Apollo said he would leave their city and go to the party of Alexander, who then besieged the town : and Apollodorus tells of some, that tied the image of Saturn with bands of wool upon his feet. So some Christians ; they think God is tied to their sect, and bound to be of their side, and the interest of their opinion ; and they think, he can never go

to the enemy's party, so long as they charm
him with certain forms of words or disguises of
their own; and then all the success they have,
and all the evils that are prosperous, all the
mischiefs they do, and all the ambitious designs
that do succeed, they reckon upon the account
of their prayers; and well they may: for their
prayers are sins, and their desires are evil;
they wish mischief, and they act iniquity, and
they enjoy their sin: and if this be a blessing
or a cursing, themselves shall then judge, and
all the world shall perceive, when the accounts
of all the world are truly stated; then, when
prosperity shall be called to accounts, and ad-
versity shall receive its comforts, when virtue
shall have a crown, and the satisfaction of all
sinful desires shall be recompensed with an intolerable sorrow, and the despair of a perishing
soul. Nero's mother prayed passionately, that
her son might be emperor; and many persons,
of whom St. James speaks, "pray to spend upon
their lusts," and they are heard too: some
were not, and very many are: and some, that
fight against a just possessor of a country, pray,
that their wars may be prosperous; and sometimes they have been heard too: and Julian
the Apostate prayed, and sacrificed, and inquired of demons, and burned man's flesh, and
operated with secret rites, and all that he
might craftily and powerfully oppose the relig-

ion of Christ; and he was heard too, and did mischief beyond the malice and the effect of his predecessors, that did swim in Christian blood. But when we sum up the accounts at the foot of their lives, or so soon as the thing was understood, we find that the effect of Agrippina's prayer was, that her son murdered her; and of those lustful petitioners, in St. James, that they were given over to the tyranny and possession of their passions and baser appetites; and the effect of Julian the Apostate's prayer was, that he lived and died a professed enemy of Christ; and the effect of the prayers of usurpers is, that they do mischief, and reap curses, and undo mankind, and provoke God, and live hated, and die miserable, and shall possess the fruit of their sin to eternal ages.

The first thing that hinders the prayer of a good man from obtaining its effects is a violent anger, and a violent storm in the spirit of him that prays. For anger sets the house on fire, and all the spirits are busy upon trouble, and intend propulsion, defence, displeasure, or revenge; it is a short madness, and an eternal enemy to discourse, and sober counsels, and fair conversation; it intends its own object with all the earnestness of perception, or activity of design, and a quicker motion of a too warm and distempered blood; it is a fever in the

heart, and a calenture in the head, and a fire
in the face, and a sword in the hand, and a
fury all over ; and therefore can never suffer a
man to be in a disposition to pray. For prayer
is an action, and a state of intercourse and
desire, exactly contrary to this character of
anger. Prayer is an action of likeness to the
Holy Ghost, the spirit of gentleness and dove-
like simplicity ; an imitation of the holy Jesus,
whose spirit is meek, up to the greatness of
the biggest example ; and a conformity to God,
whose anger is always just, and marches
slowly, and is without transportation, and often
hindered, and never hasty, and is full of mercy :
prayer is the peace of our spirit, the stillness
of our thoughts, the evenness of recollection,
the seat of meditation, the rest of our cares,
and the calm of our tempest ; prayer is the
issue of a quiet mind, of untroubled thoughts ;
it is the daughter of charity, and the sister of
meekness ; and he that prays to God with an
angry, that is, with a troubled and discomposed
spirit, is like him that retires into a battle to
meditate, and sets up his closet in the out-
quarters of an army, and chooses a frontier-
garrison to be wise in. Anger is a perfect
alienation of the mind from prayer, and therefore is contrary to that attention which pre-
sents our prayers in a right line to God. For
so have I seen a lark rising from his bed of

grass, and soaring upwards, singing as he rises, and hopes to get to heaven, and climb above the clouds; but the poor bird was beaten back with the loud sighings of an eastern wind, and his motion made irregular and inconstant, descending more at every breath of the tempest than it could recover by the libration and frequent weighing of his wings; till the little creature was forced to sit down and pant, and stay till the storm was over; and then it made a prosperous flight, and did rise and sing, as if it had learned music and motion from an angel, as he passed sometimes through the air about his ministries here below. So is the prayer of a good man; when his affairs have required business, and his business was matter of discipline, and his discipline was to pass upon a sinning person, or had a design of charity, his duty met with the infirmities of a man, and anger was its instrument, and the instrument became stronger than the prime agent, and raised a tempest, and overruled the man; and then his prayer was broken, and his thoughts were troubled, and his words went up towards a cloud, and his thoughts pulled them back again and made them without intention; and the good man sighs for his infirmity, but must be content to lose the prayer, and he must recover it when his anger is removed, and his spirit is becalmed, made even as the brow of

Jesus, and smooth like the heart of God; and then it ascends to heaven upon the wings of the holy dove, and dwells with God, till it returns, like the useful bee, laden with a blessing and the dew of heaven.

But, then, for spiritual things, for the interest of our souls, and the affairs of the kingdom, we pray to God with just such a zeal as a man begs of a surgeon to cut him of the stone, or a condemned man desires his executioner quickly to put him out of his pain, by taking away his life; when things are come to that pass, it must be done, but God knows with what little complacency and desire the man makes his request. And yet the things of religion and the spirit are the only things that ought to be desired vehemently, and pursued passionately, because God hath set such a value upon them, that they are the effects of his greatest loving-kindness; they are the purchases of Christ's blood, and the effect of his continual intercession; the fruits of his bloody sacrifice, and the gifts of his healing and saving mercy; the graces of God's spirit, and the only instruments of felicity; and if we can have fondness for things indifferent or dangerous, our prayers upbraid our spirits when we beg coldly and tamely for those things for which we ought to die, which are more precious than the globes of kings, and weightier than imperial sceptres, richer than the spoils of the sea, or the treasures of the Indian hills.

He that is cold and tame in his prayers, hath not tasted of the deliciousness of religion and the goodness of God; he is a stranger to the secrets of the kingdom, and therefore he does not know what it is either to have hunger or satiety; and therefore neither are they hungry for God nor satisfied with the world, but remain stupid and inapprehensive, without resolution and determination, never choosing clearly, nor pursuing earnestly; and therefore never enter into possession, but always stand at the gate of weariness, unnecessary caution, and perpetual irresolution. But so it is too often in our prayers; we come to God because it is civil so to do and a general custom, but neither drawn thither by love, nor pinched by spiritual necessities, and pungent apprehensions: we say so many prayers, because we are resolved so to do, and we pass through them, sometimes with a little attention, sometimes with none at all; and can we think that the grace of chastity can be obtained at such a purchase, that grace that hath cost more labors than all the persecutions of faith, and all the disputes of hope, and all the expense of charity besides, amounts to? Can we expect that our sins should be washed by a lazy prayer?

Though your person be as gracious as David

or Job, and your desire as holy as the love of
angels, and your necessities great as a new
penitent, yet it pierces not the clouds, unless
it be also as loud as thunder, passionate as the
cries of women, and clamorous as necessity.
For every prayer we make is considered by
God, and recorded in heaven ; but cold prayers
are not put into the account in order to effect
an acceptation, but are laid aside like the buds
of roses which a cold wind hath nipped into
death, and the discolored tawny face of an
Indian slave : and when, in order to your hopes
of obtaining a great blessing, you reckon up
your prayers with which you have solicited
your suit in the court of heaven, you must
reckon, not by the number of the collects, but
by your sighs and passions, by the vehemence
of your desires and the fervor of your spirit,
the apprehension of your need and the consequent prosecution of your supply. Christ
prayed " with loud cryings," and St. Paul
made mention of his scholars in his prayers
" night and day." Fall upon your knees and
grow there, and let not your desires cool nor
your zeal remit, but renew it again and again ;
and let not your offices and the custom of praying put thee in mind of thy need, but let thy
need draw thee to thy holy offices ; and remember how great a God, how glorious a Majesty
you speak to ; therefore let not your devotions

and addresses be little. Remember how great a need thou hast; let not your desires be less. Remember how great the thing is you pray for; do not undervalue it with any indifferency. Remember that prayer is an act of religion; let it, therefore, be made thy business: and, lastly, remember that God hates a cold prayer, and, therefore, will never bless it, but it shall be always ineffectual.

No prayers can prevail upon an indisposed person. For the sun himself cannot enlighten a blind eye, nor the soul move a body whose silver cord is loosed, and whose joints are untied by the rudeness and dissolutions of a pertinacious sickness. But then, suppose an eye quick and healthful, or apt to be refreshed with light and a friendly prospect; yet a glow-worm or a diamond, the shells of pearl, or a dead man's candle, are not enough to make him discern the beauties of the world, and to admire the glories of creation.

A man of an ordinary piety is like Gideon's fleece, wet in its own locks, but it could not water a poor man's garden. But so does a thirsty land drink all the dew of heaven that wets its face, and a greater shower makes no torrent, nor digs so much as a little furrow, that the drills of the water might pass into rivers, or refresh their neighbor's weariness: but when the earth is full, and hath no strange

consumptive needs, then at the next time when
God blesses it with a gracious shower, it divides
into portions, and sends it abroad in free and
equal communications, that all that stand round
about may feel the shower. So is a good
man's prayer; his own cup is full, it is crowned
with health, and overflows with blessings, and
all that drink of his cup and eat at his table
are refreshed with his joys, and divide with him
in his holy portions.

The world itself is established and kept from
dissolution by the prayers of saints; and the
prayers of saints shall hasten the day of judgment; and we cannot easily find two effects
greater. But there are many other very great
ones; for the prayers of holy men appease
God's wrath, drive away temptations, and resist
and overcome the devil: holy prayer procures
the ministry and service of angels, it rescinds
the decrees of God, it cures sicknesses and
obtains pardon, it arrests the sun in its course,
and stays the wheels of the chariot of the
moon; it rules over all God's creatures, and
opens and shuts the storehouses of rain; it
unlocks the cabinet of the womb, and quenches
the violence of fire; it stops the mouths of
lions, and reconciles our sufferance and weak
faculties with the violence of torment and
sharpness of persecution; it pleases God and
supplies all our needs.

Prayer can obtain everything; it can open the windows of heaven, and shut the gates of hell; it can put a holy constraint upon God, and detain an angel till he leave a blessing; it can open the treasures of rain, and soften the iron ribs of rocks, till they melt into tears and a flowing river; prayer can unclasp the girdles of the north, saying to a mountain of ice, Be thou removed hence, and cast into the bottom of the sea; it can arrest the sun in the midst of his course, and send the swift-winged winds upon our errand; and all those strange things, and secret decrees, and unrevealed transactions, which are above the clouds and far beyond the regions of the stars, shall combine in ministry and advantages for the praying man.

PARDON OF SIN.

IF we consider upon how trifling and inconsiderable grounds most men hope for pardon, (if at least that may be called hope, which is nothing but a careless boldness, and an unreasonable wilful confidence,) we shall see much cause to pity very many who are going merrily to a sad and intolerable death. Pardon of sins is a mercy which Christ purchased with his dearest blood, which he ministers to us upon

conditions of an infinite kindness, but yet of
great holiness and obedience, and an active
living faith. It is a grace, that the most holy
persons beg of God with mighty passion, and
labor for with a great diligence, and expect
with trembling fears, and concerning it many
times suffer sadnesses with uncertain souls, and
receive it by degrees, and it enters upon them
by little portions, and it is broken as their sighs
and sleeps. But so have I seen the returning
sea enter upon the strand; and the waters rolling towards the shore, throw up little portions
of the tide, and retire as if nature meant to
play, and not to change the abode of waters;
but still the flood crept by little steppings, and
invaded more by his progressions than he lost
by his retreat; and having told the number of
its steps, it possesses its new portion till the
angel calls it back, that it may leave its un-
faithful dwelling of the sand. So is the pardon
of our sin; it comes by slow motions, and first
quits a present death, and turns, it may be,
into a sharp sickness; and if that sickness prove
not health to the soul, it washes off, and it may
be will dash against the rock again, and proceed to take off the several instances of anger
and the periods of wrath; but all this while
it is uncertain concerning our final interest,
whether it be ebb or flood; and every hearty
prayer and every bountiful alms still enlarges

the pardon, or adds a degree of probability and hope ; and then a drunken meeting, or a covetous desire, or an act of lust, or looser swearing, idle talk, or neglect of religion, makes the pardon retire ; and while it is disputed between Christ and Christ's enemy, who shall be Lord, the pardon fluctuates like the wave, striving to climb the rock, and is washed off like its own retinue, and it gets possession by time and uncertainty, by difficulty and the degrees of a hard progression.

GODLY FEAR.

FEAR is the great bridle of intemperance, the modesty of the spirit, and the restraint of gayeties and dissolutions ; it is the girdle to the soul, and the handmaid to repentance, the arrest of sin, and the cure or antidote to the spirit of reprobation ; it preserves our apprehensions of the divine majesty, and hinders our single actions from combining to sinful habits ; it is the mother of consideration, and the nurse of sober counsels ; and it puts the soul to fermentation and activity, making it to pass from trembling to caution, from caution to carefulness, from carefulness to watchfulness, from thence to prudence ; and by the gates and progresses of repentance, it leads the soul on to

love, and to felicity, and to joys in God that
shall never cease again. Fear is the guard of
a man in the days of prosperity, and it stands
upon the watch-towers, and spies the approaching danger, and gives warning to them that
laugh loud, and feast in the chambers of rejoicing, where a man cannot consider by reason
of the noises of wine and jest and music : and
if prudence takes it by the hand, and leads it
on to duty, it is a state of grace, and a universal instrument to infant religion, and the
only security of the less perfect persons ; and
in all senses is that homage we owe to God,
who sends often to demand it, even then when
he speaks in thunder, or smites by a plague, or
awakens us by threatenings, or discomposes our
easiness by sad thoughts, and tender eyes, and
fearful hearts, and trembling considerations.

But this so excellent grace is soon abused in
the best and most tender spirits ; in those who
are softened by nature and by religion, by infelicities or cares, by sudden accidents or a sad
soul ; and the devil, observing that fear, like spare
diet, starves the fevers of lust and quenches
the flames of hell, endeavors to heighten this
abstinence so much as to starve the man, and
break the spirit into timorousness and scruple,
sadness and unreasonable tremblings, credulity
and trifling observation, suspicion and false
accusations of God ; and then vice being turned

out at the gate, returns in at the postern, and
does the work of hell and death by running
too inconsiderately in the paths which seem to
lead to heaven. But so have I seen a harmless dove, made dark with an artificial night,
and her eyes sealed and locked up with a little
quill, soaring upward and flying with amazement, fear, and an undiscerning wing; she
made towards heaven, but knew not that she
was made a train and an instrument to teach
her enemy to prevail upon her and all her defenceless kindred. So is a superstitious man,
zealous and blind, forward and mistaken; he
runs towards heaven, as he thinks, but he
chooses foolish paths, and out of fear takes anything that he is told; or fancies and guesses
concerning God by measures taken from his
own diseases and imperfections. But fear,
when it is inordinate, is never a good counsellor, nor makes a good friend; and he that fears
God as his enemy, is the most completely miserable person in the world. For if he with
reason believes God to be his enemy, then the
man needs no other argument to prove that he
is undone than this, that the fountain of blessing (in this state in which the man is) will
never issue anything upon him but cursings.
But if he fears this without reason, he makes
his fears true by the very suspicion of God,
doing him dishonor, and then doing those fond

and trifling acts of jealousy which will make God to be what the man feared he already was. We do not know God, if we can think any hard thing concerning him. If God be merciful, let us only fear to offend him; but then let us never be fearful that he will destroy us, when we are careful not to displease him. There are some persons so miserable and scrupulous, such perpetual tormentors of themselves with unnecessary fears, that their meat and drink is a snare to their consciences; if they eat, they fear they are gluttons; if they fast, they fear they are hypocrites; and if they would watch, they complain of sleep as of a deadly sin; and every temptation, though resisted, makes them cry for pardon; and every return of such an accident makes them think God is angry; and every anger of God will break them in pieces.

These persons do not believe noble things concerning God; they do not think that he is as ready to pardon them as they are to pardon a sinning servant; they do not believe how much God delights in mercy, nor how wise he is to consider and to make abatement for our unavoidable infirmities; they make judgment of themselves by the measures of an angel, and take the account of God by the proportions of a tyrant. The best that can be said concerning such persons is, that they are hugely tempted, or hugely ignorant. For although ignorance is by some persons named the mother of devotion, yet, if it falls in a hard ground, it is the mother of atheism ; if in a soft ground, it is the parent of superstition ; but if it proceeds from evil or mean opinions of God, (as such scruples and unreasonable fears do many times,) it is an evil of a great impiety, and, in some sense, if it were in equal degrees, is as bad as atheism : for so he that says there was no such man as Julius Cæsar does him less displeasure than he that says there was, but that he was a tyrant and a bloody parricide. And the Cimmerians were not esteemed impious for saying that there was no sun in the heavens ; but Anaxagoras was esteemed irreligious for saying the sun was a very stone : and though to deny there is a God is a high impiety and intolerable, yet he says worse who, believing there is a God, says he delights in human sacrifices, in miseries and death, in tormenting his servants, and punishing their very infelicities and unavoidable mischances. To be God, and to be essentially and infinitely good, is the same thing ; and therefore to deny either is to be reckoned among the greatest crimes in the world.

Let the grounds of our actions be noble, beginning upon reason, proceeding with prudence, measured by the common lines of men, and confident upon the expectation of a usual

providence. Let us proceed from causes to
effects, from natural means to ordinary events,
and believe felicity not to be a chance but a
choice ; and evil to be the daughter of sin and
the divine anger, not of fortune and fancy. Let
us fear God when we have made him angry,
and not be afraid of him when we heartily and
laboriously do our duty. Our fears are to be
measured by open revelation and certain experience, by the threatenings of God and the sayings of wise men, and their limit is reverence,
and godliness is their end ; and then fear shall
be a duty, and a rare instrument of many. In
all other cases it is superstition or folly, it is
sin or punishment, the ivy of religion, and the
misery of an honest and a weak heart ; and is
to be cured only by reason and good company,
a wise guide and a plain rule, a cheerful spirit
and a contented mind, by joy in God according
to the commandments, that is, " a rejoicing
evermore."

The illusions of a weak piety, or an unskilful
confident soul, fancy to see mountains of difficulty ; but touch them, and they seem like
clouds riding upon the wings of the wind, and
put on shapes as we please to dream. He that
denies to give alms for fear of being poor, or to
entertain a disciple for fear of being suspected
of the party, or to own a duty for fear of being
put to venture for a crown ; he that takes part

of the intemperance because he dares not displease the company, or in any sense fears the fears of the world and not the fear of God,— this man enters into his portion of fear betimes, but it will not be finished to eternal ages.　To fear the censures of men, when God is your judge; to fear their evil, when God is your defence; to fear death, when he is the entrance to life and felicity, is unreasonable and pernicious.　But if you will turn your passion into duty and joy and security, fear to offend God, to enter voluntarily into temptation; fear the alluring face of lust, and the smooth entertainments of intemperance; fear the anger of God, when you have deserved it; and, when you have recovered from the snare, then infinitely fear to return into that condition, in which whosoever dwells is the heir of fear and eternal sorrow.

HUMAN WEAKNESS.

THERE is nothing that creeps upon the earth, nothing that ever God made, weaker than man.　For God fitted horses and mules with strength, bees and pismires with sagacity, harts and hares with swiftness, birds with feathers and a light airy body; and they all know their times, and are fitted for their

work, and regularly acquire the proper end
of their creation. But man, that was designed to an immortal duration, and the fruition of God forever, knows not how to obtain it; he is made upright to look up to
heaven, but he knows no more how to purchase it than to climb it. Once, man went
to make an ambitious tower to outreach the
clouds, or the preternatural risings of the
water, but could not do it; he cannot promise himself the daily bread of his necessity
upon the stock of his own wit or industry;
and for going to heaven, he was so far from
doing that naturally, that as soon as ever he
was made, he became the son of death, and he
knew not how to get a pardon for eating of
an apple against the divine commandment.

—✦—

FAITH.

FAITH is a certain image of eternity; all
things are present to it; things past and
things to come are all so before the eyes of
faith, that he in whose eye that candle is enkindled beholds heaven as present, and sees
how blessed a thing it is to die in God's favor,
and to be chimed to our grave with the music
of a good conscience. Faith converses with

the angels, and antedates the hymns of glory; every man that hath this grace is as certain that there are glories for him, if he perseveres in duty, as if he had heard and sung the thanksgiving-song for the blessed sentence of doomsday. And therefore it is no matter if these things are separate and distant objects; none but children and fools are taken with the present trifle, and neglect a distant blessing of which they have credible and believed notices. Did the merchant see the pearls and the wealth he designed to get in the trade of twenty years? And is it possible that a child should, when he learns the first rudiments of grammar, know what excellent things there are in learning, whither he designs his labor and his hopes? We labor for that which is uncertain and distant and believed, and hoped for with many allays, and seen with diminution, and a troubled ray; and what excuse can there be that we do not labor for that which is told us by God, and preached by his only Son, and confirmed by miracles, and which Christ himself died to purchase, and millions of martyrs died to witness, and which we see good men and wise believe with an assent stronger than their evidence, and which they do believe because they do love, and love because they do believe? There is nothing to be said, but that faith which did enlighten the blind, and cleanse the lepers, and

washed the soul of the Ethiopian ; that faith
that cures the sick, and strengthens the paralytic, and baptizes the catechumens, and justi-
fies the faithful, and repairs the penitent, and
confirms the just, and crowns the martyrs ;
that faith, if it be true and proper, Christian
and alive, active and effective in us, is sufficient to appease the storm of our passions, and
to instruct all our ignorances, and to " make us
wise unto salvation."

LUKEWARMNESS AND ZEAL.

A S our duty must be whole, so it must be
fervent ; for a languishing body may have
all its parts, and yet be useless to many purposes of nature : and you may reckon all the
joints of a dead man, but the heart is cold, and
the joints are stiff, and fit for nothing but for
the little people that creep in graves.   And so
are very many men ; if you sum up the accounts of their religion, they can reckon days
and months of religion, various offices, charity
and prayers, reading and meditation, faith and
knowledge, catechism and sacraments, duty to
God and duty to princes, paying debts and provision for children, confessions and tears, discipline in families, and love of good people ; and

6

it may be, you shall not reprove their numbers,
or find any lines unfilled in their tables of
accounts. But when you have handled all
this, and considered, you will find at last you
have taken a dead man by the hand ; there is
not a finger wanting, but they are stiff as
icicles, and without flexure, as the legs of
elephants.

I have seen a fair structure begun with art
and care, and raised to half its stature, and
then it stood still by the misfortune or negligence of the owner ; and the rain descended,
and dwelt in its joints, and supplanted the con-
texture of its pillars ; and having stood a while
like the antiquated temple of a deceased ora-
cle, it fell into a hasty age, and sunk upon its
own knees, and so descended into ruin. So is
the imperfect, unfinished spirit of a man ; it
lays the foundation of a holy resolution, and
strengthens it with vows and arts of prosecution ; it raises up the walls, sacraments, and
prayers, reading, and holy ordinances ; and
holy actions begin with a slow motion, and the
building stays, and the spirit is weary, and the
soul is naked, and exposed to temptations, and
in the days of storm takes in everything that
can do it mischief ; and it is faint and sick, list-
less and tired, and it stands till its own weight
wearies the foundation, and then declines to
death and sad disorder.

However it be very easy to have our thoughts wander, yet it is our indifferency and lukewarmness that makes it so natural : and you may observe it, that so long as the light shines bright, and the fires of devotion and desires flame out, so long the mind of a man stands close to the altar, and waits upon the sacrifice : but as the fires die and desires decay, so the mind steals away, and walks abroad to see the little images of beauty and pleasure, which it beholds in the falling stars and little glow-worms of the world. The river that runs slow and creeps by the banks, and begs leave of every turf to let it pass, is drawn into little hollownesses, and spends itself in smaller portions, and dies with diversion ; but when it runs with vigorousness and a full stream, and breaks down every obstacle, making it even as its own brow, it stays not to be tempted by little avocations, and to creep into holes, but runs into the sea through full and useful channels. So is a man's prayer ; if it moves upon the feet of an abated appetite, it wanders into the society of every trifling accident, and stays at the corners of the fancy, and talks with every object it meets, and cannot arrive at heaven ; but when it is carried upon the wings of passion and strong desires, a swift motion and a hungry appetite, it passes on through all the intermedial regions of clouds, and stays not till it dwells at the foot of the throne, where mercy sits, and thence sends holy showers of refreshment. I deny not but some little drops will turn aside, and fall from the full channel by the weakness of the banks, and hollowness of the passage ; but the main course is still continued : and although the most earnest and devout persons feel and complain of some looseness of spirit, and unfixed attentions, yet their love and their desire secure the main portions, and make the prayer to be strong, fervent, and effectual.

He that is warm to-day and cold to-morrow, zealous in his resolution and weary in his practices, fierce in the beginning and slack and easy in his progress, hath not yet well chosen what side he will be of; he sees not reason enough for religion, and he hath not confidence enough for its contrary ; and therefore he is, as St. James calls him, " of a doubtful mind." For religion is worth as much to-day as it was yesterday, and that cannot change though we do ; and if we do, we have left God ; and whither he can go that goes from God, his own sorrows will soon enough instruct him. This fire must never go out, but it must be like the fire of heaven, it must shine like the stars ; though sometimes covered with a cloud, or obscured by a greater light, yet they dwell forever in their orbs, and walk in their circles, and observe their circumstances, but go not out by

day nor night, and set not when kings die, nor
are extinguished when nations change their
government. So must the zeal of a Christian
be a constant incentive of his duty ; and though
sometimes his hand is drawn back by violence
or need, and his prayers shortened by the importunity of business, and some parts omitted
by necessities and just compliances, yet still the
fire is kept alive, it burns within when the light
breaks not forth, and is eternal as the orb of
fire, or the embers of the altar of incense.

In every action of religion God expects such
a warmth, and a holy fire to go along, that it
may be able to enkindle the wood upon the
altar, and consume the sacrifice ; but God hates
an indifferent spirit. Earnestness and vivacity,
quickness and delight, perfect choice of the
service and a delight in the prosecution, is all
that the spirit of a man can yield towards his
religion : the outward work is the effect of the
body ; but if a man does it heartily and with all
his mind, then religion hath wings and moves
upon wheels of fire.

The zeal of the Apostles was this : they
preached publicly and privately, they prayed
for all men, they wept to God for the hardness
of men's hearts, they " became all things to all
men, that they might gain some," they travelled through deeps and deserts, they endured
the heat of the Syrian star and the violence of

Euroclydon, winds and tempests, seas and pris-
ons, mockings and scourgings, fastings and
poverty, labor and watching; they endured
every man and wronged no man; they would
do any good thing and suffer any evil, if they
had but hopes to prevail upon a soul; they
persuaded men meekly, they entreated them
humbly, they convinced them powerfully; they
watched for their good, but meddled not with
their interest: and this is the Christian zeal,
the zeal of meekness, the zeal of charity, the
zeal of patience.

The Jews tell that Adam, having seen the
beauties and tasted the delicacies of paradise,
repented and mourned upon the Indian mountains for three hundred years together: and we,
who have a great share in the cause of his sorrows, can by nothing be invited to a persever-
ing, a great, a passionate religion, more than
by remembering what he lost, and what is laid
up for them whose hearts are burning lamps,
and are all on fire with divine love, whose
flames are fanned with the wings of the holy
dove, and whose spirits shine and burn with
that fire which the holy Jesus came to enkindle upon the earth.

THE EPICURE'S FEAST.

LET us eat and drink; for to-morrow we die." This is the epicure's proverb, begun upon a weak mistake, started by chance from the discourses of drink, and thought witty by the undiscerning company, and prevailed infinitely, because it struck their fancy luckily, and maintained the merry-meeting; but, as it happens commonly to such discourses, so this also, when it comes to be examined by the consultations of the morning, and the sober hours of the day, it seems the most witless and the most unreasonable in the world. When Seneca describes the spare diet of Epicurus and Metrodorus, he uses this expression: " Liberaliora sunt alimenta carceris; sepositos ad capitale supplicium, non tam angustè, qui occisurus est, pascit," — The prison keeps a better table ; and he that is to kill the criminal to-morrow morning gives him a better supper over night. By this he intended to represent his meal to be very short; for as dying persons have but little stomach to feast high, so they that mean to cut their throat will think it a vain expense to please it with delicacies, which after the first alteration must be poured upon the ground, and looked upon as the worst part of the accursed thing. And there is also the same proportion of unreasonableness, that, because men shall die to-morrow, and by the sentence and unalterable decree of God they are now descending to their graves, that therefore they should first destroy their reason, and then force dull time to run faster, that they may die sottish as beasts, and speedily as a fly. But they thought there was no life after this; or if there were, it was without pleasure, and every soul thrust into a hole, and a dormitory of a span's length allowed for his rest, and for his walk; and in the shades below no numbering of healths by the numeral letters of Philenium's name, no fat mullets, no oysters of Lucrinus, no Lesbian or Chian wines. Therefore now enjoy the delicacies of nature, and feel the descending wines distilled through the limbeck of thy tongue and larynx, and suck the delicious juice of fishes, the marrow of the laborious ox, and the tender lard of Apulian swine, and the condited bellies of the scarus; but lose no time, for the sun drives hard, and the shadow is long, and the days of mourning are at hand, but the number of the days of darkness and the grave cannot be told.

Thus they thought they discoursed wisely, and their wisdom was turned into folly; for all their arts of providence, and witty securities of pleasure, were nothing but unmanly prologues to death, fear and folly, sensuality and

beastly pleasures. But they are to be excused
rather than we. They placed themselves in
the order of beasts and birds, and esteemed
their bodies nothing but receptacles of flesh
and wine, larders and pantries ; and their soul
the fine instrument of pleasure and brisk reception, of relishes and gusts, reflections and
duplications of delight ; and therefore they
treated themselves accordingly. But then why
we should do the same things, who are led by
other principles, and a more severe institution,
and better notices of immortality, who understand what shall happen to a soul hereafter,
and know that this time is but a passage to
eternity, this body but a servant to the soul,
this soul a minister to the spirit, and the whole
man in order to God and to felicity; this, I
say, is more unreasonable than to eat aconite
to preserve our health, and to enter into the
flood that we may die a dry death; this is a
perfect contradiction to the state of good
things, whither we are designed, and to all
the principles of a wise philosophy, whereby
we are instructed that we may become wise
unto salvation.

Plenty and the pleasures of the world are
no proper instruments of felicity. It is necessary that a man have some violence done to
himself before he can receive them : for nature's bounds are, " *non esurire, non sitire, non*

algere," to be quit from hunger and thirst and
cold, — that is, to have nothing upon us that
puts us to pain; against which she hath made
provisions by the fleece of the sheep and the
skins of the beasts, by the waters of the fountain and the herbs of the field; and of these
no good man is destitute, for that share that he
can need to fill those appetites and necessities
he cannot otherwise avoid. For it is unimaginable that nature should be a mother, natural
and indulgent to the beasts of the forest, and
the spawn of fishes, to every plant and fungus,
to cats and owls, to moles and bats, making
her storehouses always to stand open to them;
and that, for the Lord of all these, even to the
noblest of her productions, she should have
made no provisions, and only produced in us
appetites sharp as the stomach of wolves, troublesome as the tiger's hunger, and then run
away, leaving art and chance, violence and
study, to feed us and to clothe us. This is so
far from truth, that we are certainly more provided for by nature than all the world besides;
for everything can minister to us; and we can
pass into none of nature's cabinets, but we can
find our table spread : so that what David said
to God, " Whither shall I go from thy presence? If I go to heaven, thou art there; if I
descend to the deep, thou art there also; if I
take the wings of the morning, and flee into

the uttermost parts of the wilderness, even there thou wilt find me out, and thy right hand shall uphold me," we may say it concerning our table and our wardrobe. If we go into the fields, we find them tilled by the mercies of heaven, and watered with showers from God, to feed us, and to clothe us. If we go down into the deep, there God hath multiplied our stores, and filled a magazine which no hunger can exhaust. The air drops down delicacies, and the wilderness can sustain us; and all that is in nature, that which feeds lions, and that which the ox eats, that which the fishes live upon, and that which is the provision for the birds, all that can keep us alive. And if we consider that of the beasts and birds, for whom nature hath provided but one dish, it may be flesh or fish, or herbs or flies, and these also we secure with guards from them, and drive away birds and beasts from that provision which nature made for them, yet seldom can we find that any of these perish with hunger; much rather shall we find that we are secured by the securities proper for the more noble creatures by that Providence that disposes all things; by that mercy that gives us all things which to other creatures are ministered singly : by that labor that can procure what we need ; by that wisdom that can consider concerning future necessities ; by that power that can force it

from inferior creatures ; and by that temperance which can fit our meat to our necessities.
For if we go beyond what is needful, as we
find sometimes more than was promised, and
very often more than we need, so we disorder
the certainty of our felicity, by putting that to
hazard which nature hath secured. For it is
not certain, that, if we desire to have the
wealth of Susa, or garments stained with the
blood of the Tyrian fish, that, if we desire to
feed like Philoxenus, or to have tables laden
like the boards of Vitellius, that we shall never
want. It is not nature that desires these
things, but lust and violence ; and by a disease
we entered into the passion and the necessity,
and in that state of trouble it is likely we may
dwell forever, unless we reduce our appetites
to nature's measures. And therefore it is that
plenty and pleasures are not the proper instruments of felicity. Because felicity is not a
jewel that can be locked in one man's cabinet.
God intended that all men should be made
happy ; and he that gave to all men the same
natural desires, and to all men provision of
satisfactions by the same meats and drinks,
intended that it should not go beyond that
measure of good things, which corresponds to
those desires which all men naturally have.

He that cannot be satisfied with common
provision, hath a bigger need than he that

can; it is harder, and more contingent, and
more difficult, and more troublesome for him
to be satisfied. "I feed sweetly," said Epicurus, " upon bread and water, those sweet and
easy provisions of the body, and I defy the
pleasures of costly provisions "; and the man
was so confident that he had the advantage
over wealthy tables, that he thought himself
happy as the immortal gods. For these provisions are easy, they are to be gotten without
amazing cares; no man needs to flatter if he
can live as nature did intend: " *Magna pars
libertatis est benè moratus venter* " ; he need
not swell his accounts, and intricate his spirit
with arts of subtilty and contrivance ; he can
be free from fears, and the chances of the
world cannot concern him. And this is true,
not only in those severe and anchoretical and
philosophical persons, who lived meanly as a
sheep, and without variety as the Baptist, but
in the same proportion it is also true in every
man that can be contented with that which is
honestly sufficient. Maximus Tyrius considers
concerning the felicity of Diogenes, a poor
Sinopean, having not so much nobility as to
be born in the better parts of Greece : but he
saw that he was compelled by no tyrant to
speak or do ignobly ; he had no fields to till,
and therefore took no care to buy cattle, and
to hire servants ; he was not distracted when a

rent-day came, and feared not when the wise
Greeks played the fool and fought who should
be lord of that field that lay between Thebes
and Athens; he laughed to see men scramble
for dirty silver, and spend ten thousand Attic
talents for the getting the revenues of two
hundred philippics; he went with his staff and
bag into the camp of the Phocenses, and the
soldiers reverenced his person and despised his
poverty, and it was truce with him whosoever
had wars; and the diadem of kings and the
purple of the emperors, the mitre of high-
priests and the divining-staff of soothsayers,
were things of envy and ambition, the purchase of danger, and the rewards of a mighty
passion; and men entered into them by trouble
and extreme difficulty, and dwelt under them
as a man under a falling roof, or as Damocles
under the tyrant's sword, sleeping like a condemned man; and let there be what pleasure
men can dream of in such broken slumbers,
yet the fear of waking from this illusion, and
parting from this fantastic pleasure, is a pain
and torment which the imaginary felicity cannot pay for.

All our trouble is from within us; and if a
dish of lettuce and a clear fountain can cool all
my heats, so that I shall have neither thirst
nor pride, lust nor revenge, envy nor ambition,
I am lodged in the bosom of felicity; and, in-

deed, no men sleep so soundly as they that lay
their head upon nature's lap. For a single
dish, and a clean chalice lifted from the springs,
can cure my hunger and thirst; but the meat
of Ahasuerus's feast cannot satisfy my ambition
and my pride. He, therefore, that hath the
fewest desires and the most quiet passions,
whose wants are soon provided for, and whose
possessions cannot be disturbed with violent
fears, he that dwells next door to satisfaction,
and can carry his needs and lay them down
where he pleases, — this man is the happy
man; and this is not to be done in great designs and swelling fortunes. For as it is in
plants which nature thrusts forth from her
navel, she makes regular provisions, and dresses
them with strength and ornament, with easiness
and full stature; but if you thrust a jessamine
there where she would have had a daisy grow,
or bring the tall fir from dwelling in his own
country, and transport the orange- or the al-
mond-tree near the fringes of the north star,
nature is displeased, and becomes unnatural,
and starves her sucklings, and renders you a
return less than your charge and expectation.
So it is in all our appetites; when they are
natural and proper, nature feeds them and
makes them healthful and lusty, as the coarse
issue of the Scythian clown; she feeds them
and makes them easy without cares and costly

passions. But if you thrust an appetite into her which she intended not, she gives you sickly and uneasy banquets, you must struggle with her for every drop of milk she gives beyond her own needs; you may get gold from her entrails, and at a great charge provide ornaments for your queens and princely women : but your lives are spent in the purchase; and when you have got them you must have more ; for these cannot content you, nor nourish the spirit. A man must labor infinitely to get more than he needs ; but to drive away thirst and hunger, a man needs not sit in the fields of the oppressed poor, nor lead armies, nor break his sleep, nor suffer shame and danger, and envy and affront, and all the retinue of infelicity.

If men did but know what felicity dwells in the cottage of the poor man, how sound his sleep, how quiet his breast, how composed his mind, how free from care, how easy his provision, how healthful his morning, how sober his night, how moist his mouth, how joyful his heart, they would never admire the noises and the diseases, the throng of passions and the violence of unnatural appetites, that fill the houses of the luxurious and the heart of the ambitious. These which you call pleasures are but the imagery and fantastic appearances, and such appearances even poor men may have.

It is like felicity, that the king of Persia should come to Babylon in the winter, and to Susa in the summer; and be attended with all the servants of one hundred and twenty-seven provinces, and with all the princes of Asia. It is like this, that Diogenes went to Corinth in the time of vintage, and to Athens when winter came; and instead of courts, visited the temples and the schools, and was pleased in the society of scholars and learned men, and conversed with the students of all Asia and Europe. If a man loves privacy, the poor fortune can have that when princes cannot; if he loves noises, he can go to markets and to courts, and may glut himself with strange faces and strange voices and strange manners, and the wild design of all the world. And when that day comes in which we shall die, nothing of the eating and drinking remains, nothing of the pomp and luxury, but the sorrow to part with it, and shame to have dwelt there where wisdom and virtue seldom come, unless it be to call men to sober counsels, to a plain and a severe and more natural way of living; and when Lucian derides the dead princes and generals, and says that in hell they go up and down selling salt meats and crying mussels, or begging; and he brings in Philip of Macedon, mending of shoes in a little stall; he intended to represent, that in the shades below, and in the state of the grave,

7

the princes and voluptuous have a being different from their present plenty; but that their
condition is made contemptible and miserable
by its disproportion to their lost and perishing
voluptuousness. The result is this, that Tiresias
told the ghost of Menippus, inquiring what
state of life was nearest to felicity, the private
life, that which is free from tumult and vanity,
noise and luxury, business and ambition, nearest to nature, and a just entertainment to
our necessities; that life is nearest to felicity.
Therefore despise the swellings and the diseases of a disordered life, and a proud vanity;
be troubled for no outward thing beyond its
merit, enjoy the present temperately, and you
cannot choose but be pleased to see that you
have so little share in the follies and miseries
of the intemperate world.

INTEMPERANCE.

INTEMPERANCE in eating and drinking is
an enemy to health; which is, as one calls
it, " *ansa voluptatum et condimentum vitæ* " ;
it is that handle by which we can apprehend
and perceive pleasures, and that sauce that
only makes life delicate; for what content can
a full table administer to a man in a fever?

Health is the opportunity of wisdom, the fairest scene of religion, the advantages of the glorifications of God, the charitable ministries to men ; it is a state of joy and thanksgiving, and in every of its periods feels a pleasure from the blessed emanations of a merciful Providence. The world does not minister, does not feel, a greater pleasure, than to be newly delivered from the racks or the gratings of the stone, and the torments and convulsions of a sharp colic ; and no organs, no harp, no lute, can sound out the praises of the Almighty Father so sprightfully, as the man that rises from his bed of sorrows, and considers what an excellent difference he feels from the groans and intolerable accents of yesterday.

When Cyrus had espied Astyages and his fellows coming drunk from a banquet, laden with variety of follies and filthiness, their legs failing them, their eyes red and staring, cozened with a moist cloud, and abused by a doubled object, their tongues full of sponges, and their heads no wiser, he thought they were poisoned : and he had reason ; for what malignant quality can be more venomous and hurtful to a man than the effect of an intemperate goblet and a full stomach? It poisons both the soul and body. All poisons do not kill presently, and this will in process of time, and hath formidable effects at present.

But, therefore, methinks the temptations which men meet withal from without, are in themselves most unreasonable and soonest confuted by us. He that tempts me to drink beyond my measure, civilly invites me to a fever, and to lay aside my reason as the Persian women did their garments and their modesty at the end of feasts; and all the question then will be, which is the worst evil, to refuse your uncivil kindness, or to suffer a violent headache, or to lay up heaps big enough for an English surfeit. Creon in the tragedy said well, " It is better for me to grieve thee, O stranger, or to be affronted by thee, than to be tormented by thy kindness the next day and the morrow after."

It is reported concerning Socrates, that when Athens was destroyed by the plague, he in the midst of all the danger escaped untouched by sickness, because by a spare and severe diet he had within him no tumult of disorderly humors, no factions in his blood, no loads of moisture prepared for charnel-houses or the sickly hospitals; but a vigorous heat, and a well-proportioned radical moisture; he had enough for health and study, philosophy and religion, for the temples and the academy, but no superfluities to be spent in groans and sickly nights. Strange it is that for the stomach, which is scarce a span long, there should be provided so many furnaces and ovens, huge fires and an army of cooks, cellars swimming with wine, and granaries sweating with corn ; and that into one belly should enter the vintage of many nations, the spoils of distant provinces, and the shell-fishes of several seas. When the heathens feasted their gods, they gave nothing but a fat ox, a ram, or a kid ; they poured a little wine upon the altar, and burned a handful of gum : but when they feasted themselves, they had many vessels filled with Campanian wine, turtles of Liguria, Sicilian beeves, and wheat from Egypt, wild boars from Illyrium, and Grecian sheep ; variety, and load, and cost, and curiosity : and so do we. It is so little we spend in religion, and so very much upon ourselves, so little to the poor, and so without measure to make ourselves sick, that we seem to be in love with our own mischief, and so passionate for necessity and want, that we strive all the ways we can to make ourselves need more than nature intended. I end this consideration with the saying of the cynic : " It is to be wondered at, that men eat so much for pleasure sake ; and yet for the same pleasure should not give over eating, and betake themselves to the delights of temperance, since to be healthful and holy is so great a pleasure." However, certain it is that no man ever repented that he arose from the table sober, healthful, and with his wits about him ; but very many have repented that they sat so long, till their bellies swelled, and their health, and their virtue, and their God is departed from them.

Intemperance is the nurse of vice. It makes rage and choler, pride and fantastic principles ; it makes the body a sea of humors, and those humors the seat of violence. By faring deliciously every day, men become senseless of the evils of mankind, inapprehensive of the troubles of their brethren, unconcerned in the changes of the world, and the cries of the poor, the hunger of the fatherless, and the thirst of widows. Tyrants, said Diogenes, never come from the cottages of them that eat pulse and coarse fare, but from the delicious beds and banquets of the effeminate and rich feeders. For, to maintain plenty and luxury, sometimes wars are necessary, and oppressions and violence : but no landlord did ever grind the face of his tenants, no prince ever sucked blood from his subjects, for the maintenance of a sober and a moderate proportion of good things.

Intemperance is a perfect destruction of wisdom. A full-gorged belly never produced a sprightly mind : and therefore these kind of men are called " slow bellies " ; so St. Paul concerning the intemperate Cretans, out of their own poet. They are like the tigers of Brazil, which when they are empty are bold and swift and full of sagacity, but being full, sneak away from the barking of a village dog. So are these men, wise in the morning, quick and fit for business; but when the sun gives the sign to spread the tables, and intemperance brings in the messes, and drunkenness fills the bowls, then the man falls away and leaves a beast in his room. A full meal is like Sisera's banquet, at the end of which there is a nail struck into a man's head; it knocks a man down, and nails his soul to the sensual mixtures of the body. For what wisdom can be expected from them whose soul dwells in clouds of meat, and floats up and down in wine, like the spilled cups which fell from their hands when they could lift them to their heads no longer? It is a perfect shipwreck of a man; the pilot is drunk, and the helm dashed in pieces, and the ship first reels, and by swallowing too much is itself swallowed up at last. And therefore the madness of the young fellows of Agrigentum, who, being drunk, fancied themselves in a storm, and the house the ship, was more than the wild fancy of their cups; it was really so, they were all cast away, they were broken in pieces by the foul disorder of the storm. The senses languish, the spark of divinity that dwells within is quenched; and the mind snorts, dead with sleep and fulness in the fouler regions of the belly.

So have I seen the eye of the world looking upon a fenny bottom, and drinking up too free draughts of moisture, gathered them into a cloud, and that cloud crept about his face, and made him first look red, and then covered him with darkness and an artificial night: so is our reason at a feast. The clouds gather about the head; and according to the method and period of the children, and productions of darkness, it first grows red, and that redness turns into an obscurity and a thick mist, and reason is lost to all use and profitableness of wise and sober discourses. A cloud of folly and distraction darkens the soul, and makes it crass and material, polluted and heavy, clogged and laden like the body; and there cannot be anything said worse: reason turns into folly, wine and flesh into a knot of clouds, the soul itself into a body, and the spirit into corrupted meat. There is nothing left but the rewards and portions of a fool, to be reaped and enjoyed there, where flesh and corruption shall dwell to eternal ages; their heads are gross, their souls are emerged in matter, and drowned in the moistures of an unwholesome cloud; they are dull of hearing, slow in apprehension, and to action they are as unable as the hands of a child who too hastily hath broken the enclosures of his first dwelling.

And now, after all this, I pray consider what a strange madness and prodigious folly possess many men, that they love to swallow death and diseases and dishonor, with an appetite which no reason can restrain. We expect our servants should not dare to touch what we have forbidden to them ; we are watchful that our children should not swallow poisons and filthiness and unwholesome nourishment ; we take care that they should be well-mannered and civil and of fair demeanor ; and we ourselves desire to be, or at least to be accounted, wise, and would infinitely scorn to be called fools ; and we are so great lovers of health that we will buy it at any rate of money or observance : and then for honor ; it is that which the children of men pursue with passion, it is one of the noblest rewards of virtue, and the proper ornament of the wise and valiant ; and yet all these things are not valued or considered when a merry meeting, or a looser feast, calls upon the man to act a scene of folly and madness, and healthlessness and dishonor. We do to God what we severely punish in our servants ; we correct our children for their meddling with dangers which themselves prefer before immortality ; and though no man thinks himself fit to be despised, yet he is willing to make himself a beast, a sot, and a ridiculous monkey, with the follies and vapors of wine ; and when he is

high in drink or fancy, proud as a Grecian orator in the midst of his popular noises, at the
same time he shall talk such dirty language,
such mean low things, as may well become a
changeling and a fool, for whom the stocks are
prepared by the laws, and the just scorn of
men.

Every drunkard clothes his head with a
mighty scorn, and makes himself lower at that
time than the meanest of his servants. The
boys can laugh at him when he is led like a
cripple, directed like a blind man, and speaks,
like an infant, imperfect noises, lisping with a
full and spongy tongue, and an empty head, and
a vain and foolish heart. So cheaply does he
part with his honor for drink or loads of meat;
for which honor he is ready to die, rather than
hear it to be disparaged by another; when himself destroys it, as bubbles perish with the breath
of children. Do not the laws of all wise nations mark the drunkard for a fool, with the
meanest and most scornful punishment? And
is there anything in the world so foolish as a
man that is drunk? But, good God! what an
intolerable sorrow hath seized upon great portions of mankind, that this folly and madness
should possess the greatest spirits and the wit-
tiest men, the best company, the most sensible
of the word honor, and the most jealous of
losing the shadow, and the most careless of the

thing? Is it not a horrid thing, that a wise or a crafty, a learned or a noble person, should dishonor himself as a fool, destroy his body as a murderer, lessen his estate as a prodigal, disgrace every good cause that he can pretend to by his relation, and become an appellative of scorn, a scene of laughter or derision, and all for the reward of forgetfulness and madness? for there are in immoderate drinking no other pleasures.

I end with the saying of a wise man: He is fit to sit at the table of the Lord, and to feast with saints, who moderately uses the creatures which God hath given him: but he that despises even lawful pleasures, shall not only sit and feast with God, but reign together with him, and partake of his glorious kingdom.

MARRIAGE.

THE first blessing God gave to man was society; and that society was a marriage, and that marriage was confederate by God himself, and hallowed by a blessing: and at the same time, and for very many descending ages, not only by the instinct of nature, but by a superadded forwardness, (God himself inspiring the desire,) the world was most desirous of children, impatient of barrenness, accounting single life a curse, and a childless person hated by God. The world was rich and empty, and able to provide for a more numerous posterity than it had. When a family could drive their herds, and set their children upon camels, and lead them till they saw a fat soil watered with rivers, and there sit down without paying rent, they thought of nothing but to have great families, that their own relations might swell up to a patriarchate, and their children be enough to possess all the regions that they saw, and their grandchildren become princes, and themselves build cities and call them by the name of a child, and become the fountain of a nation.

This was the consequent of the first blessing, " Increase and multiply." The next blessing was the promise of the Messiah ; and that also increased in men and women a wonderful desire of marriage : for as soon as God had chosen the family of Abraham to be the blessed line from whence the world's Redeemer should descend according to the flesh, every of his daughters hoped to have the honor to be his mother, or his grandmother, or something of his kindred ; and to be childless in Israel was a sorrow to the Hebrew women, great as the slavery of Egypt, or their dishonors in the land of their captivity.

But when the Messiah was come, and the doctrine was published, and his ministers but few, and his disciples were to suffer persecution, and to be of an unsettled dwelling, and the nation of the Jews, in the bosom and society of which the Church especially did dwell, were to be scattered and broken all in pieces with fierce calamities, and the world was apt to calumniate and to suspect and dishonor Christians upon pretences and unreasonable jealousies, and that to all these purposes the state of marriage brought many inconveniences; it pleased God in this new creation to inspire into the hearts of his servants a disposition and strong desire to lead a single life, lest the state of marriage should in that conjunction of things become an accidental impediment to the dissemination of the gospel, which called men from a confinement in their domestic charges to travel, and flight, and poverty, and difficulty, and martyrdom. Upon this necessity the Apostles and apostolical men published doctrines, declaring the advantages of single life, not by any commandment of the Lord, but by the spirit of prudence, for the present and then incumbent necessities, and in order to the advantages which did accrue to the public ministries and private piety.

Upon this occasion it grew necessary for the Apostle to state the question right, and to do

honor to the holy rite of marriage, and to
snatch the mystery from the hands of zeal
and folly, and to place it in Christ's right hand,
that all its beauties might appear, and a present convenience might not bring in a false
doctrine, and a perpetual sin, and an intolerable mischief.

Marriage is a school and exercise of virtue ;
and though marriage hath cares, yet the single
life hath desires, which are more troublesome
and more dangerous, and often end in sin,
while the cares are but instances of duty and
exercises of piety ; and therefore, if single life
hath more privacy of devotion, yet marriage
hath more necessities and more variety of it,
and is an exercise of more graces. Here is the
proper scene of piety and patience, of the duty
of parents and the charity of relatives ; here
kindness is spread abroad, and love is united
and made firm as a centre. Marriage is the
nursery of heaven ; the virgin sends prayers
to God, but she carries but one soul to him ;
but the state of marriage fills up the numbers
of the elect, and hath in it the labor of love
and the delicacies of friendship, the blessing of
society and the union of hands and hearts ; it
hath in it less of beauty, but more of safety,
than the single life ; it hath more care, but less
danger ; it is more merry, and more sad ; is
fuller of sorrows, and fuller of joys ; it lies

under more burdens, but is supported by all the strengths of love and charity, and those burdens are delightful.

Marriage is the mother of the world, and preserves kingdoms, and fills cities and churches, and heaven itself. Celibate, like the fly in the heart of an apple, dwells in a perpetual sweetness, but sits alone, and is confined and dies in singularity; but marriage, like the useful bee, builds a house, and gathers sweetness from every flower, and labors and unites into societies and republics, and sends out colonies, and feeds the world with delicacies, and obeys their king, and keeps order, and exercises many virtues, and promotes the interest of mankind, and is that state of good things to which God hath designed the present constitution of the world.

They that enter into the state of marriage, cast a die of the greatest contingency, and yet of the greatest interest in the world, next to the last throw for eternity. Life or death, felicity or a lasting sorrow, are in the power of marriage. A woman indeed ventures most, for she hath no sanctuary to retire to from an evil husband; she must dwell upon her sorrow, and hatch the eggs which her own folly or infelicity hath produced; and she is more under it, because her tormentor hath a warrant of prerogative; and the woman may complain to

God as subjects do of tyrant princes, but otherwise she hath no appeal in the causes of unkindness. And though the man can run from
many hours of his sadness, yet he must return
to it again ; and when he sits among his neighbors, he remembers the objection that lies in
his bosom, and he sighs deeply. The boys,
and the pedlers, and the fruiterers, shall tell of
this man, when he is carried to his grave, that
he lived and died a poor wretched person.

The stags in the Greek epigram, whose
knees were clogged with frozen snow upon
the mountains, came down to the brooks of
the valleys, hoping to thaw their joints with
the waters of the stream ; but there the frost
overtook them, and bound them fast in ice
till the young herdsman took them in their
stranger snare. It is the unhappy chance of
many men, finding many inconveniences upon
the mountains of single life, they descend into
the valleys of marriage to refresh their troubles, and there they enter into fetters, and are
bound to sorrow by the cords of a man's or
woman's peevishness. And the worst of the
evil is, they are to thank their own follies ; for
they fell into the snare by entering an im-
proper way. Christ and the Church were no
ingredients in their choice. But as the Indian
women enter into folly for the price of an elephant, and think their crime warrantable, so

do men and women change their liberty for a rich fortune, (like Eriphyle the Argive, she preferred gold before a good man,) and show themselves to be less than money, by overvaluing that to all the content and wise felicity of their lives: and when they have counted the money and their sorrows together, how willingly would they buy, with the loss of all that money, modesty, or sweet nature, to their relative! The odd thousand pounds would gladly be allowed in good-nature and fair manners.

As very a fool is he that chooses for beauty principally; "*cui sunt eruditi oculi, et stulta mens*" (as one said), whose eyes are witty, and their souls sensual. It is an ill band of affections to tie two hearts together by a little thread of red and white. And they can love no longer but until the next ague comes; and they are fond of each other, but, at the chance of fancy, or the small-pox, or childbearing, or care, or time, or anything that can destroy a pretty flower.

Man and wife are equally concerned to avoid all offences of each other in the beginning of their conversation. Every little thing can blast an infant blossom; and the breath of the south can shake the little rings of the vine, when first they begin to curl like the locks of a new-weaned boy; but when by age and consolidation they stiffen into the hardness of a stem, and have by the warm embraces of the

8

sun, and the kisses of heaven, brought forth
their clusters, they can endure the storms of
the north, and the loud noises of a tempest,
and yet never be broken. So are the early
unions of an unfixed marriage; watchful and
observant, jealous and busy, inquisitive and
careful, and apt to take alarm at every unkind
word. For infirmities do not manifest themselves in the first scenes, but in the succession
of a long society; and it is not chance or weakness when it appears at first, but it is want of
love or prudence, or it will be so expounded;
and that which appears ill at first, usually af-
frights the inexperienced man or woman, who
makes unequal conjectures, and fancies mighty
sorrows by the proportions of the new and
early unkindness. It is a very great passion,
or a huge folly, or a certain want of love, that
cannot preserve the colors and beauties of
kindness so long as public honesty requires a
man to wear their sorrows for the death of a
friend.

Plutarch compares a new marriage to a vessel before the hoops are on; everything dissolves their tender compaginations: but when
the joints are stiffened and are tied by a firm
compliance and proportioned bending, scarcely
can it be dissolved without fire or the violence
of iron. After the hearts of the man and the
wife are endeared and hardened by a mutual

confidence, and experience longer than artifice and pretence can last, there are a great many remembrances, and some things present, that dash all little unkindnesses in pieces. The little boy in the Greek epigram, that was creeping down a precipice, was invited to his safety by the sight of his mother's pap, when nothing else could entice him to return: and the bond of common children, and the sight of her that nurses what is most dear to him, and the endearments of each other in the course of a long society, and the same relation, is an excellent security to redintegrate and to call that love back, which folly and trifling accidents would disturb. When it is come thus far, it is hard untwisting the knot; but be careful in its first coalition that there be no rudeness done; for if there be, it will forever after be apt to start and to be diseased.

Let man and wife be careful to stifle little things, that as fast as they spring they be cut down and trod upon; for if they be suffered to grow by numbers, they make the spirit peevish, and the society troublesome, and the affections loose and easy by an habitual aversation. Some men are more vexed with a fly than with a wound; and when the gnats disturb our sleep, and the reason is disquieted, but not perfectly awakened, it is often seen

that he is fuller of trouble than if, in the
daylight of his reason, he were to contest
with a potent enemy. In the frequent little
accidents of a family, a man's reason cannot
always be awake; and when his discourses
are imperfect, and a trifling trouble makes
him yet more restless, he is soon betrayed to
the violence of passion. It is certain that
the man or woman are in a state of weakness and folly then, when they can be troubled with a trifling accident ; and therefore
it is not good to tempt their affections when
they are in that state of danger. In this
case the caution is, to subtract fuel from the
sudden flame ; for stubble, though it be quickly
kindled, yet it is as soon extinguished, if it be
not blown by a pertinacious breath, or fed with
new materials. Add no new provocations to
the accident, and do not inflame this, and peace
will soon return, and the discontent will pass
away soon, as the sparks from the collision of
a flint ; ever remembering, that discontents
proceeding from daily little things do breed
a secret undiscernible disease, which is more
dangerous than a fever proceeding from a discerned notorious surfeit.

Let them be sure to abstain from all those
things which by experience and observation
they find to be contrary to each other. They
that govern elephants, never appear before

them in white; and the masters of bulls keep
from them all garments of blood and scarlet, as
knowing that they will be impatient of civil
usages and discipline when their natures are
provoked by their proper antipathies. The
ancients in their marital hieroglyphics used to
depict Mercury standing by Venus, to signify
that by fair language and sweet entreaties the
minds of each other should be united; and
hard by them, " *suadam et gratias descripse-
runt,*" they would have all deliciousness of
manners, compliance and mutual observance
to abide.

Let the husband and wife infinitely avoid
a curious distinction of mine and thine; for
this hath caused all the laws, and all the
suits, and all the wars in the world. Let
them who have but one person have also
but one interest. Corvinus dwells in a farm
and receives all its profits, and reaps and
sows as he pleases, and eats of the corn and
drinks of the wine; it is his own : but all that
also is his lord's, and for it Corvinus pays
acknowledgment; and his patron hath such
powers and uses of it as are proper to the
lords ; and yet for all this, it may be the king's
too, to all the purposes that he can need, and
is all to be accounted in the census, and for
certain services and times of danger. So are
the riches of a family; they are a woman's as

well as a man's; they are hers for need, and
hers for ornament, and hers for modest delight, and for the uses of religion and prudent
charity: but the disposing them into portions
of inheritance, the assignation of charges and
governments, stipends and rewards, annuities
and greater donatives, are the reserves of the
superior right, and not to be invaded by the
under-possessors.

As the earth, the mother of all creatures
here below, sends up all its vapors and proper
emissions at the command of the sun, and yet
requires them again to refresh her own needs,
and they are deposited between them both, in
the bosom of a cloud, as a common receptacle,
that they may cool his flames, and yet descend
to make her fruitful: so are the proprieties
of a wife to be disposed of by her lord; and
yet all are for her provision, it being a part of
his need to refresh and supply hers, and it
serves the interest of both while it serves the
necessities of either.

These are the duties of them both, which
have common regards and equal necessities and
obligations; and indeed there is scarce any
matter of duty, but it concerns them both alike,
and is only distinguished by names, and hath
its variety by circumstances and little accidents: and what in one is called love, in the
other is called reverence; and what in the wife

is obedience, the same in the man is duty. He provides, and she dispenses; he gives commandments, and she rules by them; he rules her by authority, and she rules him by love; she ought by all means to please him, and he must by no means displease her. For as the heart is set in the midst of the body, and though it strikes to one side by the prerogative of nature, yet those throbs and constant motions are felt on the other side also, and the influence is equal to both: so it is in conjugal duties; some motions are to the one side more than to the other, but the interest is on both, and the duty is equal in the several instances.

The next inquiry is more particular, and considers the power and duty of the man. "Let every one of you so love his wife, even as himself"; she is as himself, the man hath power over her as over himself, and must love her equally. A husband's power over his wife is paternal and friendly, not magisterial and despotic. The wife is "*in perpetuâ tutelâ*," under conduct and counsel; for the power a man hath is founded in the understanding, not in the will or force; it is not a power of coercion, but a power of advice, and that government that wise men have over those who are fit to be conducted by them. Thou art to be a father and a mother to her, and a brother: and great reason, unless the state of marriage should be no better than the condition of an orphan. For she that is bound to leave father and mother and brother for thee, either is miserable, like a poor fatherless child, or else ought to find all these, and more, in thee.

The dominion of a man over his wife is no other than as the soul rules the body; for which it takes a mighty care, and uses it with a delicate tenderness, and cares for it in all contingencies, and watches to keep it from all evils, and studies to make for it fair provisions, and very often is led by its inclinations and desires, and does never contradict its appetites but when they are evil, and then also not without some trouble and sorrow; and its government comes only to this: it furnishes the body with light and understanding, and the body furnishes the soul with hands and feet; the soul governs because the body cannot else be happy, but the government is no other than provision; as a nurse governs a child when she causes him to eat, and to be warm, and dry, and quiet. And yet even the very government itself is divided; for man and wife in the family are as the sun and moon in the firmament of heaven; he rules by day, and she by night, that is, in the lesser and more proper circles of her affairs, in the conduct of domestic provisions and necessary offices, and shines only by his light, and rules by his authority.

And as the moon in opposition to the sun shines brightest, that is, then when she is in her own circles and separate regions, so is the authority of the wife then most conspicuous when she is separate and in her proper sphere; "*in gynæceo*," in the nursery and offices of domestic employment. But when she is in conjunction with the sun her brother, that is, in that place and employment in which his care and proper offices are employed, her light is not seen, her authority hath no proper business. But else there is no difference; for they were barbarous people among whom wives were instead of servants; and it is a sign of impotency and weakness to force the camels to kneel for their load, because thou hast not spirit and strength enough to climb: to make the affections and evenness of a wife bend by the flexures of a servant, is a sign the man is not wise enough to govern when another stands by. And as amongst men and women humility is the way to be preferred, so it is in husbands; they shall prevail by cession, by sweetness and counsel, and charity and compliance. So that we cannot discourse of the man's right without describing the measures of his duty; that, therefore, follows next.

"Let him love his wife even as himself":— that is his duty, and the measure of it too; which is so plain, that, if he understands how

he treats himself, there needs nothing be added
concerning his demeanor towards her, save
only that we add the particulars in which
holy Scripture instances this general commandment.

The first is, "Be not bitter against her";
and this is the least index and signification of
love; a civil man is never bitter against a
friend or a stranger, much less to him that
enters under his roof, and is secured by the
laws of hospitality. But a wife does all that
and more: she quits all her interest for his
love; she gives him all that she can give; she
is much the same person as another can be the
same, who is conjoined by love and mystery
and religion, and all that is sacred and profane.
They have the same fortune, the same family,
the same children, the same religion, the same
interest, the same flesh; and therefore the
Apostle urges, "No man hateth his own flesh,
but nourisheth and cherisheth it"; and he certainly is strangely sacrilegious and a violator
of the rights of hospitality and sanctuary, who
uses her rudely, who is fled for protection not
only to his house, but also to his heart and
bosom.

There is nothing can please a man without
love; and if a man be weary of the wise discourses of the Apostles, and of the innocency
of an even and a private fortune, or hates peace

or a fruitful year, he hath reaped thorns and
thistles from the choicest flowers of paradise;
for nothing can sweeten felicity itself, but love.
But when a man dwells in love, then the breasts
of his wife are pleasant as the droppings upon
the hill of Hermon, her eyes are fair as the
light of heaven, she is a fountain sealed, and he
can quench his thirst, and ease his cares, and lay
his sorrow down upon her lap, and can retire
home as to his sanctuary and refectory, and his
gardens of sweetness and chaste refreshments.

No man can tell but he that loves his children, how many delicious accents make a man's
heart dance in the pretty conversation of those
dear pledges; their childishness, their stammering, their little angers, their innocence,
their imperfections, their necessities, are so
many little emanations of joy and comfort to
him that delights in their persons and society.
But he that loves not his wife and children
feeds a lioness at home, and broods a nest of
sorrows; and blessing itself cannot make him
happy: so that all the commandments of God
enjoining a man to love his wife are nothing
but so many necessities and capacities of joy.
She that is loved is safe, and he that loves is
joyful.

The husband should nourish and cherish her;
he should refresh her sorrows and entice her
fears into confidence and pretty arts of rest.

But it will concern the prudence of the husband's love to make the cares and evils as simple and easy as he can, by doubling the joys and acts of a careful friendship, by tolerating her infirmities, (because by so doing he either cures her, or makes himself better,) by fairly expounding all the little traverses of society and communication, by taking everything by the right handle, as Plutarch's expression is; for there is nothing but may be misinterpreted; and yet if it be capable of a fair construction, it is the office of love to make it. Love will account that to be well said which, it may be, was not so intended; and then it may cause it to be so, another time.

Hither also is to be referred that he secure the interest of her virtue and felicity by a fair example; for a wife to a husband is a line or superficies, — it hath dimensions of its own, but no motion or proper affections; but commonly puts on such images of virtues or vices as are presented to her by her husband's idea: and if thou beest vicious, complain not that she is infected that lies in thy bosom; the interest of whose love ties her to transcribe thy copy, and write after the character of thy manners. Paris was a man of pleasure, and Helena was an adulteress, and she added covetousness upon her own account. But Ulysses was a prudent man, and a wary counsellor, sober and severe;

and he efformed his wife into such imagery as
he desired; and she was chaste as the snows
upon the mountains, diligent as the fatal sisters,
always busy, and always faithful; she had a
lazy tongue and a busy hand.

Above all the instances of love let him preserve towards her an inviolable faith, and an
unspotted chastity; for this is the marriage-ring;
it ties two hearts by an eternal band; it is like
the cherubim's flaming sword, set for the guard
of paradise; he that passes into that garden,
now that it is immured by Christ and the
Church, enters into the shades of death. No
man must touch the forbidden tree, that in the
midst of the garden, which is the tree of knowledge and life. Chastity is the security of love,
and preserves all the mysteriousness like the
secrets of a temple. Under this lock is deposited security of families, the union of affections,
the repairer of accidental breaches. This is a
grace that is shut up and secured by all arts of
heaven and the defence of laws, the locks and
bars of modesty, by honor and reputation, by
fear and shame, by interest and high regards;
and that contract that is intended to be forever
is yet dissolved and broken by the violation of
this. Nothing but death can do so much evil
to the holy rites of marriage as unchastity and
breach of faith can; and by the laws of the Romans a man might kill his daughter or his wife,

if he surprised her in the breach of her holy
vows, which are as sacred as the threads of life,
secret as the privacies of the sanctuary, and
holy as the society of angels. God that commanded us to forgive our enemies left it in our
choice, and hath not commanded us to forgive
an adulterous husband or a wife ; but the offend-
ed party's displeasure may pass into an eternal
separation of society and friendship. Now in
this grace it is fit that the wisdom and severity
of the man should hold forth a pure taper, that
his wife may, by seeing the beauties and trans-
parency of that crystal, dress her mind and her
body by the light of so pure reflections. It is
certain he will expect it from the modesty and
retirement, from the passive nature and colder
temper, from the humility and fear, from the
honor and love, of his wife, that she be pure
as the eye of heaven : and therefore it is but
reason that the wisdom and nobleness, the love
and confidence, the strength and severity of the
man should be as holy and certain in this grace
as he is a severe exactor of it at her hands,
who can more easily be tempted by another,
and less by herself.

These are the little lines of a man's duty,
which, like threads of light from the body of
the sun, do clearly describe all the regions of
his proper obligations. Now, concerning the
woman's duty, although it consists in doing

whatsoever her husband commands, and so receives measures from the rules of his government, yet there are also some lines of life depicted upon her hands, by which she may read and know how to proportion out her duty to her husband.

The first is obedience. The man's authority is love, and the woman's love is obedience ; for this obedience is no way founded in fear, but in love and reverence. We will add, that it is an effect of that modesty which, like rubies, adorns the necks and cheeks of women. It is modesty to advance and highly to honor them who have honored us by making us to be the companions of their dearest excellencies ; for the woman that went before the man in the way of death, is commanded to follow him in the way of love ; and that makes the society to be perfect, and the union profitable, and the harmony complete. A wife never can become equal but by obeying. A ruling woman is intolerable. But that is not all ; for she is miserable, too : for it is a sad calamity for a woman to be joined to a fool or a weak person ; it is like a guard of geese to keep the capitol ; or as if a flock of sheep should read grave lec· tures to their shepherd, and give him orders when he shall conduct them to pasture. To be ruled by weaker people, to have a fool to one's master, is the fate of miserable and unblessed people: and the wife can be no ways happy unless she be governed by a prudent lord, whose commands are sober counsels, whose authority is paternal, whose orders are provisions, and whose sentences are charity.

The next line of the woman's duty is compliance, which St. Peter calls " the hidden man of the heart, the ornament of a meek and a quiet spirit " ; and to it he opposes " the outward and pompous ornament of the body"; concerning which, as there can be no particular measure set down to all persons, but the proportions were to be measured by the customs of wise people, the quality of the woman, and the desires of the man ; yet it is to be limited by Christian modesty and the usages of the more excellent and severe matrons. Menander in the comedy brings in a man turning his wife from his house because she stained her hair yellow, which was then the beauty. A wise woman should not paint. A studious gallantry in clothes cannot make a wise man love his wife the better. Such gayeties are fit for tragedies, but not for the uses of life. " *Decor occultus, et tecta venustas* " ; that is the Christian woman's fineness, the hidden man of the heart, sweetness of manners, humble comportment, fair interpretation of all addresses, ready compliances, high opinion of him, and mean of herself.

To partake secretly, and in her heart, of all his joys and sorrows; to believe him comely and fair, though the sun hath drawn a cypress over him; (for as marriages are not to be contracted by the hands and eye, but with reason and the hearts, so are these judgments to be made by the mind, not by the sight;) and diamonds cannot make the woman virtuous, nor him to value her who sees her put them off, then, when charity and modesty are her brightest ornaments.

And indeed those husbands that are pleased with indecent gayeties of their wives, are like fishes taken with ointments and intoxicating baits, apt and easy for sport and mockery, but useless for food; and when Circe had turned Ulysses's companions into hogs and monkeys, by pleasures and the enchantments of her bravery and luxury, they were no longer useful to her, she knew not what to do with them; but on wise Ulysses she was continually enamoured. Indeed the outward ornament is fit to take fools, but they are not worth the taking; but she that hath a wise husband must entice him to an eternal dearness by the veil of modesty, and the grave robes of chastity, the ornament of meekness, and the jewels of faith and charity: she must have no "*fucus*" but blushings; her brightness must be purity, and she must shine round about with sweet-

9

nesses and friendship, and she shall be pleasant while she lives, and desired when she dies. If not, her grave shall be full of rottenness and dishonor, and her memory shall be worse after she is dead : " after she is dead " ; for that will be the end of all merry meetings ; and I choose this to be the last advice to both.

Remember the days of darkness, for they are many ; the joys of the bridal chambers are quickly past, and the remaining portion of the state is a dull progress, without variety of joys, but not without the change of sorrows ; but that portion that shall enter into the grave must be eternal. It is fit that I should infuse a bunch of myrrh into the festival goblet, and after the Egyptian manner serve up a dead man's bones at a feast ; I will only show it, and take it away again ; it will make the wine bitter, but wholesome. But those married pairs that live, as remembering that they must part again, and give an account how they treat themselves and each other, shall at that day of their death be admitted to glorious espousals ; and then they shall live again, be married to their Lord, and partake of his glories, with Abraham and Joseph, St. Peter and St. Paul, and all the married saints.

All those things that now please us shall pass from us, or we from them ; but those things that concern the other life are per-

manent as the numbers of eternity : and although at the resurrection there shall be no
relation of husband and wife, and no marriage shall be celebrated but the marriage
of the Lamb ; yet then shall be remembered
how men and women passed through this
state, which is a type of that ; and from this
sacramental union all holy pairs shall pass to
the spiritual and eternal, where love shall be
their portion, and joys shall crown their heads,
and they shall lie in the bosom of Jesus, and
in the heart of God to eternal ages.

THE ATHEIST.

WHO in the world is a verier fool, a more
ignorant, wretched person, than he that
is an atheist ? A man may better believe
there is no such man as himself, and that he
is not in being, than that there is no God ;
for himself can cease to be, and once was not,
and shall be changed from what he is, and in
very many periods of his life knows not that
he is ; and so it is every night with him when
he sleeps. But none of these can happen to
God ; and if he knows it not, he is a fool.
Can anything in this world be more foolish
than to think that all this rare fabric of heaven

and earth can come by chance, when all the skill of art is not able to make an oyster? To see rare effects and no cause; an excellent government and no prince; a motion without an immovable; a circle without a centre; a time without eternity; a second without a first; a thing that begins not from itself, and therefore not to perceive there is something from whence it does begin, which must be without beginning; these things are so against philosophy and natural reason, that he must needs be a beast in his understanding that does not assent to them. This is the atheist: " The fool hath said in his heart there is no God " ; that is his character. The thing framed says that nothing framed it ; the tongue never made itself to speak, and yet talks against him that did ; saying, that which is made is, and that which made it is not. But this folly is as infinite as hell, as much without light or bound as the chaos or primitive nothing. But in this the devil never prevailed very far ; his schools were always thin at these lectures. Some few people have been witty against God, that taught them to speak before they knew how to spell a syllable ; but either they are monsters in their manners, or mad in their understandings, or ever find themselves confuted by a thunder or a plague, by danger or death.

THE TONGUE.

BY the use of the tongue, God hath distinguished us from beasts; and by the well or ill using it we are distinguished from one another; and therefore though silence be innocent as death, harmless as a rose's breath to a distant passenger, yet it is rather the state of death than life; and therefore when the Egyptians sacrificed to Harpocrates their god of silence, in the midst of their rites they cried out, " The tongue is an angel," good or bad, that is, as it happens. Silence was to them a god, but the tongue is greater; it is the band of human intercourse, and makes men apt to unite in societies and republics; and I remember what one of the ancients said, that we are better in the company of a known dog than of a man whose speech is not known. A stranger to a stranger in his language is not as a man to a man; for by voices and homilies, by questions and answers, by narratives and invectives, by counsel and reproof, by praises and hymns, by prayers and glorifications, we serve God's glory and the necessities of men; and by the tongue our tables are made to differ from mangers, our cities from deserts, our churches from herds of beasts and flocks of sheep.

But the tongue is a fountain both of bitter

waters and of pleasant; it sends forth blessing
and cursing; it praises God, and rails at men;
it is sometimes set on fire, and then it puts
whole cities in combustion; it is unruly, and no
more to be restrained than the breath of a tempest; it is volatile and fugitive: reason should
go before it; and, when it does not, repentance
comes after it; it was intended for an organ of
the divine praises, but the devil often plays
upon it, and then it sounds like the screech-
owl, or the groans of death; sorrow and shame,
folly and repentance, are the notes and formidable accents of that discord.

He that loves to talk much, must scrape
materials together to furnish out the scenes
and long orations; and some talk themselves
into anger, and some furnish out their dialogues
with the lives of others; either they detract
or censure, or they flatter themselves, and tell
their own stories with friendly circumstances;
and pride creeps up the sides of the discourse,
and the man entertains his friend with his own
panegyric; or the discourse looks one way and
rows another, and more minds the design than
its own truth; and most commonly will be so
ordered that it shall please the company.

IDLE TALK.

LET no man think it a light matter that he spends his precious time in idle words; let no man be so weary of what flies away too fast, and cannot be recalled, as to use arts and devices to pass the time away in vanity, which might be rarely spent in the interests of eternity. Time is given us to repent in, to appease the divine anger, to prepare for and hasten to the society of angels, to stir up our slackened wills, and enkindle our cold devotions, to weep for our daily iniquities, and to sigh after, and work for, the restitution of our lost inheritance; and the reward is very inconsiderable that exchanges all this for the pleasure of a voluble tongue: and indeed this is an evil that cannot be avoided by any excuse that can be made for words that are in any sense idle, though in all senses of their own nature and proper relations they be innocent. They are a throwing away something of that which is to be expended for eternity, and put on degrees of folly according as they are tedious and expensive of time to no good purposes.

Great knowledge, if it be without vanity, is the most severe bridle of the tongue. For so have I heard that all the noises and prating of the pool, the croaking of frogs and toads, is hushed and appeased upon the instant of bringing upon them the light of a candle or torch. Every beam of reason and ray of knowledge checks the dissolutions of the tongue. But, every man as he is a fool and contemptible, so his tongue is hanged loose, being like a bell, in which there is nothing but tongue and noise.

No prudence is a sufficient guard, or can always stand " *in excubiis*," still watching, when a man is in perpetual floods of talk : for prudence attends after the manner of an angel's ministry; it is despatched on messages from God, and drives away enemies, and places guards, and calls upon the man to awake, and bids him send out spies and observers, and then goes about his own ministries above : but an angel does not sit by a man, as a nurse by the baby's cradle, watching every motion, and the lighting of a fly upon the child's lip. And so is prudence ; it gives rules, and proportions out our measures, and prescribes us cautions, and by general influences orders our particulars : but he that is given to talk cannot be secured by all this; the emissions of his tongue are beyond the general figures and lines of rule ; and he can no more be wise in every period of a long and running talk than a lutanist can deliberate and make every motion of his hand by the division of his notes to be chosen and distinctly voluntary. And hence it comes, that

at every corner of the mouth a folly peeps out,
or a mischief creeps in. A little pride and a
great deal of vanity will soon escape, while the
man minds the sequel of his talk, and not that
ugliness of humor which the severe man that
stood by did observe and was ashamed of. Do
not many men talk themselves into anger,
screwing up themselves with dialogues of fancy,
till they forget the company and themselves?
And some men hate to be contradicted or interrupted, or to be discovered in their folly; and
some men being a little conscious, and not
striving to amend by silence, they make it
worse by discourse. A long story of themselves, a tedious praise of another collaterally,
to do themselves advantage; a declamation
against a sin, to undo the person or oppress the
reputation of their neighbor; unseasonable rep-
etition of that which neither profits nor delights;
trifling contentions about a goat's beard or the
blood of an oyster, anger and animosity, spite
and rage, scorn and reproach, begun upon questions which concern neither of the litigants;
fierce disputations: strivings for what is past,
and for what shall never be: these are the
events of the loose and unwary tongue, which
are like flies and gnats upon the margin of a
pool; they do not sting like an asp, or bite deep
as a bear, yet they can vex a man into a fever
and impatience, and make him incapable of
rest and counsel.

JESTING.

ECCLESIASTICAL History reports that many jests passed between St. Anthony, the father of the Hermits, and his scholar St. Paul ; and St. Hilarion is reported to have been very pleasant, and of facetious, sweet, and more lively conversation ; and indeed plaisance, and joy, and a lively spirit, and a pleasant conversation, and the innocent caresses of a charitable humanity, is not forbidden ; and here in my text our conversation is commanded to be such, that it may minister grace, that is, favor, complacence, cheerfulness, and be acceptable and pleasant to the hearer : and so must be our conversation ; it must be as far from sullenness as it ought to be from lightness, and a cheerful spirit is the best convoy for religion ; and though sadness does in some cases become a Christian, as being an index of a pious mind, of compassion, and a wise, proper resentment of things, yet it serves but one end, being useful in the only instance of repentance ; and hath done its greatest works, not when it weeps and sighs, but when it hates and grows careful against sin. But cheerfulness and a festival spirit fills the soul full of harmony, it composes music for churches and hearts, it makes and publishes glorifications of

God, it produces thankfulness and serves the
end of charity; and when the oil of gladness
runs over, it makes bright and tall emissions of
light and holy fires, reaching up to a cloud,
and making joy round about. And therefore,
since it is so innocent, and may be so pious
and full of holy advantage, whatsoever can
innocently minister to this holy joy does set
forward the work of religion and charity. And
indeed charity itself, which is the vertical top
of all religion, is nothing else but a union of
joys, concentred in the heart, and reflected
from all the angles of our life and intercourse.
It is a rejoicing in God, a gladness in our
neighbor's good, a pleasure in doing good, a
rejoicing with him; and without love we cannot have any joy at all. It is this that makes
children to be a pleasure, and friendship to be
so noble and divine a thing; and upon this
account it is certain that all that which can
innocently make a man cheerful does also
make him charitable; for grief, and age, and
sickness, and weariness, these are peevish and
troublesome; but mirth and cheerfulness is
content, and civil, and compliant, and com-
municative, and loves to do good, and swells
up to felicity only upon the wings of charity.
Upon this account here is pleasure enough for
a Christian at present; and if a facetious discourse, and an amicable friendly mirth, can

refresh the spirit, and take it off from the vile temptation of peevish, despairing, uncomplying melancholy, it must needs be innocent and commendable. And we may as well be refreshed by a clean and a brisk discourse as by the air of Campanian wines; and our faces and our heads may as well be anointed and look pleasant with wit and friendly intercourse as with the fat of the balsam-tree; and such a conversation no wise man ever did or ought to reprove. But when the jest hath teeth and nails, biting or scratching our brother, when it is loose and wanton, when it is unseasonable, and much, or many, when it serves ill purposes, or spends better time, then it is the drunkenness of the soul, and makes the spirit fly away, seeking for a temple where the mirth and the music is solemn and religious.

COMMON SWEARING.

AGAINST common swearing, St. Chrysostom spends twenty homilies: and by the number and weight of arguments hath left this testimony, that it is a foolish vice, but hard to be cured; infinitely unreasonable, but strangely prevailing; almost as much without remedy as it is without pleasure; for it enters first by

folly, and grows by custom, and dwells with
carelessness, and is nursed by irreligion and
want of the fear of God. It profanes the most
holy things, and mingles dirt with the beams of
the sun, follies and trifling talk interweaved
and knit together with the sacred name of God.
It placeth the most excellent of things in the
meanest and basest circumstances ; it brings
the secrets of heaven into the streets, dead
men's bones into the temple. Nothing is a
greater sacrilege than to prostitute the great
name of God to the petulancy of an idle
tongue, and blend it as an expletive to fill up
the emptiness of a weak discourse. The name
of God is so sacred, so mighty, that it rends
mountains ; it opens the bowels of the deepest
rocks, it casts out devils, and makes hell to
tremble, and fills all the regions of heaven
with joy. The name of God is our strength
and confidence, the object of our worshippings,
and the security of all our hopes ; and when
God had given himself a name, and immured
it with dread and reverence, like the garden
of Eden with the swords of cherubims, none
durst speak it but he whose lips were hallowed,
and that at holy and solemn times, in a most
holy and solemn place.

FLATTERY.

THIS is the mischief that is done by flattery; it is a design against the wisdom, against the repentance, against the growth and promotion of a man's soul. He that persuades an ugly, deformed man, that he is handsome, a short man that he is tall, a bald man that he hath a good head of hair, makes him to become ridiculous and a fool, but does no other mischief. But he that persuades his friend that is a goat in his manners, that he is a holy and a chaste person, or that his looseness is a sign of a quick spirit, or that it is not dangerous but easily pardonable, a trick of youth, a habit that old age will lay aside, as a man pares his nails, this man hath given great advantage to his friend's mischief; he hath made it grow in all the dimensions of the sin, till it grows intolerable, and perhaps unpardonable. And let it be considered, what a fearful destruction and contradiction of friendship or service it is, so to love myself and my little interest, as to prefer it before the soul of him whom I ought to love. Carneades said bitterly, but it had in it too many degrees of truth, that princes and great personages never learn to do anything perfectly well but to ride the great horse, because the proud beast knows not how to flatter, but

will as soon throw him off from his back as he
will shake off the son of a porter. But a flat-
terer is like a neighing horse, that neigheth
under every rider, and is pleased with everything, and commends all that he sees, and
tempts to mischief, and cares not, so his friend
may but perish pleasantly. And indeed that is
a calamity that undoes many a soul; we so
love our peace, and sit so easily upon our own
good opinions, and are so apt to flatter ourselves, and lean upon our own false supports,
that we cannot endure to be disturbed or awakened from our pleasing lethargy. For we care
not to be safe, but to be secure; not to escape
hell, but to live pleasantly; we are not solicitous of the event, but of the way thither; and
it is sufficient if we be persuaded all is well;
in the mean time we are careless whether indeed it be so or no, and therefore we give pen-
sions to fools and vile persons to abuse us, and
cozen us of felicity.

CONSOLATION.

GOD glories in the appellative that he is the
Father of mercies, and the God of all comfort, and therefore to minister in the office is to
become like God, and to imitate the charities

of heaven; and God hath fitted mankind for
it; he most needs it, and he feels his brother's
wants by his own experience; and God hath
given us speech and the endearments of society, and pleasantness of conversation, and powers of seasonable discourse, arguments to allay
the sorrow, by abating our apprehensions, and
taking out the sting, or telling the periods of
comfort, or exciting hope, or urging a precept,
and reconciling our affections, and reciting
promises, or telling stories of the divine mercy,
or changing it into duty, or making the burden
less by comparing it with greater, or by prov-
ing it to be less than we deserve, and that it is
so intended, and may become the instrument
of virtue. And certain it is, that as nothing
can better do it, so there is nothing greater
for which God made our tongues, next to reciting his praises, than to minister comfort to a
weary soul. And what greater measure can
we have than that we should bring joy to our
brother, who with his dreary eyes looks to
heaven and round about, and cannot find so
much rest as to lay his eyelids close together,
than that thy tongue should be tuned with
heavenly accents, and make the weary soul to
listen for light and ease; and when he perceives that there is such a thing in the world,
and in the order of things, as comfort and joy,
to begin to break out from the prison of his

sorrows at the door of sighs and tears, and by little and little melt into showers and refreshment? This is glory to thy voice, and employment fit for the brightest angel.

But so have I seen the sun kiss the frozen earth, which was bound up with the images of death and the colder breath of the north; and then the waters break from their enclosures, and melt with joy, and run in useful channels; and the flies do rise again from their little graves in walls, and dance a while in the air, to tell that there is joy within, and that the great mother of creatures will open the stock of her new refreshment, become useful to mankind, and sing praises to her Redeemer. So is the heart of a sorrowful man under the discourses of a wise comforter; he breaks from the despairs of the grave and the fetters and chains of sorrow, he blesses God, and he blesses thee, and he feels his life returning; for to be miserable is death, but nothing is life but to be comforted; and God is pleased with no music from below, so much as in the thanksgiving songs of relieved widows, of supported orphans, of rejoicing and comforted and thankful persons.

This part of communication does the work of God and of our neighbors, and bears us to heaven in streams of joy made by the overflowings of our brother's comfort. It is a fear-

10

ful thing to see a man despairing. None knows the sorrow and the intolerable anguish but themselves, and they that are damned; and so are all the loads of a wounded spirit, when the staff of a man's broken fortune bows his head to the ground, and sinks like an osier under the violence of a mighty tempest. But therefore in proportion to this I may tell the excellency of the employment, and the duty of that charity, which bears the dying and languishing soul from the fringes of hell to the seat of the brightest stars, where God's face shines and reflects comforts forever and ever.

THE SPIRIT OF GRACE.

IN the law, God gave his spirit in small proportions, like the dew upon Gideon's fleece; a little portion was wet sometimes with the dew of heaven, when all the earth besides was dry. And the Jews called it "*filiam vocis*," the daughter of a voice, still, and small, and seldom, and that by secret whispers, and sometimes inarticulate, by way of enthusiasm rather than of instruction; and God spake by the prophets, transmitting the sound as through an organ-pipe, things which themselves oftentimes understood not. But in the gospel, the spirit

is given without measure; first poured forth
upon our head Christ Jesus; then descending
upon the beard of Aaron, the fathers of the
Church, and, thence falling, like the tears of the
balsam of Judea, upon the foot of the plant,
upon the lowest of the people. And this is
given regularly to all that ask it, to all that can
receive it, and by a solemn ceremony, and con-
veyed by a sacrament: and is now, not the
daughter of a voice, but the mother of many
voices, of divided tongues, and united hearts;
of the tongues of prophets, and the duty of
saints: of the sermons of apostles, and the wisdom of governors. It is the parent of boldness
and fortitude to martyrs, the fountain of learning to doctors, an ocean of all things excellent
to all who are within the ship and bounds of
the catholic Church. So that old men and
young men, maidens and boys, the scribe and
the unlearned, the judge and the advocate, the
priest and the people, are full of the spirit, if
they belong to God. Moses's wish is fulfilled,
and all the Lord's people are prophets in some
sense or other.

A man that hath tasted of God's spirit can
instantly discern the madness that is in rage,
the folly and the disease that is in envy, the
anguish and tediousness that is in lust, the dishonor that is in breaking our faith and telling
a lie; and understands things truly as they

are; that is, that charity is the greatest nobleness in the world; that religion hath in it the
greatest pleasures; that temperance is the best
security of health; that humility is the surest
way to honor. And all these relishes are nothing but antepasts of heaven, where the quintes-
sence of all these pleasures shall be swallowed
forever; where the chaste shall follow the
Lamb, and the virgins sing there where the
mother of Jesus shall reign; and the zealous
converters of souls, and the laborers in God's
vineyard, shall worship eternally; where St.
Peter and St. Paul do wear their crowns of
righteousness; and the patient persons shall be
rewarded with Job, and the meek persons with
Christ and Moses, and all with God. The very
expectation of which proceeded from a hope
begotten in us by the spirit of manifestation,
and bred up and strengthened by the spirit of
obsignation, is so delicious an entertainment of
all our reasonable appetites, that a spiritual
man can no more be removed or enticed from
the love of God and of religion than the moon
from her orb, or a mother from loving the son
of her joys and of her sorrows.

I have read of a spiritual person who saw
heaven but in a dream, but such as made great
impression upon him, and was represented with
vigorous and pertinacious phantasms not easily
disbanding; and when he awaked he knew not

his cell, he remembered not him that slept in
the same dorture, nor could tell how night and
day were distinguished, nor could discern oil
from wine ; but called out for his vision again :
" *Redde mihi campos meos floridos, columnam
auream, comitem Hieronymum, assistentes ange-
los* " ; Give me my fields again, my most delicious fields, my pillar of a glorious light, my
companion St. Jerome, my assistant angels.
And this lasted till he was told of his duty,
and matter of obedience, and the fear of a
sin had disencharmed him, and caused him to
take care lest he lose the substance out of
greediness to possess the shadow.

Prayer is one of the noblest exercises of the
Christian religion ; or rather it is that duty in
which all graces are concentrated. Prayer is
charity, it is faith, it is a conformity to God's
will, a desiring according to the desires of
heaven, an imitation of Christ's intercession,
and prayer must suppose all holiness, or else
it is nothing : and therefore all that in which
men need God's spirit, all that is in order to
prayer. Baptism is but a prayer, and the holy
sacrament of the Lord's supper is but a prayer ;
a prayer of sacrifice representative, and a
prayer of oblation, and a prayer of intercession,
and a prayer of thanksgiving. And obedience
is a prayer, and begs and procures blessings.

THE DECLINE OF CHRISTENDOM.

IT is a sad calamity that is fallen upon all the Seven Churches of Asia, (to whom the spirit of God wrote seven epistles by Saint John,) and almost all the churches of Africa, where Christ was worshipped, and now Mahomet is thrust in substitution, and the people are servants, and the religion is extinguished; or where it remains it shines like the moon in an eclipse, or like the least spark of the Pleiades, seen but seldom, and that rather shining like a glowworm than a taper enkindled with a beam of the sun of righteousness.

THE GLORY OF GOD.

GOD is the eternal fountain of honor and the spring of glory; in him it dwells essentially, from him it derives originally; and when an action is glorious, or a man is honorable, it is because the action is pleasing to God, in the relation of obedience or imitation, and because the man is honored by God, and by God's vicegerent. And therefore God cannot be dishonored, because all honor comes from himself; he cannot but be glorified, because to be him-

self is to be infinitely glorious. And yet he is
pleased to say that our sins dishonor him, and
our obedience does glorify him. But as the
sun, the great eye of the world, prying into the
recesses of rocks and the hollowness of valleys,
receives species or visible forms from these
objects, but he beholds them only by that light
which proceeds from himself: so does God,
who is the light of that eye; he receives reflexes and returns from us, and these he calls
glorifications of himself, but they are such
which are made so by his own gracious acceptation. For God cannot be glorified by
anything but by himself, and by his own instruments, which he makes as mirrors to reflect
his own excellency; that, by seeing the glory
of such emanations, he may rejoice in his own
works, because they are images of his infinity.
Thus when he made the beauteous frame of
heaven and earth, he rejoiced in it and glorified himself; because it was the glass in which
he beheld his wisdom and almighty power.
And when God destroyed the old world, in
that also he glorified himself; for in those
waters he saw the image of his justice, — they
were the looking-glass for that attribute.

All the actions of a holy life do constitute
the mass and body of all those instruments
whereby God is pleased to glorify himself. For
if God is glorified in the sun and moon, in the

rare fabric of the honey-combs, in the discipline of bees, in the economy of pismires, in the little houses of birds, in the curiosity of an eye, God being pleased to delight in those little images and reflexes of himself from those pretty mirrors, which, like a crevice in a wall, through a narrow perspective transmit the species of a vast excellency; much rather shall God be pleased to behold himself in the glasses of our obedience, in the emissions of our will and understanding; these being rational and apt instruments to express him, far better than the natural, as being nearer communications of himself.

———◆———

DEATH-BED REPENTANCE.

SINCE repentance is a duty of so great and giant-like bulk, let no man crowd it up into so narrow room as that it be strangled in its birth for want of time, and air to breathe in. Let it not be put off to that time when a man hath scarce time enough to reckon all those particular duties which make up the integrity of its constitution. Will any man hunt the wild boar in his garden, or bait a bull in his closet? Will a woman wrap her child in her handkerchief, or a father send his son to school when he is fifty years old? These are indecencies of providence, and the instrument contradicts the end: and this is our case. There is no room for the repentance, no time to act all its essential parts.

When God requires nothing of us but to live soberly, justly, and godly, — which very things of themselves to man are a very great felicity, and necessary to his present well-being, — shall we think this to be a load, and an insufferable burden; and that heaven is so little a purchase at that price, that God in mere justice will take a death-bed sigh or groan, and a few unprofitable tears and promises, in exchange for all our duty? Strange it should be so; but stranger that any man should rely upon such a vanity, when from God's word he hath nothing to warrant such a confidence. But these men do like the tyrant Dionysius, who stole from Apollo his golden cloak and gave him a cloak of Arcadian homespun, saying that this was lighter in summer and warmer in winter. These men sacrilegiously rob God of the service of all their golden days, and serve him in their hoary head, in their furs and grave-clothes.

DECEITFULNESS OF THE HEART.

MAN is helpless and vain; of a condition so exposed to calamity, that a raisin is able to kill him; any trooper out of the Egyptian army, a fly, can do it, when it goes on God's errand; the most contemptible accident can destroy him, the smallest chance affright him, every future contingency, when but considered as possible, can amaze him; and he is encompassed with potent and malicious enemies, subtle and implacable.

The heart is deceitful in its strength; and when we have the growth of a man, we have the weaknesses of a child. Nay, more yet, and it is a sad consideration, the more we are in age, the weaker in our courage. It appears in the heats and forwardnesses of new converts, which are like to the great emissions of lightning, or like huge fires which flame and burn without measure, even all that they can; till from flames they descend to still fires, from thence to smoke, from smoke to embers, and from thence to ashes, — cold and pale, like ghosts, or the fantastic images of death. And the Primitive Church were zealous in their religion up to the degree of cherubims, and would run as greedily to the sword of the hangman, to die for the cause of God, as we do now

to the greatest joy and entertainment of a
Christian spirit, — even to the receiving of the
holy sacrament. A man would think it reasonable that the first infancy of Christianity
should, according to the nature of first beginnings, have been remiss, gentle, and inactive ;
and that, according as the object or evidence
of faith grew, which in every age hath a great
degree of argument superadded to its confirmation, so should the habit also and the grace ;
the longer it lasts, and the more objections it
runs through, it still should show a brighter
and more certain light to discover the divinity
of its principle ; and that, after the more examples, and new accidents and strangenesses
of Providence, and daily experience, and the
multitude of miracles, still the Christian should
grow more certain in his faith, more refreshed
in his hope, and warm in his charity ; the very
nature of these graces increasing and swelling
upon the very nourishment of experience, and
the multiplication of their own acts. And yet,
because the heart of man is false, it suffers the
fires of the altar to go out, and the flames
lessen by the multitude of fuel. But, indeed,
it is because we put on strange fire, and put
out the fire upon our hearths by letting in a
glaring sunbeam, the fire of lust, or the heats
of an angry spirit, to quench the fire of God,
and suppress the sweet cloud of incense.

There is no greater argument in the world of our spiritual weakness, and the falseness of our hearts in the matters of religion, than the backwardness which most men have always, and all men have sometimes, to say their prayers ; so weary of their length, so glad when they are done, so witty to excuse and frustrate an opportunity : and yet there is no manner of trouble in the duty, no weariness of bones, no violent labors ; nothing but begging a blessing, and receiving it ; nothing but doing ourselves the greatest honor of speaking to the greatest person, and greatest king of the world : and that we should be unwilling to do this, so unable to continue in it, so backward to return to it, so without gust and relish in the doing it, can have no visible reason in the nature of the thing but something within us, a strange sickness in the heart, a spiritual nauseating or loathing of manna, something that hath no name ; but we are sure that it comes from a weak, a faint and false heart.

Epictetus tells us of a gentleman returning from banishment, who, in his journey towards home, called at his house, told a sad story of an imprudent life, the greatest part of which being now spent, he was resolved for the future to live philosophically and entertain no business, to be candidate for no employment, not to go to the court, not to salute Cæsar with ambitious attendances, but to study, and worship the gods, and die willingly when nature or necessity called him. It may be, this man believed himself; but Epictetus did not. And he had reason : letters from Cæsar met him at the doors, and invited him to court ; and he forgot all his promises which were warm upon his lips, and grew pompous, secular, and ambitious, and gave the gods thanks for his preferment. Thus many men leave the world when their fortune hath left them ; and they are severe and philosophical, and retired forever, if forever it be impossible to return. But let a prosperous sunshine warm and refresh their sadnesses, and make it but possible to break their purposes, and there needs no more temptation ; their own false heart is enough ; they are like Ephraim in the day of battle, starting aside like a broken bow.

The heart is false, deceiving and deceived, in its intentions and designs. A man hears the precepts of God enjoining us to give alms of all we possess ; he readily obeys with much cheerfulness and alacrity, and his charity, like a fair-spreading tree, looks beauteously. But there is a canker at the heart ; the man blows a trumpet to call the poor together, and hopes the neighborhood will take notice of his bounty. Nay, he gives alms privately, and charges no man to speak of it, and yet hopes by some accident or other to be praised both for his charity and humility. And if, by chance, the fame of his alms come abroad, it is but his duty to "let his light so shine before men" that God may be glorified.

There is wrought upon the spirits of many men great impressions by education, by a modest and temperate nature, by human laws and the customs and severities of sober persons, and the fears of religion, and the awfulness of a reverend man, and the several arguments and endearments of virtue : and it is not in the nature of some men to do an act in despite of reason, and religion, and arguments, and reverence, and modesty, and fear ; but men are forced from their sin by the violence of the grace of God, when they hear it speak. But so a Roman gentleman kept off a whole band of soldiers who were sent to murder him, and his eloquence was stronger than their anger and design : but, suddenly, a rude trooper rushed upon him, who neither had nor would hear him speak ; and he thrust his spear into that throat whose music had charmed all his fellows into peace and gentleness. So do we. The grace of God is armor and defence enough against the most violent incursion of the spirits and the works of darkness ; but then we must hear its excellent charms, and consider its reasons, and remember its precepts, and dwell

with its discourses. But this the heart of man
loves not.

Theocritus tells of a fisherman that dreamed
he had taken a fish of gold, upon which being
overjoyed, he made a vow that he never would
fish more; but when he waked, he soon declared his vow to be null, because he found his
golden fish was escaped away through the holes
of his eyes when he first opened them. Just
so we do in the purposes of religion; sometimes, in a good mood, we seem to, see heaven
opened, and all the streets of the heavenly
Jerusalem paved with gold and precious stones,
and we are ravished with spiritual apprehensions, and resolve never to return to the low
affections of the world and the impure adherences of sin. But when this flash of lightning
is gone, and we converse again with the inclinations and habitual desires of our false hearts,
those other desires and fine considerations disband, and the resolutions, taken in that pious
fit, melt into indifference and old customs.

The effect of all is this, that we are ignorant
of the things of God. We make religion to be
the work of a few hours in the whole year; we
are without fancy or affection to the severities
of holy living; we reduce religion to the believing of a few articles, and doing nothing that
is considerable; we pray seldom, and then but
very coldly and indifferently; we communicate

not so often as the sun salutes both the tropics;
we profess Christ, but dare not die for him;
we are factious for a religion, and will not live
according to its precepts ; we call ourselves
Christians, and love to be ignorant of many of
the laws of Christ, lest our knowledge should
force us into shame, or into the troubles of a
holy life. All the mischiefs that you can suppose to happen to a furious, inconsiderate person, running after the wildfires of the night,
over rivers and rocks and precipices, without
sun or star, or angel or man, to guide him ; all
that, and ten thousand times worse, may you
suppose to be the certain lot of him who gives
himself up to the conduct of a passionate, blind
heart, whom no fire can warm, and no sun can
enlighten ; who hates light, and loves to dwell
in the regions of darkness.

The heart of man is strangely proud. If
men commend us, we think we have reason
to distinguish ourselves from others, since the
voice of discerning men hath already made the
separation. If men do not commend us, we
think they are stupid and understand us not ;
or envious, and hold their tongues in spite. If
we are praised by many, then " *Vox populi, vox
Dei*," Fame is the voice of God. If we be
praised but by few, then, " *Satis unus, satis
nullus* " ; we cry, These are wise, and one wise
man is worth a whole herd of the people. But

if we be praised by none at all, we resolve to be even with all the world, and speak well of nobody, and think well only of ourselves. And then we have such beggarly arts, such tricks, to cheat for praise. We inquire after our faults and failings, only to be told we have none, but did excellently ; and then we are pleased : we rail upon our actions, only to be chidden for so doing; and then he is our friend who chides us into a good opinion of ourselves, which however all the world cannot make us part with. Nay, humility itself makes us proud ; so false, so base is the heart of man. For humility is so noble a virtue that even pride itself puts on its upper garment ; and we do like those who cannot endure to look upon an ugly or a deformed person, and yet will give a great price for a picture extremely like him. Humility is despised in substance, but courted and admired in effigy. And Æsop's picture was sold for two talents, when himself was made a slave at the price of two philippics. And because humility makes a man to be honored, therefore we imitate all its garbs and postures, its civilities and silence, its modesties and condescensions. And, to prove that we are extremely proud in the midst of all this pageantry, we should be extremely angry at any man that should say we are proud; and that is a sure sign we are so. And in the midst of all our arts to seem humble, we use devices to bring ourselves into talk ; we thrust ourselves into company, we listen at doors, and, like the great beards in Rome that pretended philosophy and strict life, " we walk by the obelisk," and meditate in piazzas, that they that meet us may talk of us, and they that follow may cry out, " Behold! there goes an excellent man! He is very prudent, or very learned, or a charitable person, or a good housekeeper, or at least very humble."

When the heart of man is bound up by the grace of God, and tied in golden bands, and watched by angels, tended by those nurse-keepers of the soul, it is not easy for a man to wander; and the evil of his heart is but like the ferity and wildness of lions' whelps. But when once we have broken the hedge, and got into the strengths of youth, and the licentiousness of an ungoverned age, it is wonderful to observe what a great inundation of mischief in a very short time will overflow all the banks of reason and religion.

FAITH AND PATIENCE.

SO long as the world lived by sense and discourses of natural reason, as they were

abated with human infirmities and not at all
heightened by the spirit and divine revelations,
so long men took their accounts of good and
-bad by their being prosperous or unfortunate ;
and amongst the basest and most ignorant of
men that only was accounted honest which
was profitable, and he only wise that was
rich, and those men beloved of God who
received from him all that might satisfy their
lust, their ambition, or their revenge.

But because God sent wise men into the
world, and they were treated rudely by the
world, and exercised with evil accidents, and
this seemed so great a discouragement to virtue,
that even these wise men were more troubled
to reconcile virtue and misery than to reconcile
their affections to the suffering; God was pleased
to enlighten their reason with a little beam of
faith, or else heightened their reason by wiser
principles than those of vulgar understandings,
and taught them in the clear glass of faith, or
the dim perspective of philosophy, to look beyond the cloud, and there to spy that there
stood glories behind their curtain, to which they
could not come but by passing through the
cloud, and being wet with the dew of heaven
and the waters of affliction. And according as
the world grew more enlightened by faith, so it
grew more dark with mourning and sorrows.
God sometimes sent a light of fire, and a pillar

of a cloud, and the brightness of an angel, and
the lustre of a star, and the sacrament of a
rainbow, to guide his people through their portion of sorrows, and to lead them through
troubles to rest.   But as the sun of righteousness approached towards the chambers of the
east, and sent the harbingers of light peeping
through the curtains of the night, and leading
on the day of faith and brightest revelation ;
so God sent degrees of trouble upon wise and
good men, that now in the same degree in the
which the world "lives by faith" and not by
sense, in the same degree they might be able
to live in virtue even while she lived in trouble,
and not reject so great a beauty because she
goes in mourning, and hath a black cloud of
cypress drawn before her face.   Literally thus:
God first entertained their services, and allured
and prompted on the infirmities of the infant
world by temporal prosperity ; but by degrees
changed his method, and as men grew stronger
in the knowledge of God and the expectations
of heaven, so they grew weaker in their fortunes, more afflicted in their bodies, more
abated in their expectations, more subject to
their enemies, and were to "endure the contradiction of sinners," and the immission of the
sharpnesses of providence and divine economy.

THE HUMILIATION OF CHRIST.

JESUS entered into the world with all the circumstances of poverty. He had a star to illustrate his birth; but a stable for his bed-chamber, and a manger for his cradle. The angels sang hymns when he was born; but he was cold and cried, uneasy and unprovided. He lived long in the trade of a carpenter; he by whom God made the world had, in his first years, the business of a mean and ignoble trade. He did good wherever he went; and almost wherever he went was abused. He deserved heaven for his obedience, but found a cross in his way thither: and if ever any man had reason to expect fair usages from God, and to be dandled in the lap of ease, softness, and a prosperous fortune, he it was only that could deserve that, or anything that can be good. But after he had chosen to live a life of vir-tue, of poverty and labor, he entered into a state of death.

All that Christ came for was, or was mingled with, sufferings: for all those little joys which God sent, either to recreate his person, or to illustrate his office, were abated or attended with afflictions; God being more careful to establish in him the covenant of sufferings than to refresh his sorrows. Presently after

the angels had finished their hallelujahs, he
was forced to fly to save his life; and the air
became full of shrieks of the desolate mothers
of Bethlehem for their dying babes. God had
no sooner made him illustrious with a voice
from heaven, and the descent of the Holy
Ghost upon him in the waters of baptism, but
he was delivered over to be tempted and as-
saulted by the devil in the wilderness. His
transfiguration was a bright ray of glory; but
then also he entered into a cloud, and was told
a sad story what he was to suffer at Jerusalem.
And upon Palm-Sunday, when he rode tri-
umphantly into Jerusalem, and was adorned
with the acclamations of a king and a God, he
wet the palms with his tears, sweeter than the
drops of manna or the little pearls of heaven
that descended upon Mount Hermon; weeping
in the midst of this triumph over obstinate,
perishing, and malicious Jerusalem. For this
Jesus was like the rainbow which God set in
the clouds as a sacrament to confirm a promise
and establish a grace; he was half made of the
glories of the light, and half of the moisture of
a cloud; in his best days he was but half triumph and half sorrow: he was sent to tell of
his Father's mercies, and that God intended
to spare us; but appeared not but in the company or in the retinue of a shower, and of foul
weather.

But I need not tell that Jesus, beloved of God, was a suffering person. That which concerns this question most, is, that he made for us a covenant of sufferings; his doctrines were such as expressly and by consequence enjoin and suppose sufferings and a state of affliction; his very promises were sufferings; his beatitudes were sufferings; his rewards, and his arguments to invite men to follow him, were only taken from sufferings in this life, and the reward of sufferings hereafter. We must follow him that was crowned with thorns and sorrows, — him that was drenched in Cedron, nailed upon the cross, that deserved all good and suffered all evil: that is the sum of the Christian religion, as it distinguishes from all the religions of the world. So that if we will serve the king of sufferings, whose crown was of thorns, whose sceptre was a reed of scorn, whose imperial robe was a scarlet of mockery, whose throne was the cross, we must serve him in sufferings, in poverty of spirit, in humility and mortification. And for our reward we shall have persecution, and all its blessed consequents. "*Atque hoc est esse Christianum.*"

For as the gospel was founded in sufferings, we shall also see it grow in persecutions : and as Christ's blood did cement the corner-stones and the first foundations, so the blood and sweat, the groans and sighings, the afflictions and mortifications of saints and martyrs did make the superstructures, and must at last finish the building.

———◆———

TRIUMPHS OF CHRISTIANITY.

NOW began to work the greatest glory of the divine providence : here was the case of Christianity at stake. The world was rich and prosperous, learned and full of wise men ; the gospel was preached with poverty and persecution, in simplicity of discourse, and in demonstration of the spirit. God was on one side, and the devil on the other ; they each of them dressed up their city ; Babylon upon earth, Jerusalem from above. The devil's city was full of pleasure, triumphs, victories, and cruelty ; good news, and great wealth ; conquest over kings, and making nations tributary. They "bound kings in chains, and the nobles with links of iron ; and the inheritance of the earth was theirs." The Romans were lords over the greatest part of the world ; and God permitted to the devil the firmament and increase, the wars and the success of that people giving to him an entire power of disposing the great change of the world so as might best increase their greatness and power: and he therefore did it because all the power of the Roman greatness was a professed enemy to Christianity. And, on the other side, God was to build up Jerusalem, and the kingdom of the gospel; and he chose to build it of hewn stone, cut and broken. The Apostles he chose for preachers, and they had no learning; women and mean people were the first disciples, and they had no power. The devil was to lose his kingdom, he wanted no malice ; and therefore he stirred up, and, as well as he could, he made active, all the power of Rome, and all the learning of the Greeks. and all the malice of barbarous people, and all the prejudice and the obstinacy of the Jews, against this doctrine and institution, which preached, and promised, and brought persecution along with it. On the one side there was " *scandalum crucis,*" on the other, "*patientia sanctorum*" : and what was the event ? They that had overcome the world could not strangle Christianity. But so have I seen the sun with a little ray of distant light challenge all the power of darkness, and, without violence and noise climbing up the hill, hath made night so to retire that its memory was lost in the joys and sprightfulness of the morning. And Christianity, without violence or armies, without resistance and self-preservation, without strength or human eloquence,

without challenging of privileges or fighting
against tyranny, without alteration of government and scandal of princes, with its humility
and meekness, with toleration and patience,
with obedience and charity, with praying and
dying, did insensibly turn the world into Christian, and persecution into victory.

Presently it came to pass that men were no
longer ashamed of the cross, but it was worn
upon breasts, printed in the air, drawn upon
foreheads, carried upon banners, put upon
crowns imperial.   Presently it came to pass
that the religion of the despised Jesus did
infinitely prevail; a religion that taught men
to be meek and humble, apt to receive injuries,
but unapt to do any; a religion that gave
countenance to the poor and pitiful, in a time
when riches were adored, and ambition and
pleasure had possessed the heart of all mankind; a religion that would change the face of
things and the hearts of men, and break vile
habits into gentleness and counsel.   That such
a religion, in such a time, by the sermons and
conduct of fishermen, men of mean breeding
and illiberal arts, should so speedily triumph
over the philosophy of the world, and the arguments of the subtle, and the sermons of the
eloquent, the power of princes and the interests of States, the inclinations of nature and
the blindness of zeal, the force of custom and

the solicitation of passions, the pleasures of sin
and the busy arts of the devil ; that is, against
wit and power, superstition and wilfulness,
fame and money, nature and empire, which are
all the causes in this world that can make a
thing impossible ; — this, this is to be ascribed
to the power of God, and is the great demonstration of the resurrection of Jesus. Everything was an argument for it, and improved it ;
no objection could hinder it, no enemies destroy
it ; whatsoever was for them, it made the religion to increase ; whatsoever was against them,
made it to increase ; sunshine and storms, fair
weather or foul, it was all one as to the event
of things : for they were instruments in the
hands of God, who could make what himself
should choose to be the product of any cause ;
so that if the Christians had peace, they went
abroad and brought in converts : if they had
no peace, but persecution, the converts came
in to them. In prosperity they allured and
enticed the world by the beauty of holiness ; in
affliction and trouble they amazed all men with
the splendor of their innocence and the glories of their patience ; and quickly it was that
the world became disciple to the glorious Naza-
rene, and men could no longer doubt of the
resurrection of Jesus, when it became so de-
monstrated by the certainty of them that saw
it, and the courage of them that died for it,

and the multitude of them that believed it;
who by their sermons and their actions, by
their public offices and discourses, by festivals
and eucharists, by arguments of experience
and sense, by reason and religion, by persuad-
ing rational men and establishing believing
Christians, by their living in the obedience of
Jesus and dying for the testimony of Jesus,
have greatly advanced his kingdom, and his
power, and his glory, into which he entered
his resurrection from the dead.

AFFLICTIONS OF THE CHURCH.

IF under a head crowned with thorns, we
bring to God members circled with roses,
and softness, and delicacy, triumphant members in the militant Church, God will reject us;
he will not know us who are so unlike our
elder brother. For we are members of the
Lamb, not of the lion; and of Christ's suffering part, not of the triumphant part: and for
three hundred years together the Church lived
upon blood, and was nourished with blood, — the
blood of her own children. Thirty-three bishops of Rome in immediate succession were put
to violent and unnatural deaths; and so were
all the churches of the East and West built.

The cause of Christ and of religion was advanced by the sword, but it was the sword of the persecutors, not of resisters or warriors. They were all baptized into the death of Christ; their very profession and institution is to live like him, and, when he requires it, to die for him; that is the very formality, the life and essence, of Christianity. This, I say, lasted for three hundred years, that the prayers, and the backs, and the necks of Christians fought against the rods and axes of the persecutors, and prevailed, till the country, and the cities, and the court itself, was filled with Christians. And by this time the army of martyrs was vast and numerous, and the number of sufferers blunted the hangman's sword. For Christ had triumphed over the princes and powers of the world, before he would admit them to serve him; he first felt their malice, before he would make use of their defence; to show, that it was not his necessity that required it, but his grace that admitted kings and queens to be nurses of the Church.

Christ also promised that "all things should work together for the best to his servants," that is, he would "out of the eater bring meat, and out of the strong issue sweetness," and crowns and sceptres should spring from crosses, and that the cross itself should stand upon the globes and sceptres of princes; but he never promised to his servants that they should pursue kings and destroy armies, that they should reign over nations, and promote the cause of Jesus Christ by breaking his commandment. " The shield of faith, and the sword of the spirit, the armor of righteousness, and the weapons of spiritual warfare " ; these are they by which Christianity swelled from a small company, and a less reputation, to possess the chairs of doctors, and the thrones of princes, and the hearts of all men.

----•----

THE RIGHTEOUS OPPRESSED.

IF prosperity were the voice of God to approve an action, then no man were vicious but he that is punished, and nothing were rebellion but that which cannot be easily suppressed ; and no man were a pirate but he that robs with a little vessel ; and no man could be a tyrant but that he is no prince ; and no man an unjust invader of his neighbor's rights but he that is beaten and overthrown. Then the crime grows big and loud, then it calls to heaven for vengeance, when it hath been long a growing, when it hath thriven under the devil's managing; when God hath long suffered it, and with patience, in vain expecting the repentance of a sinner. He that "treasures up wrath against the day of wrath," that man hath been a prosperous, that is, an unpunished and a thriving sinner: but then it is the sin that thrives, not the man: and that is the mistake upon this whole question; for the sin cannot thrive, unless the man goes on without apparent punishment and restraint. And all that the man gets by it is, that by a continual course of sin he is prepared for an intolerable ruin.

The spirit of God bids us look upon the end of these men; not the way they walk, or the instrument of that pompous death. When Epaminondas was asked which of the three was happiest, himself, Chabrias, or Iphicrates, he bid the man stay till they were all dead; for till then that question could not be answered. He that had seen the Vandals besiege the city of Hippo, and had known the barbarousness of that unchristened people, and had observed that St. Austin with all his prayers and vows could not obtain peace in his own days, not so much as a reprieve for the persecution, and then had observed St. Austin die with grief that very night, would have perceived his calamity more visible than the reward of his piety and holy religion. When Lewis, surnamed Pius, went his voyage to Palestine upon a holy end, and for the glory of God, to fight against the Saracens and Turks and Mamelukes, the world did promise to themselves that a good cause should thrive in the hands of so holy a man ; but the event was far otherwise : his brother Robert was killed, and his army destroyed, and himself taken prisoner, and the money which by his mother was sent for his redemption was cast away in a storm, and he was exchanged for the last town the Christians had in Egypt, and brought home the cross of Christ upon his shoulder in a real pressure and participation of his Master's sufferings. When Charles the Fifth went to Algiers to suppress pirates and unchristened villains, the cause was more confident than the event was prosperous ; and when he was almost ruined in a prodigious storm, he told the minutes of the clock, expecting that at midnight, when religious persons rose to matins, he should be eased by the benefit of their prayers. But the providence of God trod upon those waters, and left no footsteps for discovery. His navy was beat in pieces, and his design ended in dishonor, and his life almost lost by the bargain. Was ever cause more baffled than the Christian cause by the Turks in all Asia and Africa, and some parts of Europe, if to be persecuted and afflicted be reckoned a calamity ? What prince was ever more unfortunate than Henry the Sixth of England ? and yet that age saw none more pious and devout. And the title of the house of Lancaster was advanced against the right of York for three descents. But what was the end of these things? The persecuted men were made saints, and their memories are preserved in honor, and their souls shall reign forever. And some good men were engaged in a wrong cause, and the good cause was sometimes managed by evil men; till that the suppressed cause was lifted up by God in the hands of a young and prosperous prince, and at last both interests were satisfied in the conjunction of two roses, which was brought to issue by a wonderful chain of causes managed by the divine providence. And there is no age, no history, no state, no great change in the world, but hath ministered an example of an afflicted truth, and a prevailing sin: for I will never more call that sinner prosperous, who, after he hath been permitted to finish his business, shall die and perish miserably; for at the same rate we may envy the happiness of a poor fisherman, who, while his nets were drying, slept upon the rock, and dreamt that he was made a king; on a sudden starts up, and leaping for joy, falls down from the rock, and in the place of his imaginary felicities loses his little portion of pleasure and innocent solaces he had from the sound sleep and little cares of his humble cottage.

12

REAL AND APPARENT HAPPINESS.

IF we should look under the skirt of the prosperous and prevailing tyrant, we should find even in the days of his joys such allays and abatements of his pleasure as may serve to represent him presently miserable, besides his final infelicities. For I have seen a young and healthful person warm and ruddy under a poor and thin garment, when at the same time an old rich person hath been cold and paralytic under a load of sables and the skins of foxes. It is the body that makes the clothes warm, not the clothes the body; and the spirit of a man makes felicity and content, not any spoils of a rich fortune wrapt about a sickly and an uneasy soul. Apollodorus was a traitor and a tyrant, and the world wondered to see a bad man have so good a fortune; but knew not that he nourished scorpions in his breast, and that his liver and his heart were eaten up with spectres and images of death. His thoughts were full of interruptions, his dreams of illusions; his fancy was abused with real troubles and fantastic images, imagining that he saw the Scythians flaying him alive, his daughters like pillars of fire dancing round about a caldron in which himself was boiling, and that his heart accused itself to be the cause of all these evils.

Does not he drink more sweetly that takes his beverage in an earthen vessel, than he that looks and searches into his golden chalices for fear of poison, and looks pale at every sudden noise, and sleeps in armor, and trusts nobody, and does not trust God for his safety, but does greater wickedness only to escape awhile unpunished for his former crimes? "*Auro bibitur venenum.*" No man goes about to poison a poor man's pitcher, nor lays plots to forage his little garden made for the hospital of two beehives, and the feasting of a few Pythagorean herb-eaters. They that admire the happiness of a prosperous, prevailing tyrant, know not the felicities that dwell in innocent hearts, and poor cottages, and small fortunes.

Can a man bind a thought with chains, or carry imaginations in the palm of his hand? Can the beauty of the peacock's train, or the ostrich plume, be delicious to the palate and the throat? Does the hand intermeddle with the joys of the heart? or darkness, that hides the naked, make him warm? Does the body live, as does the spirit? or can the body of Christ be like to common food? Indeed the sun shines upon the good and bad; and the vines give wine to the drunkard as well as to the sober man; pirates have fair winds and a calm sea at the same time when the just and peaceful merchantman hath them. But although the things of this world are common to good and bad, yet sacraments and spiritual joys, the food of the soul, and the blessing of Christ, are the peculiar right of saints.

MARTYRDOM.

THEY that suffer anything for Christ, and are ready to die for him, let them do nothing against him. For certainly they think too highly of martyrdom, who believe it able to excuse all the evils of a wicked life. A man may give his body to be burned, and yet have no charity; and he that dies without charity dies without God: "for God is love." And when those who fought in the days of the Maccabees for the defence of true religion, and were killed in those holy wars, yet, being dead, were found having about their necks pendants consecrated to idols of the Jamnenses; it much allayed the hope which, by their dying in so good a cause, was entertained concerning their beatifical resurrection. He that overcomes his fear of death, does well; but if he hath not also overcome his lust, or his anger, his baptism of blood will not wash him clean. Many things make a man willing to die in a good cause: public reputation, hope of reward, gallantry of spirit, a confident resolution, and a masculine courage; or a man may be vexed into a stubborn and unrelenting suffering. But nothing can make a man live well but the grace and the love of God. But those persons are infinitely condemned by their last act, who profess their religion to be worth dying for, and yet are so unworthy as not to live according to its institution. It were a rare felicity, if every good cause could be managed by good men only; but we have found that evil men have spoiled a good cause, but never that a good cause made those evil men good and holy. If the governor of Samaria had crucified Simon Magus for receiving Christian baptism, he had no more died a martyr than he lived a saint. For dying is not enough, and dying in a good cause is not enough; but then only we receive the crown of martyrdom when our death is the seal of our life, and our life is a continual testimony of our duty, and both give testimony to the excellencies of the religion, and glorify the grace of God. If a man be gold, the fire purges him; but it burns him if he be like stubble, cheap, light, and useless. For martyrdom is the consummation of love. But then it must be supposed that this grace must have had its beginning, and its several stages and periods, and must have passed through labor to zeal, through all the regions of duty to the per-

fections of sufferings. And therefore it is a sad
thing to observe how some empty souls will
please themselves with being of such a religion
or such a cause, and, though they dishonor
their religion, or weigh down the cause with
the prejudice of sin, believe all is swallowed up
by one honorable name, or the appellative of
one virtue. If God had forbid nothing but
heresy and treason, then to have been a loyal
man, or of a good belief, had been enough:
but he that forbade rebellion forbids all swearing and covetousness, rapine and oppression,
lying and cruelty. And it is a sad thing to
see a man not only to spend his time, and his
wealth, and his money, and his friends upon his
lust, but to spend his sufferings too: to let the
canker-worm of a deadly sin devour his martyrdom. He therefore that suffers in a good
cause, let him be sure to walk worthy of that
honor to which God hath called him; let him
first deny his sins, and then deny himself, and
then he may take up his cross and follow
Christ; ever remembering that no man pleases
God in his death who hath walked perversely
in his life.

THE PROGRESS OF SOULS.

AS the silk-worm eateth itself out of a seed to become a little worm; and there feeding on the leaves of mulberries, it grows till its coat be off, and then works itself into a house of silk; then casting its pearly seeds for the young to breed, it leaveth its silk for man, and dieth all white and winged in the shape of a flying creature: so is the progress of souls. When they are regenerate by baptism, and have cast off their first stains and the skin of worldly vanities by feeding on the leaves of scriptures, and the fruits of the vine, and the joys of the sacrament, they encircle themselves in the rich garments of holy and virtuous habits; then by leaving their blood, which is the Church's seed, to raise up a new generation to God, they leave a blessed memory and fair example, and are themselves turned into angels, whose felicity is to do the will of God, as their employment was in this world to suffer it.

THE INEXPERIENCED CHRISTIAN.

THE righteous is safe; but by intermedial difficulties: and he is safe in the midst of his persecutions; they may disturb his rest, and discompose his fancy, but they are like the fiery chariot to Elias; he is encircled with fire, and rare circumstances, and strange usages, but is carried up to heaven in a robe of flames. And so was Noah safe when the flood came, and was the great type and instance too of the verification of this proposition; he was put into a strange condition, perpetually wandering, shut up in a prison of wood, living upon faith, having never had the experience of being safe in floods.

And so have I often seen young and unskilful persons sitting in a little boat, when every little wave sporting about the sides of the vessel, and every motion and dancing of the barge seemed a danger, and made them cling fast upon their fellows; and yet all the while they were as safe as if they sat under a tree, while a gentle wind shaked the leaves into a refreshment and a cooling shade. And the unskilful, inexperienced Christian shrieks out whenever his vessel shakes, thinking it always a danger that the watery pavement is not stable and resident like a rock; and yet all his danger is in himself, none at all from without: for he is indeed moving upon the waters, but fastened to a rock. Faith is his foundation, and hope is his anchor, and death is his harbor, and Christ is his pilot, and heaven is his country; and all the evils of poverty, or affronts of tribunals and evil judges, of fears and sadder apprehensions, are but like the loud wind blowing from the right point: they make a noise, and drive faster to the harbor. And if we do not leave the ship and leap into the sea; quit the interests of religion, and run to the securities of the world; cut our cables, and dissolve our hopes; grow impatient, and hug a wave, and die in its embraces; we are as safe at sea, safer in the storm which God sends us, than in a calm when we are befriended with the world.

THE SORROWS OF THE GODLY.

SO much as moments are exceeded by eternity, and the sighing of a man by the joys of an angel, and a salutary frown by the light of God's countenance, a few groans by the infinite and eternal hallelujahs; so much are the sorrows of the godly to be undervalued in respect of what is deposited for them in the treasures of eternity. Their sorrows can die, but so cannot their joys. And if the blessed martyrs and confessors were asked concerning their past sufferings and their present rest, and the joys of their certain expectation, you should hear them glory in nothing but in the mercies of God, and in the cross of the Lord Jesus. Every chain is a ray of light, and every prison is a palace, and every loss is the purchase of a kingdom, and every affront in the cause of God is an eternal honor, and every day of sorrow is a thousand years of comfort, multiplied with a never-ceasing numeration; days without night, joys without sorrow, sanctity without sin, charity without stain, possession without fear, society without envying, communication of joys without lessening: and they shall dwell in a blessed country, where an enemy never entered, and from whence a friend never went away.

THE GOODNESS OF GOD.

FROM the beginning of time till now, all effluxes which have come from God have been nothing but emanations of his goodness clothed in variety of circumstances. He made man with no other design than that man should be happy, and by receiving derivations from his fountain of mercy, might reflect glory to him. And therefore God making man for his own glory, made also a paradise for man's use ; and did him good, to invite him to do himself a greater. For God gave forth demonstrations of his power by instances of mercy, and he who might have made ten thousand worlds of wonder and prodigy, and created man with faculties able only to stare upon and admire those miracles of mightiness, did choose to instance his power in the effusions of mercy, that at the same instant he might represent himself desirable and adorable, in all the capacities of amiability ; viz: as excellent in himself, and profitable to us. For as the sun sends forth a benign and gentle influence on the seed of plants, that it may invite forth the active and plastic power from its recess and secrecy, that by rising into the tallness and dimensions of a tree it may still receive a greater and more refreshing influence from its foster-father, the prince of all the bodies of light ; and in all these emanations the sun itself receives no advantage but the honor of doing benefits : so doth the Almighty Father of all the creatures ; he at first sends forth his blessings upon us, that we by using them aright should make ourselves capable of greater ; while the giving glory to God, and doing homage to him, are nothing for his advantage, but only for ours ;

our duties towards him being like vapors ascending from the earth, not at all to refresh the region of the clouds, but to return back in a fruitful and refreshing shower ; and God created us, not that we can increase his felicity, but that he might have a subject receptive of felicity from him.

What a prodigy of favor is it to us, that he hath passed by so many forms of his creatures, and hath not set us down in the rank of any of them, till we came to be "*paulo minores angelis*," a little lower than the angels? and yet from the meanest of them God can perfect his own praise. The deeps and the snows, the hail and the rain, the birds of the air and the fishes of the sea, they can and do glorify God, and give him praise in their capacity. And yet he gave them no speech, no reason, no immortal spirit, or capacity of eternal blessedness. But he hath distinguished us from them by the absolute issues of his predestination, and hath given us a lasting and eternal spirit, excellent organs of perception, and wonderful instruments of expression, that we may join in consort with the morning-star, and bear a part in the chorus with the angels of light, to sing hallelujah to the great Father of men and angels.

The poorest person amongst us, besides the blessings and graces already reckoned, hath enough about him, and the accidents of every day, to shame him into repentance. Does not God send his angels to keep thee in all thy way? Are not they ministering spirits sent forth to wait upon thee as thy guard? Art not thou kept from drowning, from fracture of bones, from madness, from deformities, by the riches of the divine goodness? Tell the joints of thy body, dost thou want a finger? and if thou dost not understand how great a blessing that is, do but remember how ill thou canst spare the use of it when thou hast but a thorn in it. The very privative blessings, the blessings of immunity, safeguard, and integrity, which we all enjoy, deserve a thanksgiving of a whole life. If God should send a cancer upon thy face, or a wolf into thy breast, if he should spread a crust of leprosy upon thy skin, what wouldest thou give to be but as now thou art? Wouldest not thou repent of thy sins upon that condition? Which is the greater blessing, — to be kept from them, or to be cured of them?

THE DANGER OF PROSPERITY.

IN the tomb of Terentia certain lamps burned under-ground many ages together; but as soon as ever they were brought into the air, and saw a bigger light, they went out, never to be reënkindled. So long as we are in the retirements of sorrow, of want, of fear, of sickness, or of any sad accident, we are " burning and shining lamps " ; but when God comes with his forbearance, and lifts us up from the gates of death, and carries us abroad into the open air, that we converse with prosperity and temptation, we go out in darkness ; and we cannot be preserved in heat and light but by still dwelling in the regions of sorrow.

——◆——

MERCY AND JUDGMENT.

IF God suffers men to go on in sins, and punishes them not, it is not a mercy, it is not a forbearance ; it is a hardening them, a consigning them to ruin and reprobation : and themselves give the best argument to prove it ; for they continue in their sin, they multiply their iniquity, and every day grow more an enemy to God ; and that is no mercy that increases their hostility and enmity with God. A prosperous iniquity is the most unprosperous condition in the whole world. " When he slew them, they sought him, and turned them early, and inquired after God " : but as long as they

prevailed upon their enemies, " they forgot
that God was their strength, and the high God
was their redeemer." It was well observed
by the Persian ambassador of old, — when he
was telling the king a sad story of the over-
throw of all his army by the Athenians, he
adds this of his own, — that the day before the
fight, the young Persian gallants, being confident they should destroy their enemies, were
drinking drunk, and railing at the timorousness
and fears of religion, and against all their gods,
saying there were no such things, and that all
things came by chance and industry, nothing
by the providence of the Supreme Power.
But the next day, when they had fought un-
prosperously, and flying from their enemies,
who were eager in their pursuit, they came to
the river Strymon, which was so frozen that
their boats could not launch, and yet it began
to thaw, so that they feared the ice would not
bear them ; then you should see the bold gallants, that the day before said there was no
God, most timorously and superstitiously fall
upon their faces, and beg of God that the
river Strymon might bear them over from their
enemies.

What wisdom and philosophy, and perpetual
experience and revelation, and promises and
blessings cannot do, a mighty fear can ; it can
allay the confidences of bold lust and imperious

sin, and soften our spirit into the lowness of a
child, our revenge into the charity of prayers,
our impudence into the blushings of a chidden
girl; and therefore God hath taken a course
proportionable: for he is not so unmercifully
merciful as to give milk to an infirm lust, and
hatch the egg to the bigness of a cockatrice.
And therefore observe how it is that God's
mercy prevails over all his works. It is even
then when nothing can be discerned but his
judgments. For as when a famine had been
in Israel in the days of Ahab for three years
and a half, when the angry prophet Elijah met
the king, and presently a great wind arose, and
the dust blew into the eyes of them that walked
abroad, and the face of the heavens was black
and all tempest, yet then the prophet was the
most gentle, and God began to forgive, and
the heavens were more beautiful than when the
sun puts on the brightest ornaments of a bride-
groom, going from his chambers of the east:
so it is in the economy of the divine mercy;
when God makes our faces black, and the
winds blow so loud till the cordage cracks,
and our gay fortunes split, and our houses
are dressed with cypress and yew, and the
mourners go about the streets, this is nothing
but the " *pompa misericordiæ*," — this is the
funeral of our sins, dressed indeed with em-
blems of mourning, and proclaimed with sad

accents of death; but the sight is refreshing as the beauties of the field which God had blessed, and the sounds are healthful as the noise of a physician.

But however we sleep in the midst of such alarms, yet know that there is not one death in all the neighborhood but is intended to thee; every crowing of the cock is to awake thee to repentance. And if thou sleepest still, the next turn may be thine; God will send his angel, as he did to Peter, and smite thee on thy side, and awake thee from thy dead sleep of sin and sottishness. But beyond this some are despisers still, and hope to drown the noises of Mount Sinai, the sound of cannons, of thunders and lightnings, with a counter-noise of revelling and clamorous roarings, with merry meetings; like the sacrifices to Moloch, they sound drums and trumpets that they might not hear the sad shriekings of their children as they were dying in the cavity of the brazen idol. And when their conscience shrieks out or murmurs in a sad melancholy, or something that is dear to them is smitten, they attempt to drown it in a sea of drink, in the heathenish noises of idle and drunken company; and that which God sends to lead them to repentance leads them to a tavern, not to refresh their needs of nature, or for ends of a tolerable civility, or innocent purposes, but, like the condemned persons among the Levantines, they tasted wine freely that they might die and be insensible.

He that is full of stripes and troubles, and decked round about with thorns, he is near to God. But he that, because he sits uneasily when he sits near the King that was crowned with thorns, shall remove thence, or strew flowers, roses and jessamine, the down of thistles and the softest gossamer, that he may die without pain, die quietly and like a lamb, sink to the bottom of hell without noise ; this man is a fool, because he accepts death if it arrests him in civil language, is content to die by the sentence of an eloquent judge, and prefers a quiet passage to hell before going to heaven in a storm.

PRIMITIVE PIETY.

WHEN Christianity, like the day-spring from the east, with a new light did not only enlighten the world, but amazed the minds of men, and entertained their curiosities, and seized upon their warmer and more pregnant affections, it was no wonder that whole nations were converted at a sermon, and multitudes were instantly professed, and their understandings followed their affections, and their wills followed their understandings, and they were convinced by miracle, and overcome by grace, and passionate with zeal, and wisely governed by their guides, and ravished with the sanctity of the doctrine and the holiness of their examples. And this was not only their duty, but a great instance of providence, that by the great religion and piety of the first professors, Christianity might be firmly planted, and unshaken by scandal, and hardened by persecution; and that these first lights might be actual precedents forever, and copies for us to transcribe in all descending ages of Christianity, that thither we might run to fetch oil to enkindle our extinguished lamps.

Men of old looked upon themselves as they stood by the examples and precedents of martyrs, and compared their piety to the life of St. Paul, and estimated their zeal by flames of the Boanerges, St. James and his brother; and the bishops were thought reprovable as they fell short of the ordinary government of St. Peter and St. John; and the assemblies of Christians were so holy that every meeting had religion enough to hallow a house and convert it to a church; and every day of feasting was a communion; and every fasting-day was a day of repentance and alms; and every day of thanksgiving was a day of joy and alms; and religion began all their actions, and prayer consecrated them; and they ended in charity and were not polluted with design: they despised the world heartily and pursued after heaven greedily; they knew no ends but to serve God and to be saved; and had no designs upon their neighbors but to lead them to God and to felicity.

———

GROWTH IN GRACE.

A MAN cannot, after a state of sin, be instantly a saint; the work of heaven is not done by a flash of lightning, or a dash of affectionate rain, or a few tears of a relenting pity. Remember that God sent you into the world for religion: we are but to pass through our pleasant fields or our hard labors, but to lodge a little while in our fair palaces or our meaner cottages, but to bait in the way at our full tables or with our spare diet; but then only man does his proper employment when he prays, and does charity, and mortifies his unruly appetites, and restrains his violent passions, and becomes like to God, and imitates his holy Son, and writes after the copies of apostles and saints.

The canes of Egypt, when they newly arise from their bed of mud and slime of Nilus, start

up into an equal and continual length, and are
interrupted but with few knots, and are strong
and beauteous with great distances and intervals : but when they are grown to their full
length, they lessen into the point of a pyramid,
and multiply their knots and joints, interrupt-
ing the fineness and smoothness of its body.
So are the steps and declensions of him that
does not grow in grace. At first, when he
springs up from his impurity by the waters
of baptism and repentance, he grows straight
and strong, and suffers but few interruptions
of piety ; and his constant courses of religion
are but rarely intermitted, till they ascend up
to a full age, or towards the ends of their life ;
then they are weak, and their devotions often
intermitted, and their breaches are frequent,
and they seek excuses and labor for dispen-
sations, and love God and religion less and
less, till their old age, instead of a crown of
their virtue and perseverance, ends in levity
and unprofitable courses ; light and useless as
the tufted feathers upon the cane, every wind
can play with it and abuse it, but no man can
make it useful. When, therefore, our piety
interrupts its greater and more solemn expressions, and upon the return of the greater
offices and bigger solemnities we find them
to come upon our spirits like the wave of a
tide, which retired only because it was natural

so to do, and yet came farther upon the strand
at the next rolling; when every new confes-
sion, every succeeding communion, every time
of separation for more solemn and intense
prayer is better spent and more affectionate,
leaving a greater relish upon the spirit, and
possessing greater portions of our affections,
our reason and our choice; then we may
give God thanks, who hath given us more
grace to use that grace, and a blessing to en-
deavor our duty, and a blessing upon our en-
deavor.

In all cases, the well-grown Christian, he
that improves or goes forward in his way to
heaven, brings virtue forth, not into discourses
and panegyrics, but into his life and manners.
His virtue, although it serves many good ends
accidentally, yet, by his intention, it only sup-
presses his inordinate passions, makes him temperate and chaste, casts out his devils of drunkenness and lust, pride and rage, malice and revenge; it makes him useful to his brother, and
a servant of God. And although these flowers
cannot choose but please his eye and delight
his smell, yet he chooses to gather honey, and
lick up the dew of heaven, and feasts his spirit
upon the manna, and dwells not in the collateral usages and accidental sweetnesses which
dwell at the gates of other senses; but, like
a bee, loads his thighs with wax and his bag

with honey, that is, with the useful parts of
virtue, in order to holiness and felicity.

Though the great physician of our souls hath
mingled profits and pleasures with virtue, to
make its chalice sweet and apt to be drank off;
yet he that takes out the sweet ingredient and
feasts his palate with the less wholesome part
because it is delicious, serves a low end of
sense or interest, but serves not God at all,
and as little does benefit to his soul. Such
a person is like Homer's bird, deplumes himself to feather all the naked callows that he
sees; and holds a taper that may light others
to heaven, while he burns his own fingers. But
a well-grown person, out of habit and choice,
out of love and virtue and just intention, goes
on his journey in straight ways to heaven, even
when the bridle and coercion of laws, or the
spurs of interest or reputation are laid aside;
and desires witnesses of his actions, not that he
may advance his fame, but for reverence and
fear, and to make it still more necessary to do
holy things.

----&----

GROWTH IN SIN.

WHEN we see a child strike a servant
rudely, or jeer a silly person, or wittingly

cheat his playfellow, or talk words light as the
skirt of a summer garment, we laugh and are
delighted with the wit and confidence of the
boy, and encourage such hopeful beginnings;
and in the mean time we consider not that from
these beginnings he shall grow up till he become a tyrant, an oppressor, a goat, and a
traitor. No man is discerned to be vicious
so soon as he is so; and vices have their
infancy and their childhood; and it cannot
be expected that in a child's age should be
the vice of a man; that were monstrous, as
if he wore a beard in his cradle; and we do
not believe that a serpent's sting does just
then grow when he strikes us in a vital part;
the venom and the little spear was there when
it first began to creep from his little shell.

For so have I seen the little purls of a spring
sweat through the bottom of a bank and inten-
erate the stubborn pavement, till it hath made
it fit for the impression of a child's foot; and it
was despised, like the descending pearls of a
misty morning, till it had opened its way and
made a stream large enough to carry away the
ruins of the undermined strand, and to invade
the neighboring gardens: but then the despised
drops were grown into an artificial river and an
intolerable mischief. So are the first entrances
of sin stopped with the antidotes of a hearty
prayer, and checked into sobriety by the eye

of a reverend man, or the counsels of a single
sermon : but when such beginnings are neg-
lected, and our religion hath not in it so
much philosophy as to think anything evil as
long as we can endure it, they grow up to
ulcers and pestilential evils ; they destroy the
soul by their abode, who at their first entry
might have been killed with the pressure of
a little finger.

I wish we lived in an age in which the
people were to be treated with concerning re-
nouncing the single actions of sin, and the seldom interruptions of piety. Certain it is, that
God hath given us precepts of such a holiness
and such a purity, such a meekness and such
humility, as hath no pattern but Christ, no prec-
edent but the purities of God : and therefore it
is intended we should live with a life whose
actions are not checkered with white and black,
half sin and half virtue. God's sheep are not
like Jacob's flock, streaked and spotted ; it is
an entire holiness that God requires, and will
not endure to have a holy course interrupted
by the dishonor of a base and ignoble action.
I do not mean that a man's life can be as pure
as the sun, or the rays of celestial Jerusalem ;
but like the moon, in which there are spots,
but they are no deformity ; a lessening only
and an abatement of light, no cloud to hinder
and draw a veil before its face, but sometimes

it is not so serene and bright as at other times.

Every man hath his indiscretions and infirmities, his arrests and sudden incursions, his neighborhoods and semblances of sin, his little violences to reason, and peevish melancholy, and humorous fantastic discourses, unaptness to a devout prayer, his fondness to judge favorable in his own cases, little deceptions, and voluntary and involuntary cozenages, ignorances and inadvertencies, careless hours and unwatchful seasons. But no good man can ever commit one act of adultery ; no godly man will, at any time, be drunk ; or if he be, he ceases to be a godly man, and is run into the confines of death, and is sick at heart, and may die of the sickness, die eternally. This happens more frequently in persons of an infant piety, when the virtue is not corroborated by a long abode, and a confirmed resolution, and an usual victory, and a triumphant grace : and the longer we are accustomed to piety, the more unfrequent will be the little breaches of folly, and a returning to sin. But as the needle of a compass, when it is directed to its beloved star, at the first addresses waves on either side, and seems indifferent in his courtship of the rising or declining sun, and when it seems first determined to the north, stands awhile trembling, as if it suffered inconvenience in the first fruition

of its desires, and stands not still in full enjoy-
ment till after first a great variety of motion,
and then in an undisturbed posture : so is
the piety and so is the conversion of a man
wrought by degrees and several steps of imperfection : and at first our choices are wavering,
convinced by the grace of God, and yet not persuaded : and then persuaded, but not resolved ;
and then resolved, but deferring to begin ; and
then beginning, but (as all beginnings are) in
weakness and uncertainty ; and we fly out
often into huge indiscretions and look back
to Sodom, and long to return to Egypt : and
when the storm is quite over, we find little bub-
blings and unevennesses upon the face of the
waters, — we often weaken our own purposes
by the returns of sin ; and we do not call ourselves conquerors, till by the long possession of
virtues it is a strange and unusual, and therefore
an uneasy and unpleasant thing, to act a crime.

He that hath passed many stages of a good
life, to prevent his being tempted to a single
sin, must be very careful that he never entertain his spirit with the remembrances of his past
sin, nor amuse it with the fantastic apprehensions of the present. When the Israelites fancied the sapidness and relish of the fleshpots,
they longed to taste and to return.

So when a Lybian tiger, drawn from his
wilder foragings, is shut up and taught to eat

civil meat, and suffer the authority of a man,
he sits down tamely in his prison, and pays to
his keeper fear and reverence for his meat.
But if he chance to come again and taste a
draught of warm blood, he presently leaps into
his natural cruelty. He scarce abstains from
eating those hands that brought him discipline
and food. So is the nature of a man made
tame and gentle by the grace of God, and reduced to reason, and kept in awe by religion
and laws, and by an awful virtue is taught to
forget those alluring and sottish relishes of sin.
But if he diverts from his path, and snatches
handfuls from the wanton vineyards, and remembers the lasciviousness of his unwholesome
food that pleased his childish palate, then he
grows sick again and hungry after unwholesome diet, and longs for the apples of Sodom.
A man must walk through the world without
eyes or ears, fancy or appetite, but such as are
created and sanctified by the grace of God;
and being once made a new man, he must
serve all the needs of nature by the appetites
and faculties of grace; nature must be wholly
a servant: and we must so look towards the
deliciousness of our religion and the ravishments of heaven, that our memory must be
forever useless to the affairs and perceptions
of sin. We cannot stand, we cannot live,
unless we be curious and watchful in this particular.

Every delay of return is, in the case of habitual sins, an approach to desperation, because the nature of habits is like that of the crocodiles, they grow as long as they live ; and if they come to obstinacy or confirmation, they are in hell already, and can never return back. For so the Pannonian bears, when they have clasped a dart in the region of their liver, wheel themselves upon the wound, and with anger and malicious revenge strike the deadly barb deeper, and cannot be quit from that fatal steel, but, in flying, bear along that which themselves make the instrument of a more hasty death. So is every vicious person struck with a deadly wound, and his own hands force it into the entertainments of the heart ; and because it is painful to draw it forth by a sharp and salutary repentance, he still rolls and turns upon his wound, and carries his death in his bowels, where it first entered by choice, and then dwelt by love, and at last shall finish the tragedy by divine judgments and an unalterable decree.

WORLDLY POSSESSIONS.

SUPPOSE a man gets all the world, what is it that he gets? It is a bubble and a phantasm, and hath no reality beyond a pres-

ent transient use ; a thing that is impossible to
be enjoyed, because its fruits and usages are
transmitted to us by parts and by succession.
He that hath all the world, (if we can suppose
such a man,) cannot have a dish of fresh summer fruits in the midst of winter, not so much
as a green fig: and very much of its possessions
is so hid, so fugacious and of so uncertain purchase, that it is like the riches of the sea to the
lord of the shore ; all the fish and wealth within
all its hollownesses are his, but he is never the
better for what he cannot get. All the shell-
fish that produce pearl, produce them not for
him ; and the bowels of the earth shall hide
her treasures in undiscovered retirements. So
that it will signify as much to this great pur-
chaser to be entitled to an inheritance in the
upper region of the air ; he is so far from possessing all its riches, that he does not so much
as know of them, nor understand the philosophy
of her minerals.

I consider, that he that is the greatest possessor in the world, enjoys its best and most
noble parts, and those which are of most excellent perfection, but in common with the inferior
persons and the most despicable of his kingdom. Can the greatest prince enclose the
sun and set one little star in his cabinet for
his own use ? Or secure to himself the gentle
and benign influences of any one constellation ?

Are not his subjects' fields bedewed with the same showers that water his gardens of pleasure?

Nay, those things which he esteems his ornament and the singularity of his possessions, are they not of more use to others than to himself? For suppose his garments splendid and shining like the robe of a cherub or the clothing of the fields, all that he that wears them enjoys, is, that they keep him warm and clean and modest; and all this is done by clean and less pompous vestments; and the beauty of them, which distinguishes him from others, is made to please the eyes of the beholders; and he is like a fair bird, or the meretricious painting of a wanton woman, made wholly to be looked on, that is, to be enjoyed by every one but himself. And the fairest face and the sparkling eye cannot perceive or enjoy their own beauties, but by reflection. It is I that am pleased with beholding his gayety, and the gay man in his greatest bravery is only pleased because I am pleased with the sight; so borrowing his little and imaginary complacency from the delight that I have, not from any inherency of his own possession.

The poorest artisan of Rome, walking in Cæsar's gardens, had the same pleasures which they ministered to their lord. And although it may be he was put to gather fruits to eat

from another place, yet his other senses were
delighted equally with Cæsar's. The birds
made him as good music, the flowers gave him
as sweet smells, he there sucked as good air,
and delighted in the beauty and order of the
place, for the same reason and upon the same
perception as the prince himself; save only
that Cæsar paid for all that pleasure vast sums
of money, the blood and treasure of a province,
which the poor man had for nothing.

Suppose a man lord of all the world, (for
still we are but in supposition,) yet since everything is received not according to its own
greatness and worth, but according to the capacity of the receiver, it signifies very little as
to our content, or to the riches of our possession. If any man should give to a lion a fair
meadow full of hay, or a thousand quince-
trees; or should give to the goodly bull, the
master and the fairest of the whole herd, a
thousand fair stags; if a man should present to
a child a ship laden with Persian carpets, and
the ingredients of the rich scarlet; all these,
being disproportionate either to the appetite or
to the understanding, could add nothing of
content, and might declare the freeness of the
presenter, but they upbraid the incapacity of
the receiver. And so it does if God should
give the whole world to any man. He knows
not what to do with it; he can use no more

but according to the capacities of a man; he can use nothing but meat and drink and clothes; and infinite riches, that can give him changes of raiment every day and a full table, do but give him a clean trencher every bit he eats; it signifies no more but wantonness, and variety to the same, not to new purposes.

He to whom the world can be given to any purpose greater than a private estate can minister, must have new capacities created in him: he needs the understanding of an angel, to take the accounts of his estate; he had need have a stomach like fire or the grave, for else he can eat no more than one of his healthful subjects; and unless he hath an eye like the sun, and a motion like that of a thought, and a bulk as big as one of the orbs of heaven, the pleasure of his eye can be no greater than to behold the beauty of a little prospect from a hill, or to look upon the heap of gold packed up in a little room, or to dote upon a cabinet of jewels, better than which there is no man that sees at all but sees every day. For, not to name the beauties and sparkling diamonds of heaven, a man's, or a woman's, or a hawk's eye is more beauteous and excellent than all the jewels of his crown. And when we remember that a beast, who hath quicker senses than a man, yet hath not so great delight in the fruition of any object, because he wants

14

understanding, and the power to make reflex acts upon his perception ; it will follow, that understanding and knowledge is the greatest instrument of pleasure, and he that is most knowing hath a capacity to become happy, which a less knowing prince or a rich person hath not ; and in this only a man's capacity is capable of enlargement. But then, although they only have power to relish any pleasure rightly, who rightly understand the nature and degrees, and essences, and ends of things ; yet they that do so, understand also the vanity and the unsatisfyingness of the things of this world, so that the relish which could not be great but in a great understanding, appears contemptible, because its vanity appears at the same time ; the understanding sees all, and sees through it.

The greatest vanity of this world is remarkable in this, that all its joys summed up together are not big enough to counterpoise the evil of one sharp disease, or to allay a sorrow. For imagine a man great in his dominion as Cyrus, rich as Solomon, victorious as David, beloved like Titus, learned as Trismegist, powerful as all the Roman greatness ; all this, and the results of all this, give him no more pleasure in the midst of a fever or the tortures of the stone, than if he were only lord of a little dish, and a dishful of fountain-water. Indeed the excellency of a holy conscience is a comfort

and a magazine of joy, so great, that it sweet-
ens the most bitter potion of the world, and
makes tortures and death not only tolerable,
but amiable ; and therefore to part with this
whose excellency is so great, for the world.
that is of so inconsiderable a worth, as not to
have in it recompense enough for the sorrows
of a sharp disease, is a bargain fit to be made
by none but fools and madmen.   Antiochus
Epiphanes, and Herod the Great, and his
grandchild Agrippa, were sad instances of this
great truth ; to every of which it happened,
that the grandeur of their fortune, the greatness of their possessions, and the increase of
their estate disappeared and expired like camphor, at their arrest by those several sharp
diseases, which covered their heads with cypress, and hid their crowns in an inglorious
grave.

For what can all the world minister to a sick
person, if it represents all the spoils of nature
and the choicest delicacies of land and sea ?
Alas! his appetite is lost, and to see a pebble-
stone is more pleasing to him ; for he can look
upon that without loathing, but not so upon
the most delicious fare that ever made famous
the Roman luxury.   Perfumes make his head
ache.   If you load him with jewels, you press
him with a burden as troublesome as his grave-
stone.   And what pleasure is in all those pos-

sessions that cannot make his pillow easy, nor
tame the rebellion of a tumultuous humor, nor
restore the use of a withered hand, or straight-
en a crooked finger? Vain is the hope of that
man whose soul rests upon vanity and such
unprofitable possessions.

Suppose a man lord of all this world, a
universal monarch, as some princes have lately
designed, — all that cannot minister content to
him; not that content which a poor contem-
plative man, by the strength of Christian philosophy and the support of a very small fortune,
daily does enjoy. All his power and greatness
cannot command the sea to overflow his shores,
or to stay from retiring to the opposite strand.
It cannot make his children dutiful or wise.
And though the world admired at the greatness of Philip the Second's fortune in the ac-
cession of Portugal and the East Indies to his
principalities, yet this could not allay the infelicity of his family and the unhandsomeness of
his condition, in having a proud and indiscreet
and a vicious young prince likely to inherit all
his greatness. And if nothing appears in the
face of such a fortune to tell all the world that
it is spotted and imperfect, yet there is in all
conditions of the world such weariness and
tediousness of spirits, that a man is ever more
pleased with hopes of going off from the present than in dwelling upon that condition which,

it may be, others admire and think beauteous, but none knoweth the smart of it but he that drank off the little pleasure and felt the ill-relish of the appendage. How many kings have groaned under the burden of their crowns, and have sunk down and died! How many have quitted their pompous cares and retired into private lives, there to enjoy the pleasures of philosophy and religion, which their thrones denied!

That is a sad condition when, like Midas, all that the man touches shall turn to gold: and his is no better to whom a perpetual full table, not recreated with fasting, not made pleasant with intervening scarcity, ministers no more good than a heap of gold does; that is, he hath no benefit of it, save the beholding of it with his eyes. Cannot a man quench his thirst as well out of an urn or chalice, as out of a whole river? It is an ambitious thirst and a pride of draught, that had rather lay his mouth to Euphrates than to a petty goblet; but if he had rather, it adds not so much to his content as to his danger and his vanity. For so I have heard of persons whom the river hath swept away, together with the turf they pressed, when they stopped to drown their pride rather than their thirst.

EXCELLENCE OF THE SOUL.

IF we consider what the soul is, in its own capacity to happiness, we shall find it to be an excellency greater than the sun, of an angelical substance, sister to a cherub, an image of the divinity, and the great argument of that mercy whereby God did distinguish us from the lower form of beasts and trees and minerals.

The soul is all that whereby we may be, and without which we cannot be, happy. It is not the eye that sees the beauties of the heaven, nor the ear that hears the sweetness of music or the glad tidings of a prosperous accident, but the soul that perceives all the relishes of sensual and intellectual perfections; and the more noble and excellent the soul is, the greater and more savory are its perceptions. And if a child beholds the rich ermine, or the diamonds of a starry night, or the order of the world, or hears the discourses of an apostle, because he makes no reflex acts upon himself, and sees not that he sees, he can have but the pleasure of a fool, or the deliciousness of a mule. But although the reflection of its own acts be a rare instrument of pleasure or pain respectively, yet the soul's excellence is upon the same reason not perceived by us, by which the sapidness

of pleasant things of nature are not understood
by a child; even because the soul cannot reflect far enough. For as the sun, which is the
fountain of light and heat, makes violent and
direct emissions of his rays from himself, but
reflects them no farther than to the bottom of
a cloud, or the lowest imaginary circle of the
middle region, and therefore receives not a
duplicate of its own heat; so is the soul of
man: it reflects upon its own inferior actions
of particular sense or general understanding;
but because it knows little of its own nature,
the manners of volition, the immediate instruments of understanding, the way how it comes
to meditate, and cannot discern how a sudden
thought arrives, or the solution of a doubt not
depending upon preceding premises ; therefore above half its pleasures are abated, and
its own worth less understood : and possibly it
is the better it is so. If the elephant knew his
strength, or the horse the vigorousness of his
own spirit, they would be as rebellious against
their rulers as unreasonable men against government: nay, the angels themselves, because
their light reflected home to their orbs, and
they understood all the secrets of their own
perfection, they grew vertiginous, and fell from
the battlements of heaven.

THE REWARDS OF VIRTUE.

THE things of God are the noblest satisfactions to those desires which ought to be cherished and swelled up to infinite ; their deliciousness is vast and full of relish ; and their very appendant thorns are to be chosen, for they are gilded, they are safe and medicinal, they heal the wound they make, and bring forth fruit of a blessed and a holy life. The things of God and of religion are easy and sweet, they bear entertainments in their hand and reward at their back ; their good is certain and perpetual, and they make us cheerful to-day, and pleasant to-morrow ; and spiritual songs end not in a sigh and a groan, but they bring us to the felicity of God, the same yesterday and to-day and forever. They do not give a private and particular delight, but their benefit is public ; like the incense of the altar, it sends up a sweet smell to heaven, and makes atonement for the religious man that kindled it, and delights all the standers-by, and makes the very air wholesome. There is no blessed soul goes to heaven but he makes a general joy in all the mansions where the saints do dwell, and in all the chapels where the angels sing ; and the joys of religion are not univocal, but productive of rare and acci-

dental and preternatural pleasures ; for the
music of holy hymns delights the ear and refreshes the spirit, and makes the very bones
of the saints to rejoice. And charity, or the
giving alms to the poor, does not only ease the
poverty of the receiver, but makes the giver
rich, and heals his sickness, and delivers from
death. And temperance, though it be in the
matter of meat and drink and pleasures, yet
hath an effect upon the understanding, and
makes the reason sober, and the will orderly.
and the affections regular, and does things be-
side and beyond their natural and proper effi-
cacy : for all the parts of our duty are watered
with the showers of blessing, and bring forth
fruit according to the influence of heaven, and
beyond the capacities of nature.

But they that will not deny a lust, nor re-
frain an appetite, they that will be drunk when
their friends do merrily constrain them, or love
a cheap religion, and a gentle and lame prayer,
short and soft, quickly said and soon passed
over, seldom returning and but little observed,
how is it possible that they should think themselves persons disposed to receive such glorious
crowns and sceptres, such excellent conditions,
which they have not faith enough to believe.
nor attention enough to consider, and no man
can have wit enough to understand ? But so
might an Arcadian shepherd look from the

rocks, or through the clifts of the valley where his sheep graze, and wonder that the messenger stays so long from coming to him to be crowned king of all the Greek islands, or to be adopted heir to the Macedonian monarchy. It is an infinite love of God that we have heaven upon conditions which we can perform with greatest diligence : but, truly, the lives of men are generally such that they do things in order to heaven, things (I say) so few, so trifling, so unworthy, that they are not proportionable to the reward of a crown of oak or a yellow ribbon, the slender reward with which the Romans paid their soldiers for their extraordinary valor. True it is, that heaven is not in a just sense of a commutation, a reward, but a gift, and an infinite favor : but yet it is not reached forth but to persons disposed by the conditions of God; which conditions when we pursue in kind, let us be very careful we do not fail of the mighty prize of our high calling for want of degrees and just measures, the measures of zeal and a mighty love.

--+--

RELIGION AND GOVERNMENT.

THOSE sects of Christians, whose professed doctrine brings destruction and diminution to government, give the most intolerable scandal and dishonor to the institution ; and it had been impossible that Christianity should have prevailed over the wisdom and power of the Greeks and Romans, if it had not been humble to superiors, patient of injuries, charitable to the needy, a great exacter of obedience to kings, even to heathens, that they might be won and convinced; and to persecutors, that they might be sweetened in their anger, or upbraided for their cruel injustice. For so doth the humble vine creep at the foot of an oak, and leans upon its lowest base, and begs shade and protection, and leave to grow under its branches, and to give and take mutual refreshment, and pay a friendly influence for a mighty patronage ; and they grow and dwell together, and are the most remarkable of friends and married pairs of all the leafy nation. Religion of itself is soft, easy, and defenceless, and God hath made it grow up with empire, and lean upon the arms of kings, and it cannot well grow alone ; and if it shall, like the ivy, suck the heart of the oak, upon whose body it grew and was supported, it will be pulled down from its usurped eminence, and fire and shame shall be its portion.

HYPOCRISY.

WE do not live in an age in which there is so much need to bid men be wary, as to take care that they be innocent. Indeed in religion we are usually too loose and ungirt, exposing ourselves to temptation, and others to offence, and our name to dishonor, and the cause itself to reproach, and we are open and ready to every evil but persecution. From that we are close enough, and that alone we call prudence; but in the matter of interest we are wary as serpents, subtle as foxes, vigilant as the birds of the night, rapacious as kites, tenacious as grappling-hooks and the weightiest anchors, and, above all, false and hypocritical as a thin crust of ice spread upon the face of a deep, smooth, and dissembling pit; if you set your foot, your foot slips, or the ice breaks, and you sink into death, and are wound in a sheet of water, descending into mischief or your grave, suffering a great fall, or a sudden death, by your confidence and unsuspecting foot. There is a universal crust of hypocrisy that covers the face of the greatest part of mankind. Their religion consists in forms and outsides, and serves reputation or a design, but does not serve God. Their promises are but fair language, and the civilities of piazzas or exchanges, and disband and untie like the air that beats upon their teeth when they speak the delicious and hopeful words. Their oaths are snares to catch men, and make them confident; their contracts are arts and stratagems to deceive, measured by profit and possibility; and everything is lawful that is gainful; and their friendships are trades of getting; and their kindness of watching a dying friend is but the office of a vulture, the gaping for a legacy, the spoil of the carcase; and their sicknesses are many times policies of state, sometimes a design to show the riches of our bedchamber: and their funeral tears are but the paranymphs and pious solicitors of a second bride. And everything that is ugly must be hid, and everything that is handsome must be seen: and that will make a fair cover for a huge deformity. And therefore it is (as they think) necessary that men should always have some pretences and forms, some faces of religion or sweetness of language, confident affirmatives or bold oaths, protracted treaties or multitude of words, affected silence or grave deportment, a good name or a good cause, a fair relation or a worthy calling, great power or a pleasant wit. Anything that can be fair or that can be useful, anything that can do good or be thought good, we use it to abuse our brother, or promote our interests. Leporina resolved to die, being troubled for her husband's danger; and he resolved to die with her that had so great a kindness for him, as not to outlive the best of her husband's fortune. It was agreed; and she tempered the poison, and drank the face of the unwholesome goblet; but the weighty poison sunk to the bottom, and the easy man drank it all off, and died, and the woman carried him forth to funeral, and after a little illness, which she soon recovered, she entered upon the inheritance, and a second marriage.

CHRIST'S DISCIPLES.

WHEN our blessed Saviour told his disciples that they should sit upon twelve thrones, they presently thought they had his bond for a kingdom, and dreamed of wealth and honor, power and a splendid court; and Christ knew they did, but did not disentangle his promise from the enfolded and intricate sense, of which his words were naturally capable; but he performed his promise to better purposes than they hoped for. They were presidents in the conduct of souls, princes of God's people, the chief in sufferings, stood nearest to the cross, had an elder brother's portion in the kingdom

of grace, were the founders of churches, and
dispensers of the mysteries of the kingdom,
and ministers of the spirit of God, and channels of mighty blessings, under-mediators in
the priesthood of their Lord, and " their names
were written in heaven " : and this was infinitely better than to groan and wake under a
head pressed with a golden crown and pungent
cares, and to eat alone, and to walk in a crowd,
and to be vexed with all the public and many
of the private evils of the people, which is the
sum total of an earthly kingdom.

———◆———

THE MIRACLES OF THE DIVINE MERCY.

THE light of the world in the morning of the
creation was spread abroad like a curtain,
and dwelt nowhere, but filled the " *expansum* "
with a dissemination great as the unfoldings of
the air's looser garment, or the wilder fringes
of the fire, without knots, or order, or combi-
nation. But God gathered the beams in his
hand, and united them into a globe of fire, and
all the light of the world became the body of
the sun ; and he lent some to his weaker sister
that walks in the night, and guides a traveller,
and teaches him to distinguish a house from a
river, or a rock from a plain field. So is the

mercy of God, a vast "*expansum*" and a huge
ocean ; from eternal ages it dwelt round about
the throne of God, and it filled all that infinite
distance and space that hath no measures but
the will of God ; until God, desiring to communicate that excellence and make it relative,
created angels, that he might have persons
capable of huge gifts, and man, who he knew
would need forgiveness. For so the angels,
our elder brothers, dwelt forever in the house
of their father, and never broke his commandments ; but we, the younger, like prodigals,
forsook our father's house, and went into a
strange country, and followed stranger courses,
and spent the portion of our nature, and forfeited all our title to the family, and came to
need another portion. For, ever since the fall
of Adam, who, like an unfortunate man, spent
all that a wretched man could need, or a happy
man could have, our life is repentance, and
forgiveness is all our portion ; and though
angels were objects of God's bounty, yet man
only is (in proper speaking) the object of his
mercy ; and the mercy which dwelt in an infinite circle, became confined to a little ring,
and dwelt here below, and here shall dwell below till it hath carried all God's portion up to
heaven, where it shall reign and glory upon
our crowned heads forever and ever.

But for him that considers God's mercies,

and dwells awhile in that depth, it is hard not
to talk wildly and without art and order of dis-
coursing. St. Peter talked he knew not what,
when he entered into a cloud with Jesus upon
Mount Tabor, though it passed over him like
the little curtains that ride upon the northwind, and pass between the sun and us. And
when we converse with a light greater than
the sun, and taste a sweetness more delicious
than the dew of heaven, and in our thoughts
entertain the ravishments and harmony of that
atonement which reconciles God to man, and
man to felicity, it will be more easily pardoned
if we should be like persons that admire much
and say but little; and indeed we can best confess the glories of the Lord by dazzled eyes,
and a stammering tongue, and a heart over-
charged with the miracles of this infinity. For
so those little drops that run over, though they
be not much in themselves, yet they tell that
the vessel was full, and could express the greatness of the shower no otherwise but by spilling,
and inartificial expressions and runnings over.

But because I have undertaken to tell the
drops of the ocean, and to span the measures
of eternity, I must do it by the great lines of
revelation and experience, and tell concerning
God's mercy as we do concerning God himself,
that he is that great fountain of which we all
drink, and the great rock of which we all eat,

15

and on which we all dwell, and under whose
shadow we are all refreshed. God's mercy is
all this; and we can only draw great lines of
it, and reckon the constellations of our hemi-
sphere instead of telling the number of the
stars; we only can reckon what we feel and
what we live by. And though there be in
every one of these lines of life enough to en-
gage us forever to do God service, and to give
him praises; yet it is certain there are very
many mercies of God upon us, and towards us,
and concerning us, which we neither feel, nor
see, nor understand as yet; but yet we are
blessed by them, and are preserved and secured, and we shall then know them when we
come to give God thanks in the festivities of
an eternal sabbath.

In this account concerning the mercies of
God, I must not reckon the miracles and graces
of the creation, or anything of the nature of
man; nor tell how great an endearment God
passed upon us, that 'he made us men, capable
of felicity, apted with rare instruments of discourse and reason, passions and desires, notices
of sense, and reflections upon that sense; that
we have not the deformity of a crocodile, nor
the motion of a worm, nor the hunger of a
wolf, nor the wildness of a tiger, nor the birth,
of vipers, nor the life of flies, nor the death of
serpents.

Our excellent bodies and useful faculties, the upright motion and the tenacious hand, the fair appetites and proportioned satisfactions, our speech and our perceptions, our acts of life, the rare invention of letters, and the use of writing, and speaking at a distance, the intervals of rest and labor, (either of which, if they were perpetual, would be intolerable,) the needs of nature and the provisions of providence, sleep and business, refreshments of the body and entertainments of the soul; these are to be reckoned as acts of bounty rather than mercy. God gave us these when he made us, and before we needed mercy; these were portions of our nature, or provided to supply our consequent necessities. But when we forfeited all God's favor by our sins, then that they were continued or restored to us became a mercy, and therefore ought to be reckoned upon this new account : for it was a rare mercy that we were suffered to live at all, or that the anger of God did permit to us one blessing, that he did punish us so gently. We looked for a judge, and behold a Saviour : we feared an accuser, and behold an advocate ; we sat down in sorrow, and rise in joy ; we leaned upon rhubarb and aloes, and our aprons were made of the sharp leaves of Indian fig-trees, and so we fed, and so were clothed ; but the rhubarb proved medicinal, and the rough leaf of the tree brought its fruit wrapped up in its foldings ; and round about our dwellings was planted a hedge of thorns and bundles of thistles, the aconite and the briony, the nightshade and the poppy ; and at the root of these grew the healing plantain, which, rising up into a tallness by the friendly invitation of heavenly influence, turned about the tree of the cross, and cured the wounds of the thorns, and the curse of the thistles, and the malediction of man, and the wrath of God.

After all this, we may sit down and reckon by great sums and conjugations of his gracious gifts, and tell the minutes of eternity by the number of the divine mercies. God hath given his laws to rule us, his word to instruct us, his spirit to guide us, his angels to protect us, his ministers to exhort us. He revealed all our duty, and he hath concealed whatsoever can hinder us ; he hath affrighted our follies with fear of death, and engaged our watchfulness by its secret coming ; he hath exercised our faith by keeping private the state of souls departed, and yet hath confirmed our faith by a promise of a resurrection, and entertained our hope by some general significations of the state of interval. His mercies make contemptible means instrumental to great purposes, and a small herb the remedy of the greatest diseases. He impedes the devil's rage, and infatuates his counsels; he diverts his malice, and defeats his purposes; he binds him in the chain of darkness, and gives him no power over the children of light; he suffers him to walk in solitary places, and yet fetters him that he cannot disturb the sleep of a child; he hath given him mighty power, and yet a young maiden that resists him shall make him flee away; he hath given him a vast knowledge, and yet an ignorant man can confute him with the twelve articles of his creed; he gave him power over the winds, and made him prince of the air, and yet the breath of a holy prayer can drive him as far as the utmost sea; and he hath so restrained him, that (except it be by faith) we know not whether there be any devil, yea or no; for we never heard his noises, nor have seen his affrighting shapes.

This is that great principle of all the felicity we hope for, and of all the means thither, and of all the skill and all the strengths we have to use those means. He hath made great variety of conditions, and yet hath made all necessary, and all mutual helpers; and by some instruments and in some respects they are all equal, in order to felicity, to content, and final and intermedial satisfaction. He gave us part of our reward in hand, that he might enable us to work for more: he taught the world arts for use, arts for entertainment of all our faculties and all our dispositions: he gives eternal gifts for temporal services, and gives us whatsoever we want for asking, and commands us to ask, and threatens us if we will not ask, and punishes us for refusing to be happy. This is that glorious attribute that hath made order and health, harmony and hope, restitutions and variety, the joys of direct possession, and the joys, the artificial joys, of contrariety and comparison. He comforts the poor, and he brings down the rich, that they may be safe, in their humility and sorrow, from the transportations of an unhappy and uninstructed prosperity. He gives necessaries to all, and scatters the extraordinary provisions so, that every nation may traffic in charity, and commute for pleasures. He was the Lord of hosts, and he is still what he was; but he loves to be called the God of peace; because he was terrible in that, but he is delighted in this.

His mercy is his glory, and his glory is the light of heaven. His mercy is the life of the creation, and it fills all the earth; and his mercy is a sea too, and it fills all the abysses of the deep; it hath given us promises for supply of whatsoever we need, and relieves us in all our fears, and in all the evils that we suffer. His mercies are more than we can tell, and they are more than we can feel. For all the world in the abyss of the divine mercies is like a man diving into the bottom of the sea, over whose head the waters run insensibly and unperceived, and yet the weight is vast, and the sum of them is unmeasurable ; and the man is not pressed with the burden, nor confounded with numbers. And no observation is able to recount, no sense sufficient to perceive, no memory large enough to retain, no understanding great enough to apprehend this infinity ; but we must admire, and love, and worship, and magnify this mercy forever and ever ; that we may dwell in what we feel, and be comprehended by that which is equal to God, and the parent of all felicity.

The result of this consideration is, that as we fear the divine judgments, so we adore and love his goodness, and let the golden chains of the divine mercy tie us to a noble prosecution of our duty and the interest of religion. For he is the worst of men whom kindness cannot soften, nor endearment oblige, whom gratitude cannot tie faster than the bands of life and death. He is an ill-natured sinner, if he will not comply with the sweetnesses of heaven, and be civil to his angel guardian, or observant of his patron, God, who made him, and feeds him, and keeps all his faculties, and takes care of him, and endures his follies, and waits on him more tenderly than a nurse, more diligently than a client ; who hath greater care of him than his

father, and whose bowels yearn over him with
more compassion than a mother; who is bountiful beyond our need, and merciful beyond our
hopes, and makes capacities in us to receive
more. Fear is stronger than death, and love is
more prevalent than fear, and kindness is the
greatest endearment of love; and yet to an
ingenuous person gratitude is greater than all
these, and obliges to a solemn duty, when love
fails, and fear is dull and unactive, and death
itself is despised. But the man who is hardened against kindness, and whose duty is not
made alive with gratitude, must be used like a
slave, and driven like an ox, and enticed with
goads and whips; but must never enter into
the inheritance of sons. Let us take heed; for
mercy is like a rainbow, which God set in the
clouds to remember mankind: it shines here as
long as it is not hindered; but we must never
look for it after it is night, and it shines not in
the other world. If we refuse mercy here, we
shall have justice to eternity.

NATIONAL ADVERSITY.

IT is a sad calamity to see a kingdom spoiled
and a church afflicted; the priests slain
with the sword, and the blood of nobles min-

gled with cheaper sand ; religion made a cause of trouble, and the best men most cruelly persecuted ; government confounded and laws ashamed ; judges decreeing causes in fear and covetousness, and the ministers of holy things setting themselves against all that is sacred, and setting fire upon the fields, and turning in little foxes on purpose to destroy the vine-yards. And what shall make recompense for this heap of sorrows, whenever God shall send such swords of fire ? Even the mercies of God, which then will be made public, when we shall hear such afflicted people sing, " *In convertendo captivitatem Sion,*" with the voice of joy and festival eucharist among such as keep holiday; and when peace shall become sweeter and dwell the longer. And in the mean time it serves religion, and the affliction shall try the children of God, and God shall crown them, and men shall grow wiser and more holy, and leave their petty interests, and take sanctuary in holy living, and be taught temperance by their want, and patience by their suffering, and charity by their persecu-tion, and shall better understand the duty of their relations; and at last the secret worm that lay at the root of the plant shall be drawn forth and quite extinguished. For so have I known a luxuriant vine swell into irregular twigs and bold excrescences, and spend itself in leaves and little rings, and afford but trifling clusters to the wine-press, and a faint return to his heart, which longed to be refreshed with a full vintage : but when the lord of the vine had caused the dressers to cut the wilder plant, and made it bleed, it grew temperate in its vain expense of useless leaves, and knotted into fair and juicy branches, and made accounts of that loss of blood by the return of fruit. So is an afflicted province cured of its surfeits, and punished for its sins, and bleeds for its long riot, and is left ungoverned for its disobedience, and chastised for its wantonness ; and when the sword hath let forth the corrupted blood, and the fire hath purged the rest, then it enters into the double joys of restitution, and gives God thanks for his rod, and confesses the mercies of the Lord in making the smoke to be changed into fire, and the cloud into a perfume, the sword into a staff, and his anger into mercy.

EVANGELICAL RIGHTEOUSNESS.

WE must know that in keeping of God's commandments every degree of internal duty is under the commandments ; and therefore whatever we do, we must do it as well as

we can. Now he that does his duty with the
biggest affection he can, will also do all that he
can; and he can never know that he hath done
what is commanded, unless he does all that is
in his power. For God hath put no limit but
love and possibility; and therefore whoever
says, Hither will I go and no farther, this I
will do and no more, thus much will I serve
God, but that shall be all, — he hath the affections of a slave, and the religion of a Pharisee,
the craft of a merchant, and the falseness of a
broker; but he hath not the proper measures
of the righteousness evangelical. But so it
happens in the mud and slime of the river
Borborus, when the eye of the sun hath long
dwelt upon it, and produces frogs and mice
which begin to move a little under a thin cover
of its own parental matter, and if they can get
loose to live half a life, that is all; but the
hinder parts, which are not formed before the
setting of the sun, stick fast in their beds of
mud, and the little moiety of a creature dies before it could be well said to live. So it is with
those Christians who will do all that they think
lawful, and will do no more than what they
suppose necessary; they do but peep into the
light of the sun of righteousness; they have
the beginnings of life; but their hinder parts,
their passions and affections, and the desires of
the lower man, are still unformed; and he

that dwells in this state is just so much of a
Christian as a sponge is of a plant, and a mush-
room of a shrub : they may be as sensible as
an oyster, and discourse at the rate of a child,
but are greatly short of the righteousness
evangelical.

———◆———

WATCHFULNESS.

HE that would be free from the slavery of
sin, and the necessity of sinning, must always watch. Ay, that's the point ; but who
can watch always ? Why, every good man can
watch always : and that we may not be deceived in this, let us know that the running
away from a temptation is a part of our watchfulness, and every good employment is another
great part of it, and a laying in provision of
reason and religion beforehand, is yet a third
part of this watchfulness : and the conversation
of a Christian is a perpetual watchfulness ; not
a continual thinking of that one, or those many
things which may endanger us ; but it is a
continual doing something directly or indirectly
against sin. He either prays to God for his
spirit, or relies upon the promises, or receives
the sacrament, or goes to his bishop for counsel
and a blessing, or to his priest for religious

offices, or places himself at the feet of good
men to hear their wise sayings, or calls for the
Church's prayers, or does the duty of his calling, or actually resists temptation, or frequently
renews his holy purposes, or fortifies himself
by vows, or searches into his danger by a daily
examination ; so that in the whole he is forever upon his guard. This duty and caution
of a Christian is like watching lest a man cut
his finger. Wise men do not often cut their
fingers, and yet every day they use a knife ;
and a man's eye is a tender thing, and everything can do it wrong, can put it out; yet because we love our eyes so well, in the midst of
so many dangers, by God's providence and a
prudent natural care, by winking when anything comes against them, and by turning aside
when a blow is offered, they are preserved so
certainly, that not one in ten thousand does by
a stroke lose one of his eyes in all his lifetime.
If we would transplant our natural care to a
spiritual caution, we might by God's grace be
kept from losing our souls, as we are from losing our eyes ; and because a perpetual watchfulness is our great defence, and the perpetual
presence of God's grace is our great security,
and that this grace never leaves us unless we
leave it, and the precept of a daily watchfulness is a thing not only so reasonable, but so
many easy ways to be performed, we see upon

what terms we may be quit of our sins, and more than conquerors over all the enemies and impediments of salvation.

———◆———

PITY.

IF you do but see a maiden carried to her grave a little before her intended marriage, or an infant die before the birth of reason, nature hath taught us to pay a tributary tear. Alas! your eyes will behold the ruin of many families, which, though they sadly have deserved, yet mercy is not delighted with the spectacle; and therefore God places a watery cloud in the eye, that when the light of heaven shines upon it, it may produce a rainbow to be a sacrament and a memorial that God and the sons of God do not love to see a man perish. God never rejoices in the death of him that dies; and we also esteem it undecent to have music at a funeral. And as religion teaches us to pity a condemned criminal, so mercy intercedes for the most benign interpretation of the laws. You must indeed be as just as the laws, and you must be as merciful as your religion; and you have no way to tie these together but to follow the pattern in the mount: do as God does, who in judgment remembers mercy.

THE HOPE OF MAN.

TRULY, what is the hope of man? It is indeed the resurrection of the soul in this world from sorrow and her saddest pressures, and like the twilight to the day, and the harbinger of joy; but still it is but a conjugation of infirmities, and proclaims our present calamity; only because it is uneasy here, it thrusts us forwards toward the light and glory of the resurrection.

For as a worm, creeping with her belly on the ground, with her portion and share of Adam's curse, lifts up its head to partake a little of the blessings of the air, and opens the junctures of her imperfect body, and curls her little rings into knots and combinations, drawing up her tail to a neighborhood of the head's pleasure and motion; but still it must return to abide the fate of its own nature, and dwell and sleep upon the dust: so are the hopes of a mortal man; he opens his eyes and looks upon fine things at a distance, and shuts them again with weakness, because they are too glorious to behold; and the man rejoices because he hopes fine things are staying for him; but his heart aches, because he knows there are a thousand ways to fail and miss of those glories; and though he hopes, yet he enjoys not; he longs, but he possesses not ; and must be content with his portion of dust, and being " a worm and no man," must lie down in this portion, before he can receive the end of his hopes, the salvation of his soul in the resurrection of the dead. For as death is the end of our lives, so is the resurrection the end of our hopes ; and as we die daily, so we daily hope. But death, which is the end of our life, is the enlargement of our spirits from hope to certainty, from uncertain fears to certain expectations, from the death of the body to the life of the soul.

THE RESURRECTION.

WHEN man was not, what power, what causes made him to be ? Whatsoever it was, it did then as great a work as to raise his body to the same being again ; and because we know not the method of nature's secret changes, and how we can be fashioned beneath " *in secreto terræ,*" and cannot handle and discern the possibilities and seminal powers in the ashes of dissolved bones, must our ignorance in philosophy be put in balance against the articles of religion, the hopes of mankind, the faith of nations, and the truth of God ? And are our opinions of the power of God so low, that our

understanding must be his measure, and he
shall be confessed to do nothing unless it be
made plain in our philosophy? Certainly we
have a low opinion of God unless we believe
he can do more things than we can understand.
But let us hear St. Paul's demonstration : if
the corn dies and lives again; if it lays its body
down, suffers alteration, dissolution and death,
but at the spring rises again in the verdure
of a leaf, in the fulness of the ear, in the kid-
neys of wheat ; if it proceeds from little to
great, from nakedness to ornament, from emptiness to plenty, from unity to multitude, from
death to life ; be a Sadducee no more, shame
not thy understanding, and reproach not the
weakness of thy faith, by thinking that corn
can be restored to life, and man cannot; especially since in every creature the obediential
capacity is infinite, and cannot admit degrees ;
for every creature can be anything under the
power of God, which cannot be less than infinite.

But we find no obscure footsteps of this
mystery even amongst the heathens. Pliny
reports that Appion the grammarian, by the
use of the plant Osiris, called Homer from his
grave : and in Valerius Maximus we find that
Ælius Tubero returned to life when he was
seated in his funeral pile ; and in Plutarch, that
Soleus, after three days' burial, did live ; and

in Valerius, that Æris Pamphilius did so after ten days. And it was so commonly believed that Glaucus, who was choked in a vessel of honey, did rise again, that it grew to a proverb; " *Glaucus poto melle surrexit,*" Glaucus having tasted honey, died and lived again. I pretend not to believe these stories to be true ; but from these instances it may be concluded, that they believed it possible that there should be a resurrection from the dead ; and natural reason and their philosophy did not wholly destroy their hopes and expectation to have a portion in this article.

For God, knowing that the great hopes of man, that the biggest endearment of religion, the sanction of private justice, the band of piety and holy courage, does wholly derive from the article of the resurrection, was pleased not only to make it credible, but easy and familiar to us; and we so converse every night with the image of death, that every morning we find an argument of the resurrection. Sleep and death have but one mother, and they have one name in common.

Charnel-houses are but cemeteries or sleeping-places, and they that die are fallen asleep, and the resurrection is but an awakening and standing-up from sleep. But in sleep our senses are as fast bound by nature as our joints are by the grave-clothes ; and unless an angel of

God awaken us every morning, we must confess ourselves as unable to converse with men
as we now are afraid to die and to converse
with spirits.

I will not now insist upon the story of the
rising bones seen every year in Egypt, nor the
pretences of the chemists, that they from the
ashes of flowers can reproduce from the same
materials the same beauties in color and figure ;
for he that proves a certain truth from an
uncertain argument, is like him that wears a
wooden leg when he hath two sound legs already ; it hinders his going, but helps him
not. The truth of God stands not in need of
such supporters; nature alone is a sufficient
preacher. Night and day, the sun returning
to the same point of east, every change of
species in the same matter, generation and
corruption, the eagle renewing her youth and
the snake her skin, the silk-worm and the
swallows, the care of posterity and the care
of an immortal name, winter and summer, the
fall and spring, the Old Testament and the
New, the words of Job and the visions of the
Prophets, the prayer of Ezekiel for the resurrection of the men of Ephraim and the return
of Jonas from the whale's belly, the histories
of the Jews and the narratives of Christians,
the faith of believers and the philosophy of the
reasonable, — all join in the verification of this

mystery. And amongst these heaps it is not of the least consideration that there was never any good man, who having been taught this article, but if he served God, he also relied upon this. If he believed God, he believed this.

RESURRECTION OF SINNERS.

SO have we seen a poor condemned criminal, the weight of whose sorrows sitting heavily upon his soul hath benumbed him into a deep sleep, till he hath forgotten his groans, and laid aside his deep sighings; but on a sudden comes the messenger of death and unbinds the poppy garland, scatters the heavy cloud that encircled his miserable head, and makes him return to acts of life, that he may quickly descend into death and be no more. So is every sinner that lies down in shame and makes his grave with the wicked; he shall indeed rise again and be called upon by the voice of the archangel; but then he shall descend into sorrows greater than the reason and the patience of a man, weeping and shrieking louder than the groans of the miserable children in the valley of Hinnom.

THE DIVINE BOUNTY.

THAT our desires are so provided for by nature and art, by ordinary and extraordinary, by foresight and contingency, according to necessity and up unto conveniency, until we arrive at abundance, is a chain of mercies larger than the bow in the clouds, and richer than the trees of Eden, which were permitted to feed our miserable father. Is not all the earth our orchard and our granary, our vineyard and our garden of pleasure? And the face of the sea is our traffic, and the bowels of the sea is our "*vivarium*," a place for fish to feed us, and to serve some other collateral appendant needs; and all the face of heaven is a repository for influences and breath, fruitful showers and fair refreshments. And when God made provision for his other creatures, he gave it of one kind, and with variety no greater than the changes of day and night, one devouring the other, or sitting down with his draught of blood, or walking upon his portion of grass. But man hath all the food of beasts, and all the beasts themselves that are fit for food, and the food of angels, and the dew of heaven, and the fatness of the earth; and every part of his body hath a provision made for it. And the smoothness of the olive and the juice

of the vine refresh the heart, and make the face
cheerful, and serve the ends of joy and the fes-
tivity of man ; and are not only to cure hunger
or to allay thirst, but appease a passion and
allay a sorrow.   It is an infinite variety of
meat with which God furnishes out the table
of mankind.   And in the covering our sin and
clothing our nakedness, God passed from fig-
leaves to the skins of beasts, from aprons to
long robes, from leather to wool, and from
thence to the warmth of furs and the coolness
of silks.   He hath dressed not only our needs,
but hath fitted the several portions of the year,
and made us to go dressed like our mother,
leaving off the winter sables when the florid
spring appears, and as soon as the tulip fades
we put on the robe of summer, and then shear
our sheep for winter : and God uses us as Joseph did his brother Benjamin ; we have many
changes of raiment, and our mess is five times
bigger than the provision made for our brothers
of the creation.

But that which I shall observe in this whole
affair is, that there are, both for the provision
of our tables and the relief of our sicknesses,
so many miracles of providence that they give
plain demonstration what relation we bear to
heaven.   And the poor man need not be troubled that he is to expect his daily portion after
the sun is up ; for he hath found to this day

he was not deceived; and then he may rejoice,
because he sees, by an effective probation, that
in heaven a decree was made, every day to send
him provisions of meat and drink. And that is
a mighty mercy, when the circles of heaven are
bowed down to wrap us in a bosom of care and
nourishment, and the wisdom of God is daily
busied to serve his mercy, as his mercy serves
our necessities. Does not God plant remedies
there where the diseases are most popular?
And every country is best provided against its
own evils. Is not the rhubarb found where the
sun most corrupts the liver, and the scabious
by the shore of the sea, that God might cure
as soon as he wounds? And the inhabitants
may see their remedy against the leprosy and
the scurvy, before they feel their sickness. And
then to this we may add nature's commons and
open fields, the shores of rivers and the strand
of the sea, the unconfined air, the wilderness
that hath no hedge; and that in these every
man may hunt and fowl and fish respectively;
and that God sends some miracles and extraordinary blessings so for the public good, that he
will not endure they should be enclosed and
made several. Thus he is pleased to dispense
the manna of Calabria, the medicinal waters of
Germany, the muscles at Sluce at this day,
and the Egyptian beans in the marshes of Al-
bania, and the salt at Troas of old; which

God, to defeat the covetousness of man, and
to spread his mercy over the face of the indi-
gent, as the sun scatters his beams over the
bosom of the whole earth, did so order that, as
long as every man was permitted to partake,
the bosom of heaven was open; but when man
gathered them into single handfuls and made
them impropriate, God gathered his hand into
his bosom, and bound the heavens with ribs of
brass, and the earth with decrees of iron, and
the blessing reverted to him that gave it, since
they might not receive it to whom it was sent.
And in general, this is the excellency of this
mercy that all our needs are certainly supplied
and secured by a promise which God cannot
break. But he that cannot break the laws of
his own promises, can break the laws of nature
that he may perform his promise, and he will
do a miracle rather than forsake thee in thy
needs: so that our security and the relative
mercy is bound upon us by all the power and
the truth of God.

Temporal advantage is a great ingredient in
the constitution of every Christian grace. For
so the richest tissue dazzles the beholder's eye
when the sun reflects upon the metal, the silver and the gold weaved into fantastic imagery
or a wealthy plainness; but the rich wire and
shining filaments are wrought upon cheaper
silk, the spoil of worms and flies. So is the

embroidery of our virtue. The glories of the spirit dwell upon the face and vestment, upon the fringes and the borders, and there we see the beryl and onyx, the jasper and the sardonyx, order and perfection, love, and peace, and joy, mortification of the passions and ravishment of the will, adherences to God and imitation of Christ, reception and entertainment of the Holy Ghost, and longings after heaven, humility and chastity, temperance and sobriety. These make the frame of the garment, the clothes of the soul, that it may " not be found naked in the day of the Lord's visitation." But through these rich materials a thread of silk is drawn, some compliance with worms and weaker creatures, something that shall please our bowels and make the lower man to rejoice ; they are wrought upon secular content and material satisfactions : and now we cannot be happy unless we be pious ; and the religion of a Christian is the greatest security, and the most certain instrument of making a man rich, and pleasing, and healthful, and wise, and beloved, in the whole world.

SYMPATHY.

A FRIEND shares my sorrow, and makes it but a moiety; but he swells my joy, and makes it double. For so two channels divide the river, and lessen it into rivulets, and make it fordable, and apt to be drunk up at the first revels of the Sirian star; but two torches do not divide, but increase the flame : and though my tears are the sooner dried up when they run upon my friend's cheeks in the furrows of compassion, yet when my flame hath kindled his lamp, we unite the glories and make them radiant, like the golden candlesticks that burn before the throne of God, because they shine by numbers, by unions, and confederations of light and joy.

RESTRAINT OF THE PASSIONS.

SO have I seen a busy flame, sitting upon a sullen coal, turn its point to all the angles and portions of its neighborhood, and reach at a heap of prepared straw, which, like a bold temptation, called it to a restless motion and activity; but either it was at too big a distance, or a gentle breath from heaven diverted the sphere and the ray of the fire to the other side, and so prevented the violence of the burning, till the flame expired in a weak consumption, and died turning into smoke, and the coolness of death, and the harmlessness of a cinder. And when a man's desires are winged with sails and a lusty wind of passion, and pass on in a smooth channel of opportunity, God oftentimes hinders the lust and the impatient desire from passing on to its port and entering into action, by a sudden thought, by a little remembrance of a word, by a fancy, by a sudden disability, by unreasonable and unlikely fears, by the sudden intervening of company, by the very weariness of the passion, by curiosity, by want of health, by the too great violence of the desire, bursting itself with its fulness into dissolution and a remiss easiness, by a sentence of Scripture, by the reverence of a good man, or else by the proper interventions of the spirit of grace chastising the crime, and representing its appendant mischiefs, and its constituent disorder and irregularity: and after all this, the very anguish and trouble of being defeated in the purpose hath rolled itself into so much uneasiness and unquiet reflections, that the man is grown ashamed and vexed into more sober counsels.

GOD will restore the soul to the body, and raise the body to such a perfection that it shall be an organ fit to praise him upon ; it shall be made spiritual to minister to the soul, when the soul is turned into a spirit ; then the soul shall be brought forth by angels from her incomparable and easy bed, from her rest in Christ's holy bosom, and be made perfect in her being, and in all her operations. And this shall first appear by that perfection which the soul shall receive as instrumental to the last judgment; for then she shall see clearly all the records of this world, all the register of her own memory. For all that we did in this life is laid up in our memories ; and though dust and forgetfulness be drawn upon them, yet when God shall lift us from our dust, then shall appear clearly all that we have done, written in the tables of our conscience, which is the soul's memory. We see many times, and in many instances, that a great memory is hindered and put out, and we thirty years after come to think of something that lay so long under a curtain ; we think of it suddenly, and without a line of deduction or proper consequence. And all those famous memories of Simonides and Theodectes, of Hortensius and

Seneca, of Sceptius, Metrodorus, and Carneades, of Cyneas the ambassador of Pyrrhus, are
only the records better kept, and less disturbed
by accident and disease. For even the memory
of Herod's son, of Athens, of Bathyllus, and
the dullest person now alive, is so great, and by
God made so sure a record of all that ever he
did, that as soon as ever God shall but tune our
instrument, and draw the curtains, and but
light up the candle of immortality, there we
shall find it all, there we shall see all, and the
whole world shall see all. Then we shall be
made fit to converse with God after the manner of spirits; we shall be like to angels.

———◆———

FEMALE PIETY.

I HAVE seen a female religion that wholly
dwelt upon the face and tongue; that, like
a wanton and an undressed tree, spends all its
juice in suckers and irregular branches, in
leaves and gum; and after all such goodly outsides, you should never eat an apple, or be
delighted with the beauties or the perfumes of
a hopeful blossom. But the religion of this
excellent lady was of another constitution; it
took root downward in humility, and brought
forth fruit upward in the substantial graces of
a Christian, in charity and justice, in chastity

and modesty, in fair friendships and sweetness of society. She had not very much of the forms and outsides of godliness, but she was hugely careful for the power of it, for the moral, essential, and useful parts, such which would make her be. not seem to be, religious.

In all her religion, in all her actions of relation towards God, she had a strange evenness and untroubled passage, sliding toward her ocean of God and of infinity with a certain and silent motion. So have I seen a river deep and smooth passing with a still foot and a sober face, and paying to the "*fiscus*," the great exchequer of the sea, the prince of all the watery bodies, a tribute large and full; and hard by it a little brook skipping and making a noise upon its unequal and neighbor bottom ; and after all its talking and braggart motion, it paid to its common audit no more than the revenues of a little cloud, or a contemptible vessel. So have I sometimes compared the issues of her religion to the solemnities and famed outsides of another's piety. It dwelt upon her spirit, and was incorporated with the periodical work of every day: she did not believe that religion was intended to minister to fame and reputation, but to pardon of sins, to the pleasure of God, and the salvation of souls. For religion is like the breath of heaven : if it goes abroad into the open air, it scatters and dissolves like

camphor ; but if it enters into a secret hollowness, into a close conveyance, it is strong and
mighty, and comes forth with vigor and great
effect at the other end, at the other side of this
life, in the days of death and judgment.

The other appendage of her religion, which
also was a great ornament to all the parts of
her life, was a rare modesty and humility of
spirit, a confident despising and undervaluing
of herself. For though she had the greatest
judgment, and the greatest experience of things
and persons that I ever yet knew in a person
of her youth and sex and circumstances, yet,
as if she knew nothing of it, she had the meanest opinion of herself; and like a fair taper,
when she shined to all the room, yet round
about her own station she had cast a shadow
and a cloud, and she shined to everybody but
herself. But the perfectness of her prudence
and excellent parts could not be hid ; and all
her humility and arts of concealment made
the virtues more amiable and illustrious. For
as pride sullies the beauty of the fairest virtues
and makes our understanding but like the craft
and learning of a devil, so humility is the
greatest eminency and art of publication in the
whole world ; and she, in all her arts of secrecy
and hiding her worthy things, was but " like
one that hideth the wind, and covers the oint-
ment of her right hand."

She lived as we all should live, and she died as I fain would die. I pray God I may feel those mercies on my death-bed that she felt, and that I may feel the same effect of my repentance which she feels of the many degrees of her innocence. Such was her death, that she did not die too soon; and her life was so useful and excellent, that she could not have lived too long. And as now in the grave it shall not be inquired concerning her, how long she lived, but how well, so to us who live after her, to suffer a longer calamity, it may be some ease to our sorrows, and some guide to our lives, and some security to our conditions, to consider that God hath brought the piety of a young lady to the early rewards of a never-ceasing and never-dying eternity of glory: and we also, if we live as she did, shall partake of the same glories; not only having the honor of a good name, and a dear and honored memory, but the glories of these glories, the end of all excellent labors and all prudent counsels and all holy religion, even the salvation of our souls, in that day when all the saints, and among them this excellent woman, shall be shown to all the world to have done more, and more excellent things, than we know of or can describe. Death consecrates and makes sacred that person whose excellency was such that they that are not displeased at the death cannot dispraise the life ; but they that mourn sadly, think they can never commend sufficiently.

———◆———

THE SHORTNESS OF LIFE.

A MAN is a bubble," said the Greek proverb; which Lucian represents with advantages, and its proper circumstances, to this purpose, saying : All the world is a storm, and men rise up in their several generations like bubbles descending " *à Jove pluvio*," from God and the dew of heaven, from a tear and drop of rain, from nature and providence; and some of these instantly sink into the deluge of their first parent, and are hidden in a sheet of water, having had no other business in the world but to be born, that they might be able to die ; others float up and down two or three turns, and suddenly disappear and give their place to others ; and they that live longest upon the face of the waters are in perpetual motion, restless and uneasy, and being crushed with a great drop of a cloud, sink into flatness and a froth ; the change not being great, it being hardly possible it should be more a nothing than it was before.

So is every man : he is born in vanity and

sin; he comes into the world like morning
mushrooms, soon thrusting up their heads into
the air, and conversing with their kindred of
the same production, and as soon they turn
unto dust and forgetfulness; some of them
without any other interest in the affairs of the
world, but that they made their parents a little
glad and very sorrowful: others ride longer in
the storm, it may be until seven years of vanity be expired, and then peradventure the sun
shines hot upon their heads, and they fall into
the shades below, into the cover of death and
darkness of the grave to hide them. But if
the bubble stands the shock of a bigger drop
and outlives the chances of a child, of a careless nurse, of drowning in a pail of water, of
being overlaid by a sleepy servant, or such
little accidents, then the young man dances
like a bubble empty and gay, and shines like a
dove's neck, or the image of a rainbow, which
hath no substance, and whose very imagery
and colors are fantastical; and so he dances
out the gayety of his youth, and is all the
while in a storm, and endures only because
he is not knocked on the head by a drop of
bigger rain, or crushed by the pressure of a
load of indigested meat, or quenched by the
disorder of an ill-placed humor; and to preserve a man alive, in the midst of so many
chances and hostilities, is as great a miracle as

to create him; to preserve him from rushing
into nothing, and at first to draw him up from
nothing, were equally the issues of an almighty
power.

And therefore the wise men of the world
have contended who shall best fit man's condition with words signifying his vanity and
short abode. Homer calls a man "a leaf," the
smallest, the weakest piece of a short-lived,
unsteady plant. Pindar calls him "the dream
of a shadow"; another, "the dream of a shadow of smoke." But St. James spake by a
more excellent spirit, saying, "Our life is but
a vapor," drawn from the earth by a celestial
influence, made of smoke, or the lighter parts
of water, tossed with every wind, moved by
the motion of a superior body, without virtue
in itself, lifted up on high or left below, according as it pleases the sun, its foster-father. But
it is lighter yet. It is but "appearing"; a
fantastic vapor, an apparition, nothing real; it
is not so much as a mist, not the matter of
a shower, nor substantial enough to make a
cloud; but it is like Cassiopeia's chair, or
Pelops's shoulder, or the circles of heaven, "appearing," for which you cannot have a word
that can signify a verier nothing.

And yet the expression is one degree more
made diminutive; a vapor, and fantastical, or
a mere appearance, and this but "for a little

while " neither; the very dream, the phantasm disappears in a small time, " like the shadow that departeth, or like a tale that is told, or as a dream when one awaketh." A man is so vain, so unfixed, so perishing a creature, that he cannot long last in the scene of fancy; a man goes off and is forgotten like the dream of a distracted person. The sum of all is this: that thou art a man, than whom there is not in the world any greater instance of heights and declensions, of lights and shadows, of misery and folly, of laughter and tears, of groans and death.

And because this consideration is of great usefulness and great necessity to many purposes of wisdom and the spirit, all the succession of time, all the changes in nature, all the varieties of light and darkness, the thousand thousands of accidents in the world, and every contingency to every man and to every creature doth preach our funeral sermon, and calls us to look and see how the old sexton, Time, throws up the earth and digs a grave where we must lay our sins or our sorrows, and sow our bodies, till they rise again in a fair or in an intolerable eternity. Every revolution which the sun makes about the world divides between life and death; and death possesses both those portions by the next morrow; and we are dead to all those months which we have already lived, and we shall never live them over again; and still God makes little periods of our age.

First we change our world when we are born and feel the warmth of the sun. Then we sleep and enter into the image of death, in which state we are unconcerned in all the changes of the world: and if our mothers or our nurses die, or a wild boar destroy our vine-yards, or our king be sick, we regard it not, but during that state are as disinterested as if our eyes were closed with the clay that weeps in the bowels of the earth. At the end of seven years our teeth fall and die before us, representing a formal prologue to a tragedy; and still every seven years it is odd but we shall finish the last scene; and when nature, or chance, or vice takes our body in pieces, weakening some parts and loosening others, we taste the grave, and the solemnities of our own funerals, first, in those parts that ministered to vice, and next, in them that served for orna-ment; and in a short time even they that served for necessity become useless and en-tangled like the wheels of a broken clock.

Baldness is but a dressing to our funerals, the proper ornament of mourning, and of a person entered very far into the regions and possession of death; and we have many more of the same signification; gray hairs, rotten

teeth, dim eyes, trembling joints, short breath,
stiff limbs, wrinkled skin, short memory, decayed appetite. Every day's necessity calls
for a reparation of that portion which death
fed on all night, when we lay in his lap and
slept in his outer chambers. The very spirits
of a man prey upon the daily portion of bread
and flesh, and every meal is a rescue from one
death, and lays up for another; and while we
think a thought we die ; and the clock strikes,
and reckons on our portion of eternity ; we
form our words with the breath of our nostrils ;
we have the less to live upon for every word
we speak.

Thus nature calls us to meditate of death by
those things which are the instruments of act-
ing it; and God, by all the variety of his providence, makes us see death everywhere, in all
variety of circumstances, and dressed up for
all the fancies and the expectation of every
single person. Nature hath given us one harvest every year, but death hath two; and the
spring and the autumn send throngs of men
and women to charnel-houses ; and all the
summer long, men are recovering from the
evils of the spring, till the dog-days come and
the Sirian star makes the summer deadly; and
the fruits of autumn are laid up for all the
year's provision, and the man that gathers
them eats and surfeits and dies, and needs

them not, and himself is laid up for eternity;
and he that escapes till winter, only stays for
another opportunity, which the distempers of
that quarter minister to him with great variety.
Thus death reigns in all the portions of our
time.   The autumn with its fruits provides disorders for us, and the winter's cold turns them
into sharp diseases, and the spring brings flowers to strew our hearse, and the summer gives
green turf and brambles to bind upon our
graves.   Calentures and surfeit, cold and agues,
are the four quarters of the year, and all minister to death; and you can go no whither but
you tread upon a dead man's bones.

The wild fellow in Petronius that escaped
upon a broken table from the furies of a shipwreck, as he was sunning himself upon the
rocky shore espied a man rolling upon his
floating bed of waves, ballasted with sand in
the folds of his garment, and carried by his
civil enemy, the sea, towards the shore to
find a grave; and it cast him into some sad
thoughts: that peradventure this man's wife
in some part of the continent, safe and warm,
looks next month for the good man's return;
or it may be his son knows nothing of the tempest; or his father thinks of that affectionate
kiss, which still is warm upon the good old
man's cheek, ever since he took a kind fare-
well, and he weeps with joy to think how

blessed he shall be when his beloved boy
returns into the circle of his father's arms.
These are the thoughts of mortals, this the
end and sum of all their designs ; a dark
night and an ill guide, a boisterous sea and a
broken cable, a hard rock and a rough wind,
dashed in pieces the fortune of a whole family ;
and they that shall weep loudest for the accident are not yet entered into the storm, and
yet have suffered shipwreck. Then looking
upon the carcass, he knew it, and found it to
be the master of the ship, who the day before
cast up the accounts of his patrimony and his
trade, and named the day when he thought to
be at home. See how the man swims who
was so angry two days since ; his passions are
becalmed by the storm, his accounts are cast
up, his cares at an end, his voyage done,
and his gains are the strange events of death,
which, whether they be good or evil, the men
that are alive seldom trouble themselves concerning the interest of the dead.

But seas alone do not break our vessel in
pieces ; everywhere we may be shipwrecked.
A valiant general, when he is to reap the harvest of his crowns and triumphs, fights unpros-
perously, or falls into a fever with joy and
wine, and changes his laurel into cypress, his
triumphant chariot to a hearse ; dying the
night before he was appointed to perish in

the drunkenness of his festival joys. It was a sad arrest of the loosenesses and wilder feasts of the French court, when their king, Henry the Second, was killed really by the sportive image of a fight. And many brides have died under the hands of paranymphs and maidens, dressing them for the new and undiscerned chains of marriage. Some have been paying their vows, and giving thanks for a prosperous return to their own house, and the roof hath descended upon their heads, and turned their loud religion into the deeper silence of a grave. And how many teeming mothers have rejoiced, and pleased themselves in becoming channels of blessing to a family; and the midwife hath quickly bound their heads and feet, and carried them forth to burial. Or else the birthday of an heir hath seen the coffin of the father brought into the house, and the divided mother hath been forced to travail twice, with a painful birth, and a sadder death.

There is no state, no accident, no circumstance of our life but it hath been soured by some sad instance of a dying friend; a friendly meeting often ends in some sad mischance and makes an eternal parting; and when the poet Æschylus was sitting under the walls of his house, an eagle hovering over his bald head mistook it for a stone, and let fall his oyster, hoping there to break the shell, but pierced the poor man's skull.

Death meets us everywhere, and is procured by every instrument, and in all chances, and enters in at many doors; by violence and secret influence, by the aspect of a star and the scent of a mist, by the emissions of a cloud and the meeting of a vapor, by the fall of a chariot and the stumbling at a stone, by a full meal or an empty stomach, by watching at the wine or by watching at prayers, by the sun or the moon, by a heat or a cold, by sleepless nights or sleeping days, by water frozen into the hardness and sharpness of a dagger, or water thawed into the floods of a river, by a hair or a raisin, by violent motion or sitting still, by severity or dissolution, by God's mercy or God's anger, by everything in providence and everything in manners, by everything in nature and by everything in chance. " *Eripitur persona, manet res* "; we take pains to heap up things useful to our life, and get our death in the purchase; and the person is snatched away, and the goods remain. And all this is the law and constitution of nature; it is a punishment to our sins, the unalterable event of providence, and the decree of heaven. The chains that confine us to this condition are strong as destiny and immutable as the eternal laws of God.

I have conversed with some men who rejoiced in the death or calamity of others, and accounted it as a judgment upon them for being on the other side and against them in the contention; but within the revolution of a few months, the same man met with a more uneasy and unhandsome death; which, when I saw, I wept and was afraid; for I knew it must be so with all men, for we also shall die, and end our quarrels and contentions by passing to a final sentence.

It is a mighty change that is made by the death of every person, and it is visible to us who are alive. Reckon but from the sprightfulness of youth and the fair cheeks and the full eyes of childhood, from the vigorousness and strong flexure of the joints of five-and-twenty to the hollowness and dead paleness, to the loathsomeness and horror of a three days' burial, and we shall perceive the distance to be very great and very strange. But so have I seen a rose newly springing from the clefts of its hood, and at first it was as fair as the morning, and full with the dew of heaven as a lamb's fleece; but when a ruder breath had forced open its virgin modesty and dismantled its too youthful and unripe retirements, it began to put on darkness and to decline to softness and the symptoms of a sickly age; it bowed the head and broke its stalk, and at night, having lost some of its leaves and all its beauty, it fell into the portion of weeds and outworn faces.

The same is the portion of every man and every woman ; the heritage of worms and serpents, rottenness and cold dishonor, and our beauty so changed that our acquaintance quickly know us not ; and that change mingled with so much horror, or else meets so with our fears and weak discoursings, that they who six hours ago tended upon us, either with charitable or ambitious services, cannot without some regret stay in the room alone where the body lies stripped of its life and honor. I have read of a fair young German gentleman, who, living, often refused to be pictured, but put off the importunity of his friends' desire by giving way that after a few days' burial they might send a painter to his vault, and, if they saw cause for it, draw the image of his death unto the life. They did so, and found his face half eaten, and his midriff and backbone full of serpents ; and so he stands pictured amongst his armed ancestors. So does the fairest beauty change ; and it will be as bad with you and me ; and then what servants shall we have to wait upon us in the grave ? what friends to visit us ? what officious people to cleanse away the moist and unwholesome cloud reflected upon our faces from the sides of the weeping vaults, which are the longest weepers for our funeral ?

A man may read a sermon, the best and

most passionate that ever man preached, if he shall but enter into the sepulchres of kings. In the same Escurial where the Spanish princes live in greatness and power, and decree war or peace, they have wisely placed a cemetery, where their ashes and their glory shall sleep till time shall be no more; and where our kings have been crowned, their ancestors lie interred, and they must walk over their grand-sire's head to take his crown. There is an acre sown with royal seed, the copy of the greatest change, from rich to naked, from ceiled roofs to arched coffins, from living like gods to die like men. There is enough to cool the flames of lust, to abate the heights of pride, to appease the itch of covetous desires, to sully and dash out the dissembling colors of a lustful, artificial, and imaginary beauty. There the warlike and the peaceful, the fortunate and the miserable, the beloved and the despised princes mingle their dust, and pay down their symbol of mortality, and tell all the world that, when we die, our ashes shall be equal to kings', and our accounts easier, and our pains for our crowns shall be less.

Let no man extend his thoughts, or let his hopes wander towards future and far-distant events and accidental contingencies. This day is mine and yours, but ye know not what shall be on the morrow: and every morning creeps

out of a dark cloud, leaving behind it an ignorance and silence deep as midnight, and undiscerned as are the phantasms that make a chris-
om child to smile ; so that we cannot discern
what comes hereafter, unless we had a light
from heaven brighter than the vision of an
angel, even the spirit of prophecy. Without
revelation we cannot tell whether we shall eat
to-morrow, or whether a squinancy shall choke
us ; and it is written in the unrevealed folds of
divine predestination, that many who are this
day alive shall to-morrow be laid upon the cold
earth, and the women shall weep over their
shroud, and dress them for their funeral.

This descending to the grave is the lot of
all men ; neither doth God respect the person
of any man. The rich is not protected for
favor, nor the poor for pity ; the old man is not
reverenced for his age, nor the infant regarded
for his tenderness ; youth and beauty, learning and prudence, wit and strength lie down
equally in the dishonors of the grave. All
men, and all natures, and all persons resist the
addresses and solemnities of death, and strive
to preserve a miserable and unpleasant life ;
and yet they all sink down and die. For so
have I seen the pillars of a building assisted
with artificial props bending under the pressure of a roof, and pertinaciously resisting the
infallible and prepared ruin, till the determined

day comes, and then the burden sunk upon the
pillars, and disordered the aids and auxiliary
rafters into a common ruin and a ruder grave.
So are the desires and weak arts of man; with
little aids and assistances of care and physic we
strive to support our decaying bodies, and to
put off the evil day; but quickly that day will
come, and then neither angels nor men can
rescue us from our grave; but the roof sinks
down upon the walls, and the walls descend to
the foundation; and the beauty of the face
and the dishonors of the belly, the discerning
head and the servile feet, the thinking heart
and the working hand, the eyes and the guts
together shall be crushed into the confusion of
a heap, and dwell with creatures of an equivocal production, with worms and serpents, the
sons and daughters of our own bones, in a
house of dirt and darkness.

THE MISERIES OF LIFE.

HOW few men in the world are prosperous!
What an infinite number of slaves and
beggars, of persecuted and oppressed people,
fill all corners of the earth with groans, and
heaven itself with weeping, prayers, and sad
remembrances! How many provinces and king-

doms are afflicted by a violent war, or made
desolate by popular diseases! Some whole
countries are remarked with fatal evils, or
periodical sicknesses. Grand Cairo in Egypt
feels the plague every three years returning
like a quartan ague, and destroying many thousands of persons. All the inhabitants of Arabia
the Desert are in continual fear of being buried
in huge heaps of sand ; and therefore dwell in
tents and ambulatory houses, or retire to un-
fruitful mountains, to prolong an uneasy and
wilder life. And all the countries round about
the Adriatic Sea feel such violent convulsions
by tempests and intolerable earthquakes, that
sometimes whole cities find a tomb, and every
man sinks with his own house made ready to
become his monument, and his bed is crushed
into the disorders of a grave.

Or if you please in charity to visit an hospital, which is indeed a map of the whole world,
there you shall see the effects of Adam's sin,
and the ruins of human nature ; bodies laid up
in heaps, like the bones of a destroyed town ;
men whose souls seem to be borrowed, and
are kept there by art and the force of medi-
cine, whose miseries are so great that few
people have charity or humanity enough to
visit them, fewer have the heart to dress them ;
and we pity them in civility or with a transient
prayer, but we do not feel their sorrows by the

mercies of a religious pity; and therefore, as
we leave their sorrows in many degrees unre-
lieved and uneased, so we contract, by our
unmercifulness, a guilt by which ourselves become liable to the same calamities. Those
many that need pity, and those infinities of
people that refuse to pity, are miserable upon a
several charge, but yet they almost make up
all mankind.

But these evils are notorious and confessed;
even they also whose felicity men stare at and
admire, besides their splendor and the sharpness of their light, will, with their appendant
sorrows, wring a tear from the most resolved
eye: for not only the winter quarter is full of
storms and cold and darkness, but the beauteous spring hath blasts and sharp frosts; the
fruitful teeming summer is melted with heat,
and burnt with the kisses of the sun, her friend,
and choked with dust; and the rich autumn
is full of sickness; and we are weary of that
which we enjoy, because sorrow is its bigger
portion. For look upon kings and conquerors.
I will not tell that many of them fall into the
condition of servants, and their subjects rule
over them, and stand upon the ruins of their
families, and that to such persons the sorrow
is bigger than usually happens in smaller fortunes. But let us suppose them still conquerors, and see what a goodly purchase they get.

18

by all their pains, and amazing fears, and continual dangers. They carry their arms beyond Ister, and pass the Euphrates, and bind the Germans with the bounds of the river Rhine: I speak in the style of the Roman greatness; for nowadays the biggest fortune swells not beyond the limits of a petty province or two, and a hill confines the progress of their prosperity, or a river checks it. But whatsoever tempts the pride and vanity of ambitious persons, is not so big as the smallest star which we see scattered in disorder and unregarded upon the pavement and floor of heaven. And if we would suppose the pismires had but our understanding, they also would have the method of a man's greatness, and divide their little molehills into provinces and exarchates; and if they also grew as vicious and as miserable, one of their princes would lead an army out, and kill his neighbor-ants, that he might reign over the next handful of a turf. But then if we consider at what price and with what felicity all this is purchased, the sting of the painted snake will quickly appear, and the fairest of their fortunes will properly enter into this account of human infelicities.

We must look for prosperity, not in palaces or courts of princes, not in the tents of conquerors, or in the gayeties of fortunate and prevailing sinners; but something rather in the cottages of honest, innocent, and contented persons, whose mind is no bigger than their fortune, nor their virtue less than their security. As for others, whose fortune looks bigger, and allures fools to follow it, like the wandering fires of the night, till they run into rivers, or are broken upon rocks with staring and running after them, they are all in the condition of Marius, than whose condition nothing was more constant, and nothing more mutable. If we reckon them amongst the happy, they are the most happy men; if we reckon them amongst the miserable, they are the most miserable. For just as is a man's condition, great or little, so is the state of his misery. All have their share; but kings and princes, great generals and consuls, rich men and mighty, as they have the biggest business and the biggest charge, and are answerable to God for the greatest accounts, so they have the biggest trouble; that the uneasiness of their appendage may divide the good and evil of the world, making the poor man's fortune as eligible as the greatest: and also restraining the vanity of man's spirit, which a great fortune is apt to swell from a vapor to a bubble: but God in mercy hath mingled wormwood with their wine, and so restrained the drunkenness and follies of prosperity.

He that is no fool, but can consider wisely,

if he be in love with this world, we need not
despair but that a witty man might reconcile
him with tortures, and make him think charitably of the rack, and be brought to dwell with
vipers and dragons, and entertain his guests
with the shrieks of mandrakes, cats, and
screech-owls, with the filing of iron, and the
harshness of rending silk, or to admire the
harmony that is made by a herd of evening
wolves, when they miss their draught of blood
in their midnight revels. The groans of a man
in a fit of the stone are worse than all these;
and the distractions of a troubled conscience
are worse than those groans: and yet a careless merry sinner is worse than all that.

But if we could from one of the battlements
of heaven espy how many men and women at
this time lie fainting and dying for want of
bread, how many young men are hewn down
by the sword of war, how many poor orphans
are now weeping over the graves of their
father, by whose life they were enabled to
eat; if we could but hear how many mariners
and passengers are at this present in a storm,
and shriek out because their keel dashes against
a rock or bulges under them, how many people there are that weep with want and are
mad with oppression, or are desperate by too
quick a sense of a constant infelicity; in all
reason we should be glad to be out of the noise

and participation of so many evils. This is a place of sorrows and tears, of great evils and a constant calamity : let us remove from hence, at least in affections and preparation of mind.

———◆———

REASON AND DISCRETION.

WE must not think that the life of a man begins when he can feed himself or walk alone, when he can fight or beget his like ; for so he is contemporary with a camel or a cow : but he is first a man, when he comes to a certain steady use of reason, according to his proportion ; and when that is, all the world of men cannot tell precisely. Some are called at age at fourteen, some at one-and-twenty, some never ; but all men late enough, for the life of a man comes upon him slowly and insensibly. But as when the sun approaching towards the gates of the morning, he first opens a little eye of heaven and sends away the spirits of darkness, and gives light to a cock, and calls up the lark to matins, and by and by gilds the fringes of a cloud, and peeps over the eastern hills, thrusting out his golden horns, like those which decked the brows of Moses when he was forced to wear a veil, because himself had seen the face of God ; and still while a man tells the story, the sun gets up higher, till he shows a fair face and a full light, and then he shines one whole day, under a cloud often, and sometimes weeping great and little showers, and sets quickly: so is a man's reason and his life. He first begins to perceive himself to see or taste, making little reflections upon his actions of sense, and can discourse of flies and dogs, shells and play, horses and liberty : but when he is strong enough to enter into arts and little institutions, he is at first entertained with trifles and impertinent things, not because he needs them, but because his understanding is no bigger, and little images of things are laid before him, like a cockboat to a whale, only to play withal : but before a man comes to be wise, he is half dead with gouts and consumption, with catarrhs and aches, with sore eyes and a worn-out body. So that if we must not reckon the life of a man but by the accounts of his reason, he is long before his soul be dressed; and he is not to be called a man without a wise and an adorned soul, a soul at least furnished with what is necessary towards his well-being. But by the time his soul is thus furnished, his body is decayed; and then you can hardly reckon him to be alive, when his body is possessed by so many degrees of death.

But there is yet another arrest. At first he wants strength of body, and then he wants the

use of reason; and when that is come, it is ten
to one but he stops by the impediments of vice,
and wants the strength of the spirit; and we
know that body and soul and spirit are the
constituent parts of every Christian man. And
now let us consider what that thing is which
we call years of discretion. The young man
is past his tutors, and arrived at the bondage
of a caitiff spirit; he is run from discipline,
and is let loose to passion; the man by this
time hath wit enough to choose his vice, to act
his lust, to court his mistress, to talk confidently and ignorantly and perpetually, to despise his betters, to deny nothing to his appetite, to do things that, when he is indeed a
man, he must forever be ashamed of. For this
is all the discretion that most men show in the
first stage of their manhood; they can discern
good from evil; and they prove their skill by
leaving all that is good, and wallowing in the
evils of folly and an unbridled appetite. And
by this time the young man hath contracted
vicious habits, and is a beast in manners, and
therefore it will not be fitting to reckon the beginning of his life; he is a fool in his understanding, and that is a sad death; and he is
dead in trespasses and sins, and that is a sadder: so that he hath no life but a natural, the
life of a beast or a tree; in all other capacities
he is dead; he neither hath the intellectual nor

the spiritual life, neither the life of a man nor of a Christian; and this sad truth lasts too long. For old age seizes upon most men while they still retain the minds of boys and vicious youth, doing actions from principles of great folly and a mighty ignorance, admiring things useless and hurtful, and filling up all the dimensions of their abode with businesses of empty affairs, being at leisure to attend no virtue. They cannot pray, because they are busy and because they are passionate; they cannot communicate, because they have quarrels and intrigues of perplexed causes, complicated hostilities, and things of the world; and therefore they cannot attend to the things of God, little considering that they must find a time to die in; when death comes, they must be at leisure for that. Such men are like sailors loosing from a port, and tost immediately with a perpetual tempest lasting till their cordage crack, and either they sink or return back again to the same place: they did not make a voyage, though they were long at sea.

CHARITY.

CHARITY, with its twin-daughters, alms and forgiveness, is especially effectual for the procuring God's mercies in the day and the manner of our death. Repentance without alms is dead and without wings, and can never soar upwards to the element of love. A long experience hath observed God's mercies to descend upon charitable people, like the dew upon Gideon's fleece, when all the world was dry. When faith fails, and chastity is useless, and temperance shall be no more, then charity shall bear you upon wings of cherubim to the eternal mountain of the Lord.

I do not mean this should only be a deathbed charity, any more than a death-bed repentance; but it ought to be the charity of our life and healthful years, a parting with portions of our goods then when we can keep them. We must not first kindle our lights when we are to descend into our houses of darkness, or bring a glaring torch suddenly to a dark room that will amaze the eye and not delight it, or instruct the body; but if our tapers have, in their constant course, descended into their grave, crowned all the way with light, then let the death-bed charity be doubled, and the light burn brightest when it is to deck our hearse.

TIME.

IT is very remarkable that God who giveth plenteously to all creatures, — he hath scattered the firmament with stars, as a man sows corn in his fields, in a multitude bigger than the capacities of human order; he hath made so much variety of creatures, and gives us great choice of meats and drinks, although any one of both kinds would have served our needs; and so in all instances of nature, — yet in the distribution of our time, God seems to be straight-handed; and gives it to us, not as nature gives us rivers, enough to drown us, but drop by drop, minute after minute; so that we never can have two minutes together, but he takes away one when he gives us another. This should teach us to value our time since God so values it, and by his so small distribution of it tells us it is the most precious thing we have.

IMMODERATE GRIEF.

SOLEMN and appointed mournings are good expressions of our dearness to the departed soul, and of his worth and our value of him; and it hath its praise in nature and in manners and public customs. Something is to be given to custom, something to fame, to nature, and to civilities, and to the honor of the deceased friends; for that man is esteemed to die miserable for whom no friend or relative sheds a tear or pays a solemn sigh. I desire to die a dry death, but am not very desirous to have a dry funeral. Some showers sprinkled upon my grave would do well and comely; and a soft shower to turn those flowers into a springing memory or a fair rehearsal, that I may not go forth of my doors as my servants carry the entrails of beasts.

But that which is to be faulted in this particular is when the grief is immoderate and unreasonable; and Paula Romana deserved to have felt the weight of St. Hierom's severe reproof, when at the death of every of her children she almost wept herself into her grave. But it is worse yet when people, by an ambitious and a pompous sorrow, and by ceremonies invented for the ostentation of their grief, fill heaven and earth with exclamations, and grow troublesome because their friend is happy or themselves want his company. It is certainly a sad thing in nature to see a friend trembling with a palsy, or scorched with fevers, or dried up like a potsherd with immoderate heats, and rolling upon his uneasy bed without sleep, which cannot be invited with music, or pleasant murmurs, or a decent stillness : nothing but the servants of cold death, poppy and weariness, can tempt the eyes to let their curtains down, and then they sleep only to taste of death, and make an essay of the shades below : and yet we weep not here. The period and opportunity for tears we choose when our friend is fallen asleep, when he hath laid his neck upon the lap of his mother, and let his head down to be raised up to heaven. This grief is ill-placed and indecent. But many times it is worse ; and it hath been observed that those greater and stormy passions do so spend the whole stock of grief that they presently admit a comfort and contrary affection ; while a sorrow that is even and temperate goes on to its period with expectation and the distances of a just time.

THE EPHESIAN MATRON.

THE Ephesian woman, that the soldier told of in Petronius, was the talk of all the town, and the rarest example of a dear affection to her husband. She descended with the corpse into the vault, and there being attended with her maiden, resolved to weep to death, or die with famine or a distempered sorrow ; from

which resolution nor his nor her friends, nor
the reverence of the principal citizens, who
used the entreaties of their charity and their
power, could persuade her. But a soldier that
watched seven dead bodies hanging upon trees
just over against this monument, crept in, and
awhile stared upon the silent and comely disorders of the sorrow; and having let the wonder awhile breathe out at each other's eyes, at
last he fetched his supper and a bottle of wine,
with purpose to eat and drink, and still to feed
himself with that sad prettiness. His pity and
first draught of wine made him bold and curious to try if the maid would drink; who, having many hours since felt her resolution faint
as her wearied body, took his kindness; and
the light returned into her eyes, and danced
like boys in a festival; and fearing lest the per-
tinaciousness of her mistress's sorrows should
cause her evil to revert, or her shame to approach, assayed whether she would endure to
hear an argument to persuade her to drink and
live. The violent passion had laid all her
spirits in wildness and dissolution, and the maid
found them willing to be gathered into order at
the arrest of any new object, being weary
of the first, of which, like leeches, they had
sucked their fill, till they fell down and burst.
The weeping woman took her cordial, and was
not angry with her maid, and heard the soldier

talk. And he was so pleased with the change, that he, who first loved the silence of the sorrow, was more in love with the music of her returning voice, especially which himself had strung and put in tune ; and the man began to talk amorously, and the woman's weak head and heart were soon possessed with a little wine, and grew gay, and talked, and fell in love ; and that very night, in the morning of her passion, in the grave of her husband, in the pomps of mourning, and in her funeral garments, married her new and stranger guest.

For so the wild foragers of Lybia being spent with heat, and dissolved by the too fond kisses of the sun, do melt with their common fires, and die with faintness, and descend with motions slow and unable to the little brooks that descend from heaven in the wilderness ; and when they drink, they return into the vigor of a new life, and contract strange marriages; and the lioness is courted by a panther, and she listens to his love, and conceives a monster that all men call unnatural, and the daughter of an equivocal passion and of a sudden refreshment. And so also was it in the cave at Ephesus ; for by this time the soldier began to think it was fit he should return to his watch, and observe the dead bodies he had in charge ; but when he ascended from his mourning bridal chamber, he found that one of

the bodies was stolen by the friends of the
dead, and that he was fallen into an evil condition, because by the laws of Ephesus his
body was to be fixed in the place of it. The
poor man returns to his woman, cries out bitterly, and in her presence resolves to die to
prevent his death, and in secret to prevent his
shame. But now the woman's love was raging
like her former sadness, and grew witty, and
she comforted her soldier, and persuaded him
to live, lest by losing him, who had brought
her from death and a more grievous sorrow,
she should return to her old solemnities of dying, and lose her honor for a dream, or the
reputation of her constancy without the change
and satisfaction of an enjoyed love. The man
would fain have lived, if it had been possible;
and she found out this way for him: that he
should take the body of her first husband,
whose funeral she had so strangely mourned,
and put it upon the gallows in the place of the
stolen thief. He did so, and escaped the present danger, to possess a love which might
change as violently as her grief had done.

But so have I seen a crowd of disordered
people rush violently and in heaps till their
utmost border was restrained by a wall, or had
spent the fury of their first fluctuation and watery progress, and by and by it returned to the
contrary with the same earnestness, only be-

cause it was violent and ungoverned. A raging passion is this crowd, which, when it is not
under discipline and the conduct of reason, and
the proportions of temperate humanity, runs
passionately the way it happens, and by and
by as greedily to another side, being swayed
by its own weight, and driven anywhither by
chance, in all its pursuits having no rule but
to do all it can, and spend itself in haste, and
expire with some shame and much indecency.

———◆———

EDUCATION.

OTHERWISE do fathers, and otherwise do
mothers handle their children. These
soften them with kisses and imperfect noises,
with the pap and breast-milk of soft endearments; they rescue them from tutors, and snatch
them from discipline; they desire to keep them
fat and warm, and their feet dry, and their
bellies full ; and then the children govern and
cry, and prove fools and troublesome, so long
as the feminine republic does endure. But
fathers, because they design to have their children wise and valiant, apt for counsel or for
arms, send them to severe governments, and
tie them to study, to hard labor, and afflictive
contingencies. They rejoice when the bold

boy strikes a lion with his hunting-spear, and shrinks not when the beast comes to affright his early courage. Softness is for slaves and beasts, for minstrels and useless persons, for such who cannot ascend higher than the state of a fair ox, or a servant entertained for vainer offices; but the man that designs his son for nobler employments, to honors and to triumphs, to consular dignities and presidencies of councils, loves to see him pale with study, or panting with labor, hardened with sufferance, or eminent by dangers.

And so God dresses us for heaven. He loves to see us struggling with a disease, and resisting the devil, and contesting against the weaknesses of nature, and against hope to believe in hope, resigning ourselves to God's will, praying him to choose for us, and dying in all things but faith and its blessed consequents; and the danger and the resistance shall endear the office. For so have I known the boisterous northwind pass through the yielding air, which opened its bosom, and appeased its violence by entertaining it with easy compliance in all the regions of its reception; but when the same breath of heaven hath been checked with the stiffness of a tower, or the united strength of a wood, it grew mighty and dwelt there, and made the highest branches stoop and make a smooth path for it on the top of all its glories.

19

ADVANTAGES OF SICKNESS.

I CONSIDER one of the great felicities of heaven consists in an immunity from sin. Then we shall love God without mixtures of malice ; then we shall enjoy without envy ; then we shall see fuller vessels running over with glory, and crowned with bigger circles ; and this we shall behold without spilling from our eyes (those vessels of joy and grief) any sign of anger, trouble, or any repining spirit. Our passions shall be pure, our charity without fear, our desire without lust, our possessions all our own ; and all in the inheritance of Jesus, in the richest soil of God's eternal kingdom. Now half of this reason which makes heaven so happy by being innocent, is also in the state of sickness, making the sorrows of old age smooth, and the groans of a sick heart apt to be joined to the music of angels ; and though they sound harsh to our untuned ears and discomposed organs, yet those accents must needs be in themselves excellent which God loves to hear, and esteems them as prayers and arguments of pity, instruments of mercy and grace, and preparatives to glory.

In sickness the soul begins to dress herself for immortality. At first, she unties the strings of vanity that made her upper garment cleave to the world and sit uneasy. First, she puts off the light and fantastic summer robe of lust and wanton appetite.

Next to this, the soul by the help of sickness knocks off the fetters of pride and vainer complacencies. Then she draws the curtains and stops the light from coming in, and takes the pictures down, — those fantastic images of self-love, and gay remembrances of vain opinion and popular noises. Then the spirit stoops into the sobrieties of humble thoughts, and feels corruption chiding the forwardness of fancy, and allaying the vapors of conceit and factious opinions. For humility is the soul's grave, into which she enters, not to die, but to meditate and inter some of its troublesome appendages. There she sees the dust, and feels the dishonor of the body, and reads the register of all its sad adherences ; and then she lays by all her vain reflections, beating upon her crystal and pure mirror from the fancies of strength and beauty, and little decayed prettinesses of the body.

Next to these, as the soul is still undressing, she takes off the roughness of her great and little angers and animosities, and receives the oil of mercies and smooth forgiveness, fair interpretations and gentle answers, designs of reconcilement and Christian atonement, in their places. The temptations of this state, such I mean which are proper to it, are little and inconsiderable ; the man is apt to chide a servant too bitterly, and to be discontented with his nurse or not satisfied with his physician, and he rests uneasily, and (poor man !) nothing can please him ; and indeed these little indecencies must be cured and stopped lest they run into an inconvenience. But sickness is in this particular a little image of the state of blessed souls, or of Adam's early morning in paradise, free from the troubles of lust and violences of anger, and the intricacies of ambition or the restlessness of covetousness. For though a man may carry all these along with him into his sickness. yet there he will not find them ; and in despite of all his own malice, his soul shall find some rest from laboring in the galleys and baser captivity of sin.

At the first address and presence of sickness, stand still and arrest thy spirit that it may, without amazement or affright, consider that this was that thou lookedst for and wert always certain should happen, and that now thou art to enter into the actions of a new religion, the agony of a strange constitution ; but at no hand suffer thy spirits to be dispersed with fear or wildness of thought, but stay their looseness and dispersion by a serious consideration of the present and future employment. For so doth the Lybian lion, spying the fierce huntsman ;

he first beats himself with the strokes of his
tail and curls up his spirits, making them strong
with union and recollection, till, being struck
with a Mauritanian spear, he rushes forth into
his defence and noblest contention ; and either
escapes into the secrets of his own dwelling, or
else dies the bravest of the forest. Every
man, when shot with an arrow from God's
quiver, must then draw in all the auxiliaries
of reason, and know that then is the time to
try his strength and to reduce the words of his
religion into action, and consider that, if he
behaves himself weakly and timorously, he suffers never the less of sickness; but if he returns to health, he carries along with him the
mark of a coward and a fool ; and if he de-
scends into his grave, he enters into the state
of the faithless and unbelievers. Let him set
his heart firm upon this resolution: " I must
bear it inevitably, and I will, by God's grace,
do it nobly."

—◆—

DAILY PRAYER.

SHORT passes, quick ejections, concise forms
and remembrances, holy breathings, prayers
like little posies, may be sent forth without
number on every occasion, and God will note

them in his book. But all that have a care to walk with God fill their vessels more largely as soon as they rise, before they begin the work of the day, and before they lie down again at night; which is to observe what the Lord appointed in the Levitical ministry, a morning and an evening lamb to be laid upon the altar. So with them that are not stark irreligious, prayer is the key to open the day and the bolt to shut in the night. But as the skies drop the early dew and the evening dew upon the grass, yet it would not spring and grow green by that constant and double falling of the dew, unless some great showers at certain seasons did supply the rest; so the customary devotion of prayer twice a day is the falling of the early and the latter dew; but if you will increase and flourish in the works of grace, empty the great clouds sometimes and let them fall into a full shower of prayer; choose out the seasons in your own discretion when prayer shall overflow like Jordan in the time of harvest.

———◆———

TOLERATION.

ANY zeal is proper for religion but the zeal of the sword and the zeal of anger; this

is the bitterness of zeal, and it is a certain temptation to every man against his duty ; for if the
sword turns preacher and dictates propositions
by empire instead of arguments, and engraves
them in men's hearts with a poignard, that it
shall be death to believe what I innocently and
ignorantly am persuaded of, it must needs be
unsafe to " try the spirits," to " try all things,"
to make an inquiry ; and yet without this liberty no man can justify himself before God or
man, nor confidently say that his religion is
best.   This is inordination of zeal ; for Christ,
by reproving St. Peter drawing his sword even
in the cause of Christ for his sacred and yet
injured person. teaches us not to use the sword,
though in the cause of God or for God himself.
I end with a story which I find in the Jews'
books.

When Abraham sat at his tent-door, according to his custom, waiting to entertain stran-
gers, he espied an old man stooping and leaning
on his staff, weary with age and travel, coming
towards him. who was an hundred years of age.
He received him kindly, washed his feet. provided supper, caused him to sit down ; but observing that the old man ate, and prayed not,
nor begged for a blessing on his meat. he asked
him why he did not worship the God of heaven.
The old man told him that he worshipped the
fire only, and acknowledged no other God.   At

which answer Abraham grew so zealously angry that he thrust the old man out of his tent and exposed him to all the evils of the night and an unguarded condition. When the old man was gone, God called to Abraham and asked him where the stranger was. He replied, I thrust him away because he did not worship thee. God answered him, I have suffered him these hundred years, although he dishonored me ; and couldst thou not endure him one night when he gave thee no trouble ? Upon this, saith the story, Abraham fetched him back again, and gave him hospitable entertainment and wise instruction. Go thou and do likewise, and thy charity will be rewarded by the God of Abraham.

THE PRESENCE OF GOD.

THAT God is present in all places, that he sees every action, hears all discourses, and understands every thought, is no strange thing to a Christian ear who hath been taught this doctrine, not only by right reason and the consent of all the wise men in the world, but also by God himself in holy Scripture. God is wholly in every place, included in no place, not bound with cords, (except those of love,) not

divided into parts nor changeable into several
shapes, filling heaven and earth with his present power and with his never absent nature.
So that we may imagine God to be as the air
and the sea, and we all enclosed in his circle,
wrapt up in the lap of his infinite nature ; and
we can no more be removed from the presence
of God than from our own being.

God is present by his essence, which because
it is infinite cannot be contained within the
limits of any place ; and because he is of an
essential purity and spiritual nature, he cannot
be undervalued by being supposed present in
the places of unnatural uncleanness ; because
as the sun, reflecting upon the mud of strands
and shores, is unpolluted in its beams, so is God
not dishonored when we suppose him in every
of his creatures, and in every part of every
one of them, and is still as unmixed with any
unhandsome adherence as is the soul in the
bowels of the body.

God is everywhere present by his power.
He rolls the orbs of heaven with his hand, he
fixes the earth with his foot, he guides all the
creatures with his eye, and refreshes them with
his influence ; he makes the powers of hell to
shake with his terrors, and binds the devils with
his word, and throws them out with his command, and sends the angels on embassies with
his decrees ; he hardens the joints of infants,

and confirms the bones when they are fashioned beneath secretly in the heart. He it is that assists at the numerous productions of fishes; and there is not one hollowness in the bottom of the sea but he shows himself to be Lord of it, by sustaining there the creatures that come to dwell in it; and in the wilderness, the bittern and the stork, the dragon and the satyr, the unicorn and the elk, live upon his provisions and revere his power and feel the force of his almightiness.

God is, by grace and benediction, specially present in holy places, and in the solemn assemblies of his servants. If holy people meet in grots and dens of the earth when persecution or a public necessity disturbs the public order, circumstance, and convenience, God fails not to come thither to them; but God is also by the same or greater reason present there where they meet ordinarily.

God is especially present in the hearts of his people by his Holy Spirit; and indeed the hearts of holy men are temples in the truth of things, and in type and shadow they are heaven itself; for God reigns in the hearts of his servants; there is his kingdom. The power of grace hath subdued all his enemies; there is his power. They serve him night and day, and give him thanks and praise; that is his glory. This is the religion and worship of

God in the temple. The temple itself is the heart of man.

God is especially present in the consciences of all persons, good and bad, by way of testimony and judgment; that is, he is there a remembrancer to call our actions to mind, a witness to bring them to judgment, and a judge to acquit or condemn. And although this manner of presence is in this life after the manner of this life, that is, imperfect, and we forget many actions of our lives, yet the greatest changes of our state of grace or sin, our most considerable actions, are always present, like capital letters to an aged and dim eye ; and at the day of judgment, God shall draw aside the cloud and manifest this manner of his presence more notoriously, and make it appear that he was an observer of our very thoughts ; and that he only laid those things by which, because we covered with dust and negligence, were not then discerned. But when we are risen from our dust and imperfections, they all appear plain and legible.

Now the consideration of this great truth is of a very universal use in the whole course of the life of a Christian. All the consequents and effects of it are universal. He that remembers that God stands a witness and a judge, beholding every secrecy, besides his impiety, must have put on impudence if he be not much restrained in his temptation to sin. He is to be feared in public, he is to be feared in private : if you go forth, he spies you ; if you go in, he sees you ; when you light the candle, he observes you ; when you put it out, then also God marks you. Be sure that while you are in his sight, you behave yourself as becomes so holy a presence. But if you will sin, retire yourself wisely, and go where God cannot see ; for nowhere else can you be safe. And certainly, if men would always actually consider and really esteem this truth, that God is the great eye of the world, always watching over our actions, and an ever-open ear to hear all our words, and an unwearied arm ever lifted up to crush a sinner into ruin, it would be the readiest way in the world to make sin to cease from among the children of men, and for men to approach to the blessed state of the saints in heaven, who cannot sin, for they always walk in the presence and behold the face of God.

Let everything you see represent to your spirit the presence, the excellency, and the power of God, and let your conversation with the creatures lead you unto the Creator ; for so shall your actions be done more frequently with an actual eye to God's presence by your often seeing him in the glass of the creation. In the face of the sun you may see God's beauty ; in the fire you may feel his heat

warming; in the water his gentleness to refresh you : he it is that comforts your spirits
when you have taken cordials; it is the dew of
heaven that makes your field give you bread;
and the breasts of God are the bottles that
minister drink to your necessities.

In your retirement make frequent colloquies
or short discoursings between God and thy
own soul. "Seven times a day do I praise
thee, and in the night season also I thought
upon thee while I was waking." So did David;
and every act of complaint or thanksgiving,
every act of rejoicing or of mourning, every
petition and every return of the heart in these
intercourses, is a going to God, an appearing in
his presence, and a representing him present
to thy spirit and to thy necessity. And this
was long since by a spiritual person called
"a building to God a chapel in our heart."
It reconciles Martha's employment with Mary's
devotion, charity and religion, the necessities
of our calling and the employments of devotion. For thus, in the midst of the works of
your trade, you may retire into your chapel
(your heart), and converse with God by frequent addresses and returns.

Let us remember that God is in us, and that
we are in him. We are his workmanship, let
us not deface it : we are in his presence, let us
not pollute it by unholy and impure actions.

God is in every creature ; be cruel towards none, neither abuse any by intemperance. Remember that the creatures, and every member of thy own body, is one of the lesser cabinets and receptacles of God. They are such which God hath blessed with his presence, hallowed by his touch, and separated from unholy use by making them belong to his dwelling.

He walks as in the presence of God that converses with him in frequent prayer and frequent communion, that runs to him in all his necessities, that asks counsel of him in all his doubtings, that opens all his wants to him, that weeps before him for his sins, that asks remedy and support for his weakness, that fears him as a Judge, reverences him as a Lord, obeys him as a Father, and loves him as a Patron.

QUIET RELIGION.

IT is not altogether inconsiderable to observe that the holy Virgin came to a great perfection and state of piety by a few, and those modest and even, exercises and external actions. St. Paul travelled over the world, preached to the Gentiles, disputed against the Jews, confounded heretics, wrote excellently learned letters, suffered dangers, injuries, af-

fronts, and persecutions to the height of wonder, and by these violences of life, action, and
patience obtained the crown of an excellent
religion and devotion. But the holy Virgin,
although she was engaged sometimes in an
active life, and in the exercise of an ordinary
and small economy and government, or ministries of a family, yet she arrived to her perfections by the means of a quiet and silent
piety, the internal actions of love, devotion,
and contemplation; and instructs us that not
only those who have opportunity and powers
of a magnificent religion, or a pompous charity,
or miraculous conversion of souls, or assiduous
and effectual preachings, or exterior demonstrations of corporal mercy, shall have the
greatest crowns, and the addition of degrees
and accidental rewards; but the silent affections, the splendors of an internal devotion,
the unions of love, humility, and obedience,
the daily offices of prayer and praises sung to
God, the acts of faith and fear, of patience and
meekness, of hope and reverence, repentance
and charity, and those graces which walk in a
veil and silence, make great ascents to God,
and as sure progress to favor and a crown, as
the more ostentatious and laborious exercises
of a more solemn religion. No man needs to
complain of want of power or opportunities for
religious perfections: a devout woman in her

closet, praying with much zeal and affections for the conversion of souls, is in the same order to a " shining like the stars in glory," as he who, by excellent discourses, puts it into a more forward disposition to be actually performed. And possibly her prayers obtained energy and force to my sermon, and made the ground fruitful, and the seed spring up to life eternal. Many times God is present in the still voice and private retirements of a quiet religion, and the constant spiritualities of an ordinary life ; when the loud and impetuous winds, and the shining fires of more laborious and expensive actions, are profitable to others only, like a tree of balsam, distilling precious liquor for others, not for its own use.

THE IMITATION OF CHRIST.

IT is reported in the Bohemian story that St. Wenceslaus, their king, one winter night going to his devotions, in a remote church, barefooted in the snow and sharpness of unequal and pointed ice, his servant Podavivus, who waited upon his master's piety and endeavored to imitate his affections, began to faint through the violence of the snow and cold, till the king commanded him to follow

him, and set his feet in the same footsteps
which his feet should mark for him : the servant did so, and either fancied a cure or found
one; for he followed his prince, helped forward
with shame and zeal to his imitation and by
the forming footsteps for him in the snow.   In
the same manner does the blessed Jesus; for,
since our way is troublesome, obscure, full of
objection and danger, apt to be mistaken and
to affright our industry, he commands us to
mark his footsteps, to tread where his feet have
stood, and not only invites us forward by the
argument of his example, but he hath trodden
down much of the difficulty, and made the way
easier and fit for our feet.   For he knows our
infirmities, and himself hath felt their experience in all things but in the neighborhoods of
sin ; and therefore he hath proportioned a way
and a path to our strengths and capacities, and,
like Jacob, hath marched softly and in evenness with the children and the cattle, to entertain us by the comforts of his company and
the influences of a perpetual guide.

He that gives alms to the poor, takes Jesus
by the hand; he that patiently endures injuries
and affronts, helps him to bear his cross ; he
that comforts his brother in affliction, gives an
amiable kiss of peace to Jesus ; he that bathes
his own and his neighbor's sins in tears of
penance and compassion, washes his Master's

feet : we lead Jesus into the recesses of our heart by holy meditations ; and we enter into his heart when we express him in our actions : for so the apostle says, " He that is in Christ, walks as he also walked." But thus the actions of our life relate to him by way of worship and religion ; but the use is admirable and effectual when our actions refer to him as to our copy, and we transcribe the original to the life.

THE END.